HEART QUEST.

PRAISE FOR *AUTUMN'S SHADOW*

"Lyn Cote does it again. *Autumn's Shadow* has a great balance—a heartwarming romance coupled with enough suspense to keep the pages turning, plus a hero and heroine you can't help but love. I highly recommend this wonderful, fast-paced book!"

› **LENORA WORTH** ›

author of Lacey's Retreat

"Cote makes use of her experienced writing skills to weave an inspiring story that keeps the pages turning. The combined elements of romance, intrigue, and Christian faith result in a suspenseful tale that holds the reader's interest to the end."

› **IRENE B. BRAND** ›

author of Summer's Promise *and* Love at Last

"Lyn Cote takes a good story, adds a hook, a twist, and a kink or two, then pulls it all together into a great finale. *Autumn's Shadow* is a puzzle you'll love unravelling."

› **LOIS RICHER** ›

author of Inner Harbor *and* Blessings in Disguise

HEART
QUEST®

PRAISE FOR *WINTER'S SECRET*

"Lyn Cote owes me a night's sleep . . . because I didn't get ANY until I'd finished this book. A special mix of romance, whodunit, and personal faith."

› STEPHANIE GRACE WHITSON ›

*Christy Award finalist and best-selling author
of* Heart of the Sandhills

"*Winter's Secret* by Lyn Cote has a hero guaranteed to make any woman's heart flutter and a mystery that will keep you guessing."

› DEANNA JULIE DODSON ›

author of In Honor Bound, By Love Redeemed,
and To Grace Surrendered

Winter's Secret

Lyn Cote/Tyndale House Publishers
SUBJECT: *Romance/Suspense Fiction*
p $9.99 ISBN: 0-8423-1927

This first in the "Northern Intrigue" series will leave readers impatient for the second installment. Cote introduces believable protagonists whose characters develop as readers move through *Winter's Secret*.

When a series of robberies plagues her town and the new sheriff, Rodd Durand, discovers a connection to her, contentedly single Wendy Carey is confronted with her past; forced to accept present, unexpected change; and must overcome both to look to a bright future.

As local clinic nurse, Wendy becomes involved in Rodd's plan to trap the thief who's been targeting the sleepy Wisconsin town's elderly residents. Working through failed attempts, Wendy and Rodd learn valuable lessons. While Wendy encourages Rodd to rely on God, he shows her how to live in the present, leaving her troubled family heritage behind her.

Winter's Secret is a captivating story, blanketed with biblical truths not only for its fictional characters, but also for its readers.

—*Elizabeth Wisz*
CBA Marketplace

HEART QUEST®

romance the way it's meant to be

HeartQuest brings you romantic fiction
with a foundation of biblical truth.
Adventure, mystery, intrigue, and suspense
mingle in these heartwarming stories of
men and women of faith striving to build
a love that will last a lifetime.

May HeartQuest books sweep you
into the arms of God, who longs for you
and pursues you always.

AUTUMN'S *Shadow*

LYN COTE

HEART
QUEST®

Romance fiction from
Tyndale House Publishers, Inc., Wheaton, Illinois
www.heartquest.com

Visit Tyndale's exciting Web site at www.tyndale.com

HeartQuest is a registered trademark of Tyndale House Publishers, Inc.

Edited by Lorie Popp

Designed by Kelly Bennema

This novel is a work of fiction. Names, characters, places, and incidents are either the product of the author's imagination or are used fictitiously. Any resemblance to actual events, locales, organizations, or persons, living or dead, is entirely coincidental and beyond the intent of either the author or publisher.

Library of Congress Cataloging-in-Publication Data

Cote, Lyn.
  Autumn's shadow / Lyn Cote.
    p. cm. — (Northern intrigue #2)
  ISBN 0-8423-3557-9 (sc)
  1. Women school principals—Fiction. 2. School vandalism—Fiction.
3. Wisconsin—Fiction. 4. Sheriffs—Fiction. I. Title.

PS3553.O76378 A94 2002
813'.54—dc21   2002011989

Printed in the United States of America

07 06 05 04 03 02
 7   6   5   4   3   2   1

To Eileene Sauer, thanks for your gentle spirit and sweet smile.

*The Family Closet (named by Gail Gaymer Martin)
was inspired by Treasures on Second, the thrift shop that supports
Aid to Women, the Women's Crisis Center in Cedar Rapids, Iowa,
and also by the St. Matthias Thrift Shop in Minocqua, Wisconsin.*

Thanks to Terry Jackson, fire chief of Marion, Iowa, for his expertise.

"Am I my brother's keeper?"

Genesis 4:9b, KJV

CHAPTER ONE

KEELY TURNER INTENDED to send a clear message. So far, the pranks hadn't resulted in serious consequences, but who was behind them? And where would they end? *I'm not overreacting, am I, Lord?* She frowned. No, at tonight's school board meeting, she'd set a no-nonsense tone for the year.

The tension in her jaw finally leaked its way into her consciousness. A full day at school and now volunteering here. Flexing her jaw and neck, she realized she'd been staring at one page of the dilapidated spiral notebook lying open on the counter. The late summer sunshine glowed through the dusty windows, giving a golden cast to the Family Closet Thrift Shop, a two-bedroom bungalow that had been transformed into a snug store. Its main room, the former living room, was crammed with full shelves and rows of clothing racks. Tonight . . .

A baby toy squeaked. "Sorry, Ms. Turner," a young woman, one of Keely's former students, apologized. She tossed the faded pink bunny back into a large wicker basket full of toys.

Keely smiled and nodded, but inside she grimaced at the

narrow trend of her thoughts. *Sorry, Lord, I'm not remembering the reason for my being here.* She shut the notebook.

Dressed in a wrinkled pink blouse and worn jeans, the very young mother carried her newborn cuddled close in a denim pouch. For over an hour, Keely had tracked the girl's progress as she roamed the shop with its polished maple floors and cheery, pale yellow walls stenciled with a border of daisies.

One by one the other shoppers had made their choices and left, along with the other volunteers who staffed the charity shop, which provided help primarily for single parents. Still, the teen had continued fingering baby clothes and toys along the perimeter of the store. Until only the two of them remained. Keely had seen this pattern before—a young client awkward about asking for help.

Keely spoke quietly in the silent store. "It's almost time for me to close up for the day. Have you decided on anything?"

From behind a stack of baby blankets, the teen walked toward Keely. "I need a lot of stuff, Ms. Turner," she muttered.

A flash of memory arced through Keely's mind—this girl as a belligerent student in her high school English class, Keely's second year of teaching. This thought pulled school back into Keely's mind, but she shook it off. A young mother did need a lot of stuff—much more than baby clothes.

Keely grinned. "Babies have a way of needing things." Single motherhood had deflated this girl's trademark cockiness. The urge to wrap her arms around this child-mother drew Keely forward. *Lord, give me the right words. She's open now, needing direction, love. Don't let me waste this opportunity to slip a wedge in to keep open this breach in her defenses.* But Keely only voiced, "What did you name her?"

"Evie. She'll be two weeks old on Friday." A smile of pride and tenderness spread over the mother's pinched face.

"Bring her closer." Keely met the girl in the aisle and stroked the infant's corn-silk, baby fine hair. "Oh, what a sweetheart," Keely cooed.

Such perfection awed her. The wonder of creation, of new life, never palled. She bent and placed an angel-soft kiss on Evie's pert nose. "So tiny," she murmured. "I never get over how tiny, how perfect every little feature is." She glanced up and smiled.

"That's right," the girl observed. "You never had any kids."

The careless words slapped Keely in the heart. She caught herself and swallowed her automatic reply: *No, I'm not married.* This young mother wasn't married either. Nearly half the Family Closet clients weren't married.

"Not yet," Keely said, smoothing the baby's collar. To an eighteen-year-old girl, Keely must look well past marriage and childbearing years. After all, weren't teachers ancient creatures who'd ridden on the backs of dinosaurs?

The round black-and-white wall clock ticked over to 6 P.M., an hour till the meeting. She needed to help this single mom and get out of the shop on time. "Come to the office." Without waiting for a response, Keely led the way to the small kitchen in the rear that also served as an office and volunteer lounge where they wouldn't be interrupted in case someone came in.

The nagging thought that the sheriff hadn't returned her voice mail about tonight's meeting bobbed to the surface of Keely's mind again. She pushed it back down. Later.

Motioning the teen toward a nubby brown couch along the wall, Keely sat in the red-vinyl-seated chair by the chrome kitchen table piled high with clothing ready to be priced or pressed. The peculiar and somewhat depressing scent of the thrift shop—two parts fabric softener and one part musty basement—was always more intense in here.

"Now how can the Family Closet help you?"

The girl didn't answer; she kept her gaze on the donated industrial-grade tile on the floor.

Keely waited, then prompted, "Please?"

The sound of a sob erupted, and the girl's shoulders shook.

Keely slid from her chair onto the couch beside the girl and paused. She couldn't treat the teen like that mouthy freshman she remembered. As Keely patted the baby's back through the denim carrier, she avoided the mother's eyes. "Don't worry, little sweetheart, your mama's just having a little postpartum blues."

Gasping, the teen struggled with her tears, wiping them away with her hands.

Still not making eye contact, afraid that showing sympathy would embarrass the girl more, Keely continued to murmur to the child—knowing it was the mother who needed her comfort and more. But probably she wouldn't accept any from "Ms. Turner."

The teen sucked in her tears. "I'm sorry. I've just been feeling blue lately."

From the local gossip, Keely knew why the girl was feeling a little blue lately. "Now how can Family Closet help you?" she asked again gently.

"I heard you give clothes and stuff . . . if someone needs it." The mother kept her eyes on the top of her baby's blonde head.

"That's right—if you'd like to be one of our regular clients."

The girl looked up. "I gotta work here, right?"

"Yes, you have to take your turn helping out here at the

shop, and you have to keep your well-baby checkups at the clinic with the nurse practitioner. And you have to attend the Happy Mother's Class at the church two afternoons a month—"

The front door opened with a bang. "Hey! You ready?"

The young mother flinched. "I think that's my boyfriend. He said he'd pick me up here."

Keeping her opinion of the notorious boyfriend to herself, Keely rose and tucked a donated bag of newborn diapers under the girl's arm. She murmured a subdued thank-you and followed Keely out of the kitchen and to the front door.

"You ready to go?" the young man standing in the doorway demanded. Turning, he tossed his cigarette toward the bushes outside.

Keely motioned the teen through the exit and waved good-bye. "And congratulations," she called after them in an easy tone, "on the baby."

When she closed and locked the door, she had to shake herself. She'd been feeling a little blue lately too.

※ ※ ※

KEELY WAS LATE. Closing up the Family Closet had delayed her. The teen mother's wan face and uneasiness around her baby's father lingered in Keely's mind. Parking in the nearly empty school parking lot, she noted that no sheriff's car graced the lot and grumbled silently.

The school, built in the small town of LaFollette in the 1950s, was a solid two-story, redbrick building that looked more like a factory than a high school. Entering the glossy kelly green doors, she headed down the quiet, scuffed hallway to the student cafeteria. The long wide room's only adornments were its posters—a chart of the food pyramid and a few in gold and green announcing upcoming football games and homecoming events.

The custodian had upended all its seventies orange-plastic chairs on the tables except for some grouped around a table near the windows. The LaFollette-Steadfast Consolidated High School monthly board meeting had waited for her.

The school board members—three men and one silver-haired woman—sat around a chipped Formica table. The same five senior citizens and the local newspaper editor, who attended every school meeting and whom Keely privately called "the watchdogs," sat in a semicircle of uncomfortable chairs in front of the board. Everything was the same except . . . her empty stomach rumbled, giving sound to her tension.

Gus Feeney, a wiry World War II vet and chairman of the board, settled into his chair and patted her shoulder in greeting. Then the door opened, and every head turned to see who else had decided to attend. Keely's gaze froze on the stranger who entered, her interest quickening.

A little over six feet, he was powerfully, compactly built, and he moved as though unaware of the attention focused on him. He removed his hat, revealing close-cropped tawny hair. Nearing the table, the newcomer looked directly into Keely's eyes. His were the same shade as a June sky. Blue. Cloudless blue. Then she realized the blue eyes were assessing her—coolly and thoroughly.

As casually as she could, she sat straighter. She hoped no one else had noticed her gawking. Then it dawned on her that he wore a khaki-and-brown sheriff's department uniform. So the sheriff hadn't ignored her request after all. Or had he?

The officer nodded in greeting to the room in general. Then with his right hand, he swung down a chair from a nearby tabletop in one flowing motion and sat down on it at the end of the semicircle.

Caught by this completely natural and particularly male action, Keely frowned. She looked down at the brief agenda in front of her, aware that the law officer continued to scrutinize her. She shrugged off her reaction to his arrival. She'd been expecting the sheriff—someone she knew—not this stranger. That was all.

With a side glance toward Keely that she ignored, Gus brought the meeting to order and opened discussion about whom to hire temporarily to replace a teacher who had just had a heart attack. She slid to the edge of her stiff chair and propped one elbow on the table, an attitude of attention.

But the voices around her got lost on their way to Keely. Her traitorous eyes kept shifting to the newcomer, his tanned-to-golden skin acting on her like a magnet. However, what impressed her most was his unconcern at being among strangers. Sitting easily in the uncomfortable molded plastic chair, his attention never wandered. He didn't fidget. He just waited.

The discussion of possible replacements for the teacher flowed around her. She tried to be interested, tried to oust the stranger from her mind, but failed. She glanced down at the agenda again in confusion. What gives?

After the dismally short list of possible replacements had been exhausted, Gus brought up plans for the homecoming weekend. Topic followed topic until finally the agenda had been covered and all attention turned to Keely, then to the deputy and back to Keely.

Why did she feel . . . as though she'd been overwhelmed? The man had just come to a public meeting. He hadn't said one word yet.

Gus was the last one to glance her way. "Okay, Keely, I take it by looking at you that you invited the new deputy sheriff here tonight?"

Stifling a fluttering in her stomach, Keely sent a pointed glance to the deputy and he stood up. She also rose and offered him her hand. "Deputy, we haven't met. I'm Keely Turner, the LaFollette principal."

"Deputy Burke Sloan, Ms. Turner." A large warm hand enclosed hers briefly.

His touch upset her balance again, but she only showed him a stage frown, meant to register disappointment. She had her plan and she'd stick to it. "I was expecting Sheriff Durand to come to our meeting tonight."

He betrayed no reaction to her negative comment. "Rodd has assigned me to your school—whatever help you need you'll get."

"If that's true, I'm glad you came," she said. When Sloan's blue eyes connected with hers, sparks danced through her veins. She went on with resolve. "I want to make it clear, crystal clear, that we're not going to tolerate any more mean-spirited pranks."

She paused, not knowing whether she should express more of her vague disquiet. Had this rash of pranks started because she'd assumed her new position as principal this fall? Or . . . her brother's sullen face flashed in her mind. Would he be the problem she expected him to be?

"Stuff like this happens every year," one board member said. "You're overreacting."

"Then you don't think," the seventy-something news-paper editor interjected gruffly and without preamble, "that the cheerleader's fall was an accident?"

Everyone turned to look at the man. He'd put his finger on what had ignited Keely's concern. She pursed her lips. Tonight she and the board had avoided mentioning the incident that had taken place this afternoon during cheerleading practice.

"I heard that someone dug some holes in the football

field and concealed them with sod." Sloan's even voice heightened rather than softened the challenge in his words. "How could that be an accident?"

"My point exactly." She tried to match his assurance.

"Fletcher," Gus growled, addressing the newspaperman by his first name, "you're just trying to get a contentious headline for Monday morning. We have some smart-alecky kid doing mischief. But I think Keely's made it clear we're going to nip this right now. Will someone make a motion to adjourn?" he concluded.

The motion was made, seconded, and carried. The meeting broke up. The crusty newspaperman hurried out without speaking—as usual. The deputy stationed himself at the back of the room, nodding to each person as he or she left.

While Keely stalled, everyone else left. She wanted a private moment to touch base with this deputy. But first, she had to get her unusual awareness of him under control. Still, her unruly gaze refused to obey; she tracked the stranger's every expression and move. Irritating.

She'd seen handsome men before, but this one was definitely too handsome for his own good—and Keely's, judging by her reaction to him. Was she especially vulnerable this fall? *I've just weathered the first week of the school year—loud chaos as usual. That's it.*

Finally prepared to meet him one-on-one, Keely gathered her purse and walked with him to the building's exit.

With a polite nod, he followed her outside into the dusk. They paused under the entrance's overhang by a redbrick pillar. "So someone dug holes right where they knew the cheerleaders would be practicing?" Sloan's deep voice rumbled through her.

She was glad of his direct approach. It helped her focus on the topic, not him. "Yes, during their first cheer, one of the girls jumped high and unfortunately landed in one of the hidden holes. She twisted and severely sprained her ankle." *Just as some twisted mind had hoped.*

"Not exactly a felony." He arched an eyebrow at her.

"I know, but . . . ." How to put her unsubstantiated dread into words that this no-nonsense officer would credit.

He waited for her answer—not shifting, not prompting.

She made a face. "It's just that it isn't the usual kind of prank. I mean, a dead skunk left on the front seat of a car would have been unpleasant, but just . . . funny."

"This wasn't funny," he said, straight-faced but watchful.

She eyed him, wondering if he was making fun of her or trying to glean whatever grain of evidence he could from her vague reply. "No, it wasn't." She looked away, momentarily distracted by the birds that were chirping and flitting around the long-needled boughs in the nearby fir trees. "It took some thinking, and it was meant to harm not just embarrass. Embarrassing someone is the aim of most pranks. I can't really explain it better than that." She shrugged, glancing downward. The shadows from the evergreens were at their longest now. Day was nearly done.

He studied her—she felt it, a kind of stirring of her senses, a disquiet rippling through her.

"Rodd said that you've taught here for five years."

"I'm starting my sixth year at LaFollette."

"Aren't you a little young to be principal?"

"Maybe." She met his gaze without flinching or explanation. Soon enough he'd figure out how after a year as village board chair, she'd become principal. Or, at least, what everyone in the county thought.

"Did the cheerleader have any particular enemies?" Sloan asked.

"No, and how could anyone predict which cheerleader would take the fall?"

He nodded. "Do you think some former student might have a grudge against you? Want to make you look bad?"

Considering this, she worried her lower lip. "No." *But someone could have a grudge against my family.* That was fairly common in the county.

"We'll be patrolling your school grounds more often. And I'll be attending most of your school functions. I would anyway. My nephew is one of your new students."

"Well, that means he must be Nicholas Fleming?" The crickets were singing. She suddenly felt tired.

"Yes. He hasn't gotten into trouble with you already, has he?"

"No." Why had he asked that about his nephew? Just teasing or not? Nicholas had struck her as unhappy about being in school, but that was normal. Would she have more than just her brother to worry about? *Oh, please, I don't need another troublemaker in my school.*

"I need to be going," she said, cutting off the exchange. "I have to drop off a textbook at the clinic tonight for the cheerleader. Doc Erickson is keeping her overnight, pending some lab test." She held out her hand and then regretted it when his large palm closed around hers again. She let go. His intriguing combination of businesslike manner and disturbing presence was enough for one night.

"The principal delivers books for students?" He lifted an eyebrow.

"The clinic's on my way home."

"I guess I'll have to get used to this small-town friendliness. Let me walk you to your car."

This time she raised an eyebrow at him. "Let me guess—you're from a big city? You must be or you'd know I don't need an escort here."

A grin teased one corner of his mouth. "Milwaukee. And my car's parked right by yours."

She smiled ruefully. "Got me."

※ ※ ※

JUST AS KEELY was turning onto Highway 27 to go to the clinic for her injured cheerleader, her cell phone rang. "Keely Turner."

"Ms. Turner—" the young male voice on the line shook—"could you come? Carrie Walachek, you know, my girlfriend—"

"Who is this?" The fear in his voice put her on alert.

"Ma'am, I volunteer in the school store—"

She recognized the voice and interrupted, "What's wrong?"

"Shane gave me your cell phone number and told me to call you. I'm really scared for Carrie. This lady down the street from Carrie's trailer said I could use her phone. Carrie went inside. . . ." The teen was obviously fighting to control his emotions. "There's been a lot of shouting and—"

The line clicked.

Her pulse thudding in her head, Keely looked at the phone and then hung up. She stopped on the side of the road and snapped on her map light. Reaching into her glove compartment, she took out the student directory and located Carrie's name and address.

Resolutely, she turned her car back onto the road. Her student had sounded panicked. She'd go, assess the problem, and then call social services. She sped all the way to the edge of town where a few trailers huddled together.

When she pulled up at Carrie's address, she saw Shane Blackfeather and the teen who'd called her pounding on the trailer door, shouting Carrie's name.

Mounting dread chilled her. Keely got out and

approached the bottom of the metal steps up to the trailer. She could hear things being broken inside—ominous. She asked, "What are you two doing?"

Shane's friend knotted his hands into fists. "This is all my fault." He turned back to Shane. "Let's break down the door—"

"Shane!" Keely snapped, trying to keep the two teens from making matters worse. "What's happening?"

Shane, tall and dark, ran down to her. "We're afraid Carrie's dad is beating her. We can't get him to open up—"

She held up her hand. Muffled shouts and groans came from inside the trailer, then a thud like something heavy—a body?—hitting the inside wall. This went beyond what she could handle. Her adrenaline starting, she pulled the cell phone from her purse and speed-dialed the sheriff's department.

The trailer door burst open.

Keely dropped her phone.

"*You!*" the large man shouted. "Who invited you, Turner?"

"Mr. Walachek—," she began.

"Get out of here!" Alcohol slurred his voice. "Off my property!"

Carrie appeared just behind her father. She tried to squeeze around him. But the big man pinned her under one arm.

"Mr. Walachek," Keely spoke calmly, playing for time. Would the sheriff's dispatcher recognize her cell phone number on the caller ID? Could they do that? "The boys called me. What seems to be the problem? Can I be of any help?"

"I told you! This ain't your business, lady! Just 'cause you're a Turner don't give you the right to meddle! Get off my property—"

Carrie tried to twist out of her father's grip. The man slammed his fist into her face.

Screaming inside, Keely stooped and grabbed up her phone. *Why did I let that deputy get away so quickly!*

The teens made a rush for the girl. The father dragged his daughter inside, but he couldn't get the door shut in time. The boys rushed into the trailer—yelling.

"Get her out of there!" Keely screamed.

A police siren drowned out her voice.

Shane and his friend burst out with Carrie between them. They hustled down the steps, half carrying the girl.

"Get her into my car!" Keely shouted.

"Don't move!" Walachek bellowed at the top of the steps. "Don't move, any of you!" He held a rifle and pointed it deliberately at Keely's head.

The three teens froze halfway down the steps.

Staring into the rifle barrel, Keely couldn't draw breath.

"Mr. Walachek?" a calm voice came from behind Keely. "What seems to be the problem here?"

It was that new deputy, Burke Sloan! His voice shocked Keely out of her paralysis. She gasped for air.

"Get off my property!" the man bellowed again, the sound vibrating inside Keely, making her tremble.

"Mr. Walachek, you know I can't do that," Sloan said in a calm tone. "Not when you're pointing a weapon at Ms. Turner. I can't leave until you put that rifle away—"

"I didn't ask her to come. She's on my property. I got a right to shoot trespassers!"

"I don't want to argue with you, but if you think you can shoot Ms. Turner as a trespasser, you'll find out it won't hold up in court."

"Yeah, but if she's dead, she won't care. And it would serve her father right!" The man cursed.

"Mr. Walachek," the deputy said in the same tone he

might have used to request a weather report, "you still haven't told me what the problem is."

"This kid got my girl pregnant! And he's going to marry her or—"

"This be your first grandchild?" Sloan asked.

The man stared at him. "What?"

"I said, will this be your first grandchild?"

"Yeah! What about it?"

"I just thought you might want to be around when the baby's born." The deputy's tone continued matter-of-factly.

"What's that mean?" Walachek glared and tightened his grip on his deer rifle.

"That means this is no time to be pointing guns at people."

"Get that Turner off my property then! Her lousy father has been running this county since before I was born!"

Keely tried to block out the nasty words and the hateful tone. Her father's high-handed actions were making matters difficult for her once again.

"I don't see how that has anything to do with Ms. Turner. Now, Mr. Walachek, put down your rifle."

The intoxicated man glared at Keely.

"Mr. Walachek, my Beretta's safety is off and it's racked. I can hit you before you can aim and fire once. This is no time to be firing guns. Your daughter is in the line of fire and she's expecting a child. Now you wouldn't want anything to hurt your little girl, would you?"

Keely held her breath. Walachek stared into her eyes, seeing her fear, feeding on it—she thought. But she couldn't hide it.

"Mr. Walachek, put your gun down." The deputy's easy-going tone hardened to forged steel.

The drunken man's glare turned murderous.

CHAPTER TWO

A SUPPRESSED SCREAM vibrated in Keely's throat.

Walachek dropped his rifle. He swore at them and backed inside. The door slammed.

Frozen in place, Keely heard footsteps. Sloan grabbed her, shoved her behind him, and hustled her sideways the few feet to his Jeep. He pressed her down behind his vehicle. "Don't move," he ordered in an undertone.

"Walachek!" he called. "I'm taking your daughter to the clinic in Steadfast!"

Another stream of cursing exploded. Then the sound of breaking glass. Still crouching, Keely bent her head against the back of Sloan's neck, seeking his protection. She gripped the shoulders of his jacket with both hands.

As though they were in a war movie, the three teens who had been crouching on the bottom step ran doubled-over toward the deputy's Jeep. They crowded around Sloan like he was their campfire on a chilly night.

Sloan glanced toward Carrie. "Is there anyone in there with—"

"No," Carrie moaned. The girl began sobbing.

Keely reached for her, pulling her close.

With a few pointed words, Burke told the two boys to get in the vehicles—one would drive Keely's car and the other would drive the truck they'd come in to the Erickson Clinic.

Still crouched beside Sloan, Shane objected. "Are you going to let him just point a gun at Ms. Turner without—"

"I'm just one officer. My first duty—once Walachek put his weapon down—is to get all of you out of harm's way." He handed Keely's keys to Shane and then tugged her hand, pulling her and Carrie along with him.

Opening the back door of his Jeep, he lifted Carrie into the backseat; then he urged Keely to keep her head down while she got into the front seat. He hurried around to let himself in behind the wheel. "You two, get going."

As the teens ran to the other vehicles, Sloan started his Jeep. Instead of turning around in front of the trailer as Keely expected, he gunned it in reverse down the road. At the end of the line of trailers, he executed a U-turn and headed toward 27.

Keely hooked her seat belt with trembling hands. Pulling herself together, she turned to look through the grill that separated the front and back seats. Carrie's long black hair fell over her face, and the girl's narrow shoulders shook with her weeping. "Carrie, how badly hurt are you?"

"I'm so embarrassed. . . ."

Carrie's anguished words and forlorn sobs cut right to Keely's heart. She knew just how Carrie felt. How many times had her father's ill temper and contempt for others humiliated Keely? But no one would believe that. If you had money, you didn't have problems, right?

❖ ❖ ❖

A FEW HOURS later, Burke remained in a hard seat in the ER reception area. Ms. Turner sat beside him even though he'd tried to get her to go home. They were waiting for someone from county social services to take charge of Carrie for the night. The young girl, who fortunately hadn't suffered anything worse than bruised ribs and a battered face, was resting in a bed.

Burke's jaw hardened. During his years as a cop in Milwaukee, he'd seen all too many domestic abuse victims. Thinking of his sister and his failure to come to her and his nephew's aid stirred smoldering embers inside him. He was grateful that tonight Nick was safely in bed at Harlan's.

Ms. Turner sighed and shifted in her seat. Now that he had time, out of the corner of his eye, he studied her. His first glimpse of her at the school meeting had disconcerted him. On his way to the meeting, he'd expected to be dealing with a middle-aged woman in orthopedic shoes. Instead, he'd come up against a classy lady with long brown hair streaked with blonde and large hazel eyes.

Did she even realize how incongruous it was to him that she was a principal? At tonight's meeting, she'd behaved like the ultraprofessional type—even looked it with all that hair pulled up into a severe topknot and dressed in a white blouse, gray vest, and skirt. But when she stood up to leave the school cafeteria, he'd been caught up short—by the long elegant calves showing beneath her hem.

Nothing had been immodest about her skirt length. He'd just expected a principal's hem to be nearer her ankles than her knees. How had such a young woman become the high school principal? He'd have to ask Rodd because she sure hadn't been forthcoming.

Beside him, Ms. Turner sighed softly again. The sound curled through him, sensitizing him to her, an unusual reaction for him. Maybe it was because she didn't fit his stereotype. More likely it was because of all the changes he'd survived this past month—moving, Nicky, everything. He glanced at her again. One thing about her intrigued him: a small incongruous white scar at the corner of her lower lip. It lent an unexpected vulnerability to her calm, assured manner.

She stretched as though her back muscles were tight, showing her fatigue. He was impressed by her genuine concern over one of her students. She didn't act like she was staying because she thought it wouldn't look right to leave. In Milwaukee, he couldn't remember any incident like this where a principal ever behaved out of personal compassion as Ms. Turner had.

The principals he was used to dealing with were concerned more about liability and negative news coverage. Maybe this was more evidence of small-town differences in action. Certainly no Milwaukee principal would have contacted the sheriff over a malicious prank that hadn't resulted in bloodshed. Keely Turner was certainly showing herself as a caring principal. His job was a world away from the MPD. Would he adjust to this or not?

The woman beside him tugged at his curiosity—against his will. He had enough on his mind right now. To keep his gaze from straying to her again, Burke went over tonight's episode in his mind, making sure he'd tied up all the loose ends. On his way to the ER, he'd arranged for the sheriff to take Walachek into custody for the night. The man would be arraigned sometime tomorrow and be behind bars for a while.

He'd been putting it off, but he had to discourage Ms. Turner from getting herself in dangerous situations like the one with Walachek tonight. Might as well be now. "I've been meaning to ask you, Ms. Turner," he said, glancing at her, "why did the boys call their principal instead of their parents or the police?"

"When I was his teacher, Shane had some difficulties settling in when he was a freshman. That's when I gave him my cell phone number and that's probably why he called me." She gave him an even look. "I want you to know that

I've never done anything like this before. And I promise you I won't again."

He studied her. Her pat answer revealed that she'd been anticipating this question. He hoped she'd keep her promise. "Good."

A county social worker bustled into the ER. Within minutes, she left, taking Carrie with her.

"Come on." Sloan stood and said, "I'll walk you to your car."

Without reply, she walked beside him out into the cooler August night. "You really don't need to walk me—"

"We had this conversation before, didn't we?" He paused. "Ms. Turner, you've just been a target of someone pretty nasty. He should be in custody by now, but I'm going to follow you home just to be safe."

She gave him a guarded look. "All right."

※ ※ ※

WAVING ONE HAND behind her head to thank Sloan for his escort, Keely pushed the garage door opener on her dash and drove inside her family's four-car garage. Trying to be quiet in the late hour, she made her way through the dim garage around her mother's white BMW, her dad's dark green Tahoe, and her brother's red Jeep Wrangler.

She opened the kitchen door and was greeted by angry voices from the front hall. She halted, suddenly wishing she had somewhere else to go tonight. Ever since spring when Grady had been sent home from his fourth prep school, life at Chez Turner had become increasingly volatile.

"Where have you been, Grady? You know you were supposed to head straight home after we'd finished at the target range," her father shouted, sprinkling his accusations liberally with curses. "Don't make me ask again!"

Keely stayed where she was. She didn't want to get caught in the cross fire between her father and brother.

"Franklin, it's not that late."

Keely caught her mother's coaxing voice and cringed. Did the three of them realize that they were playing a scene from some 1950s melodrama—overbearing father enforcing will on rebel-without-a-cause son with interference from coddling mother? Keely thought about driving to a friend's house. But at half-past midnight now, it was too late to bother anyone. She leaned her forehead against a kitchen cabinet.

The three voices rattled on, sticking to the same old boring script. Did they have to fight at the bottom of the only staircase to her suite? *This could go on all night. I have to work tomorrow.*

Making a sound of disgust, Keely headed into the battle zone. Without a word, she walked around the three of them—her tall ramrod-straight father, her fashionably thin mother, and Grady—a younger version of their father but with his blond hair spiked in a bristling hairstyle. She mounted the stairs.

"Well, Keely!" her mother called after her. "You could say something—not just walk right past your parents—"

"Good night, Mother, Father, and Grady." She kept on climbing.

"Don't be flippant," her father barked.

"I'm tired and I wish you all a good night." She reached the second-floor landing and looked out the huge arched window over the front door. She glimpsed Sloan walking away from the house to his vehicle. Had he come to the door? Why? Why hadn't he just driven away as she'd expected?

She paused and watched him drive away from the house into the darkness. Whatever his business had been, she didn't blame him for turning tail. She couldn't wait for the day she moved into her first home. Sweet independence.

All I want is some peace, sweet uncomplicated peace. Please, Lord, don't let my father think of any more ways to delay my move!

❉ ❉ ❉

LATE THE NEXT afternoon, Burke hid his aggravation under a noncommittal mask. How could the judge justify what he'd done? He and Rodd would have trouble with Walachek again. It was just a matter of time.

A dapper, silver-haired man interrupted Burke's thoughts, showing a reluctant Nicky and him the utility room of the cabin that Burke was thinking of renting. Rodd had arranged for Burke and Nicky to stay with Harlan Carey till they found something else. But they couldn't board at Harlan's forever.

"Here's the water heater and propane furnace. I usually heat with the wood in the hearth. It saves money and I enjoy watching the fire. But you're both young and you'll be out on the job and at school."

Burke nodded.

"Well, I'm going out to the garage and pack some tools I want to move over to my bride's. I'll let you get a feel for the place. You could move in the day of my wedding. In fact, I wish you would, so the place will be occupied." In his seventies, the man was going to marry a second time.

Wondering why a man would chance marriage twice, Burke thanked him as he left. Burke looked over his shoulder. "So what do you think, Nicky?"

"I'm not Nicky. I haven't been Nick-y for years."

"Sorry. I'll try to remember it's Nick." He didn't want to irritate his nephew. The years had gone so fast. His slip in calling him the childish nickname showed just how far he'd kept himself from his nephew in the recent past. "We would be renting it furnished—"

"It only has one bedroom." Nick glared at him—as usual.

The three-room cabin was just a large kitchen-sitting room, a bedroom, and a bath. "I was going to get myself a daybed for that wall in the living room." Burke pointed to the back wall. "You'd have the bedroom."

His nephew looked surprised. "How come?"

"Because you're at that age. You need privacy."

Nick snorted. "Yeah, right. This little house will be private all right."

Burke ignored Nick's sarcasm. The cabin with its log walls had a cozy feel and was spotless, scrubbed to within an inch of its life. "You're staying for the year with me so get used to it."

Nick lifted a shoulder to him. "Harlan says he's been really lonely since his dog died this summer. He likes having us. Why can't we stay at Harlan's?"

"Because we need to have a place of our own." That wasn't exactly accurate. Burke was the one who needed a place of his own.

After living alone for a decade, he couldn't get used to living in someone else's house with two other people. It made him jumpy—never being by himself. If he rented this place, then he'd only have to deal with Nick. Better odds. "My crazy hours aren't good for Harlan. I know he waits up for me when I'm on night duty." Burke relented. "I know you'll have to give up using Harlan's truck and ride the bus to school—"

"No, I won't. He says I can have his truck."

"What?" The image of the battered red truck that Nick had driven here came to Burke's mind.

"He's gotta have cataract surgery sometime soon. He can't drive until he recovers from that. He says I can use his pickup for school if I come over and cook him dinner when you're on evening duty, and I gotta take him to the clinic when he has an appointment and drive him to the grocery store. But I think we should stay with him. It's a bigger house." Nick glared at Burke, looking as though he expected a fight.

Something in Nicky's—Nick's—voice alerted Burke. *Should* they stay with Harlan? The only time Nick smiled was when he talked with the older man. Burke recalled that Nick still got along with his grandfather in Milwaukee. Maybe he shouldn't uproot Nick a second time. "We can talk about this again later. We don't have to make a snap decision."

Nick's face showed his surprise at his uncle's accommodating reply. "You mean it? You're not just saying it?"

"I never 'just say' anything."

"Okay." Nick studied him.

"How's it going at school?" Burke ventured to ask, the sensation akin to walking into an unfamiliar darkened room.

Nick shrugged. "There's a kid who thinks he owns the place. A real jerk."

"The kind you want to steer clear of?" Burke offered his advice in an offhand voice.

"Don't worry about that. He's related to some big shot in town. I'm not impressed. Hey, I'm heading into town then. I gotta get some more school supplies."

"Go ahead. Just remember we're expected at the sheriff's for supper tonight with Harlan."

Nick nodded and left.

Watching Nick drive away in Harlan's truck, Burke was grateful that Nick had taken a liking to Harlan. Maybe the older man would have better luck reaching Nick. Burke's conscience crimped painfully. *I hope I can still make a difference with Nick. I know, Lord, you're not going to let me get off that easy. Reconnecting with Nick is my job.* The local pastor's Sunday sermon had reminded him of that.

Burke hadn't thought about attending church here. Not until Sheriff Rodd Durand, Burke's friend who'd asked him to interview for the deputy sheriff position here, had invited him to go that first Sunday.

In Milwaukee, Burke had attended church infrequently, chalking it up to his crazy work schedule. But here, Nicky's presence had made it necessary for him to change that. So Burke—with Nicky in tow—had accepted Rodd's invitation to church.

And the sermon had been like a finger pointed straight into Burke's heart. The pastor had recounted the story of Cain and Abel, a story of a man who hadn't wanted any restraints from God or family.

Guilt stirred the embers in Burke's stomach. Cain's disrespectful question to God reared in his mind: *"Am I my brother's keeper?"* It echoed Burke's own previous excuses for not helping Nick. In the past two years, he'd failed his sister and Nick. Would Burke's attention now be too little, too late? Would Nick settle into the high school here? How would this all end?

※ ※ ※

THAT EVENING, KEELY walked to the busy LF Café from the high school and ordered a chef's salad to go.

Complaining of frazzled nerves, her mother had flown out of the small airport in the next county this afternoon—her destination: her favorite California spa for a week's stay. At home, her father would be brooding about Grady, who'd been grounded tonight for staying out too late. Who could blame her from steering clear of home sweet home? Besides, she had enough paperwork to keep her busy all evening. For no reason at all, Burke Sloan's face came to mind—again.

The plump, middle-aged cashier bagged the salad and packets of dressing and handed over the sack and Keely's change. "I really appreciate all the extra work you do, like this—working late."

The woman's compliment took Keely by surprise. "Thank you."

"No, thank you! You really came through for my niece Carrie last night. Maybe you didn't remember, but her mother was my sister." The woman pursed her lips as though checking a show of emotion and then continued. "Anyway, I'm glad her father had to cool his heels in jail last night."

Pushing aside the sinking feeling the mention of Walachek triggered, Keely nodded. "Bye."

"Night!" The woman waved. "Take care of yourself. Don't work too hard!"

The kind words lifted Keely's spirits. Burke Sloan's voice played in her mind. Not the words, just his calm tone and even delivery. As she walked through the quiet dusky streets back to school, a red truck sped by, swirling up a few dry leaves in the gutter.

Reaching the school, she unlocked one of the front doors, the one nearest her office and locked herself inside. Tonight was one of those rare nights when no school practice or activity was being held. After last night, she looked forward to a peaceful evening. It would be good to get some work done—all alone in the school—even if the quiet was almost eerie. . . .

❉ ❉ ❉

THAT EVENING, BURKE lounged at the table in the Durand kitchen, trying not to show his worry.

Rodd and Wendy Durand, newlyweds, had invited Harlan—who happened to be Wendy's grandfather—Nicky . . . Nick and him over for supper. While Burke and Nick boarded with Harlan, they both had been taken in like family.

Wendy put a pan of biscuits into the oven, and Rodd took the opportunity to steal a kiss. Though blushing, Wendy paused to kiss him back.

"You two youngsters," Harlan scolded with a big grin, "hold up on that lovey-dovey stuff."

Burke felt like rubbing his eyes and taking another look. Rodd Durand had been one of his closest buddies in Milwaukee. A good part of that had come from the fact that neither of them was married or looking for a wife. But that had changed. Rodd was "definitely" a married man now. For some reason, Ms. Turner's face popped into Burke's mind. Maybe since she was Nick's principal?

In this cozy setting, Burke was having a hard time not letting his irritation and anxiety show. So far, Nick had yet to show up for supper. He should have been back by now. After leaving the cabin they'd been looking at, Nick had gone AWOL in Harlan's old red truck. Why? And where was he? Should Burke go after him? Being responsible for another person, a teen, was new to Burke. *Is this just the usual with teens or should I be concerned?* Who knew the answer to that?

Shaking these questions off, he stood up, walked over to the stove, and poured himself another cup of coffee from the percolator.

"I could have done that for you, Burke," Wendy said, stirring the fragrant beef stew in the skillet.

"No problem." Burke reached for the creamer. Rodd's wife had short, golden brown hair. The image of Keely Turner with her long hair came to Burke's mind again. Where was she, and was she having a better evening than he was? He hoped so. He'd wanted to ask Rodd for more background about Ms. Turner but hesitated. He didn't pry into people's lives.

But Keely Turner had made him curious. She'd been on

his mind all day. What had all the shouting he'd overheard last night at her door been about? He'd simply been trying to return a tube of lipstick that must have dropped out of her pocket. But the sound of raised voices and a glimpse through the side glass by the front door had revealed who— Keely's parents? A teenaged brother?

Their loud discussion had turned him around and back to his Jeep. He hadn't wanted to embarrass them by knocking. And judging from the heated exchange at the Turners' last night, he wasn't the only one having trouble handling a teen. But yelling didn't help. *Where are you, Nick, and what are you up to?*

※ ※ ※

LISTENING TO HER footsteps echo in the silent hallway, Keely entered the outer office in the principal's reception area. She locked that door before going into her own office. Taking these precautions in a little town like LaFollette was probably ludicrous. But the contrast between busy, noisy daytime and quiet evening at the school made her nerves edgy. During school hours, this building didn't feel large enough for all the young people who ran through the hallways, calling to each other, slamming lockers, racing to class before the raucous bell rang. Empty now, it felt like a mausoleum.

She shook her head and smiled. *At least my imagination is still working.* She laid out her supper on her desk. Her cell phone rang.

"Hi, Keely? Penny here. Just wanted to let you know that the girl you called me about came in today and signed up."

"Great." Satisfaction flowed through Keely. *Thank you, Father, for bringing her back. Let us help her.*

"Yes, she asked to volunteer when you're on duty."

"Poor girl," Keely quipped. "You'd think she'd remember what a slave driver I am."

"You would say that." Pause. "I thank God every day—" Penny's voice had become serious—"for the Family Closet, Keely. It's doing so much good for so many. I wish you'd let me tell people that you're the one—"

"You're the one," Keely said, cutting Penny off, "who had the idea for it, and some anonymous donor bought the house. I'm just the organizer, right?"

"Very well." Penny Weaver, the local pastor's wife, sounded resigned. "If that's what you say."

"That's what I say."

"Keely, I'm concerned about how much you're trying to do this year. Maybe you should work fewer hours at the Family Closet. It's your first year as principal—"

"But I'm done with grad school, Penny!"

"But you're moving into your first home! You don't know how much work and stress that is!"

Keely laughed. "You're scaring me!"

"Oh, you! But if I see you getting run down—"

"Yes, mother." Keely chuckled. "Bye. I've got work to do."

After Penny's good-bye, Keely began eating forkfuls of the crisp salad. She thought about Penny's caution. Her friend wasn't the only one who'd mentioned this to her. How could she explain how much seeing the Family Closet help those who were in real need blessed her? For the first time in her life, she felt as though she was fulfilling those verses in Matthew 25: "When did we ever see you . . . naked and give you clothing? . . . When you did it to one of the least of these my brothers and sisters, you were doing it to me!"

Maybe now as principal of the high school and with Family Closet carrying out its purpose, she could banish the irrational feeling that she had more to do—always more to do! She remembered the words from Luke 12: *"Much is required from those to whom much is given."*

Out of the blue she wondered where Burke Sloan was

tonight. Pushing away this errant thought and a few others about what else needed to be done at the thrift shop, Keely began reading the latest education bulletin from the State of Wisconsin. . . .

※ ※ ※

"MY STOMACH'S BEGINNING to rumble, Wendy," Harlan complained—with a big grin.

Wendy pointed her wooden spoon at her grandfather. "You keep talking like that and you're washing the dishes."

Looking pleased, Harlan grumbled unconvincingly.

With his coffee cup in hand, Burke sat back down. The kitchen was warm from the oven and from the obvious love that Rodd, Wendy, and Harlan had for each other. He'd recently become aware of things like this again. Tonight he felt strange, cut off, just as he'd suddenly realized he had been from his parents and brothers and sister for years. His disconnecting from his family had crept up on him over the past decade, and he hadn't realized just how isolated he'd become until his decision to move had unleashed such furor.

At the end of July, his parents and five siblings had been stunned and then very vocal about his decision to take Rodd's offer and move here to Steadfast. He'd been taken aback by their reaction. After all, they were adults and had their own lives, right? But they had told him it was the final betrayal, that he hadn't been a part of the family since Sharon . . .

Burke had gone ahead with his plans. He wanted to join Rodd up here. But the move hadn't gone quite as he had planned. His father had taken the gloves off, confronting Burke about his dereliction in hesitating to help his sister when she'd asked him to take Nick. At least, that's how his dad had seen it.

In the end, Nick had come with him to Steadfast. Why had everyone thought Burke could make a difference with

Nick? He hadn't had a relationship with his nephew since the kid had been in kindergarten. A twinge of guilt ended this line of thought.

How had he let himself get so cut off from his family? The answer to that was all too easy. He turned back to the present, tuning in on the conversation flowing around him.

"The Weavers only kept Carrie one night." Wendy was slicing tomatoes from Harlan's garden. "She went to live with an aunt in LaFollette this morning so she'd remain in the same school district." She glanced at Burke. Had she noticed his attention wandering? "The aunt is going to try to get custody. And I'm afraid that it will take a few days before Carrie's face heals. Poor kid."

"I'm sorry to report her dad was able to post bail. Walachek walked late this afternoon," Rodd added. "It was his first offense. The DA couldn't persuade the judge that Walachek was dangerous. I couldn't believe it when the judge let him out. Why would he set a man free who pointed a gun at the local principal?"

Burke burned inside again. Walachek should have been locked up for a few days at least. His temper would still be high. Would he play it cool or stir up more trouble? Burke thought trouble was the answer.

Wendy and her grandfather exchanged glances. "That judge and Ms. Turner's father have been feuding a long time," Wendy said. "Turner knows how to make enemies."

Harlan shook his head sadly at Wendy's comment and said, "Just because Turner has money doesn't mean he's had no problems—"

"I'm just telling the truth, Grandpa." Wendy turned back to her skillet.

"You didn't know Mr. Turner's father. Old Turner was a hard man. He demanded too much from his son."

Wendy turned and kissed her grandfather's cheek.

"You're too sweet sometimes." Harlan patted her cheek; then she went back to her cooking.

Burke grimly recalled Carrie's bleeding face and that moment when he drove up and found Walachek pointing a rifle at Keely Turner. The judge obviously hadn't given his decision much thought.

"Rodd," Harlan said, "how's the Weaver baby's investigation going?"

Wendy frowned. "Grandpa, Penny keeps reminding everyone not to call Rachel that. She's only their foster child. Until Rodd finds the parents, they can't adopt her."

"I'm starting to wonder—" Rodd leaned against the kitchen counter—"if I'll ever find out who that little one belongs to."

Burke heard the frustration in his old friend's tone. Rodd had told him the story. Early this year in January, Rodd had rescued a baby girl from a car just before it had exploded. A male and female in the front seat had died in the explosion, and their bodies had been burned too badly for easy identification. A local couple, Bruce and Penny Weaver, who were the pastor and his wife at the Steadfast Community Church, had taken the baby in as a foster child.

"Well—" Rodd drew in a long breath—"the car had been stolen in Milwaukee. So that seemed to be a dead end. Then I started trying to match dental records of my two victims to any missing persons from the Milwaukee area. No luck."

"Nothing came through the fire?" Burke probed. "Not even the man's billfold?"

"No, that puzzled me too. Often a man's billfold will come through a fire—the way a man sits on his billfold, the seat back will protect it. But the most peculiar thing is that neither of them had any identification on them."

"That's odd." Burke frowned. "No one around the county reported expecting friends or family to visit that didn't show up?"

Rodd shook his head.

Burke loved this kind of back and forth. He and Rodd had had these brainstorming sessions before—trying to think of every possible angle—spurring each other on to solve a crime. This had been one of the main reasons Burke had left Milwaukee when Rodd had asked him to hire on as one of his deputies. He and Rodd had clicked—they'd worked on so many cases as a team. "Could the two of them have been mugged, had their IDs lifted in the Milwaukee area or somewhere south?"

"That's a possibility."

"Anything else?"

Rodd shook his head again. "No fingerprints from the bodies because of the fire. A stolen vehicle. No matches yet for the teeth. This case is like walking in quicksand—no bottom."

Burke had no further leads to offer. Nicky popped back into his mind. So far his attempts to reconnect with his nephew matched Rodd's description of the case. Getting close to Nicky was like walking in quicksand with no bottom.

※ ※ ※

KEELY FROWNED. WHERE were those figures she needed for this form? She glanced toward the outer office where her secretary kept all the school data in bound folders. If only she could get Freda to learn how to set up databases on the computer.

She sighed and rose. In the other room, she snagged a step stool and dragged it to the corner. Of course, the folder she needed had to be on the top shelf! She mounted the step stool.

※ ※ ※

"IT'S DONE!" WENDY announced, carrying the skillet over to the table.

"Hmm. Hmm. That does look good!" Harlan rubbed his gnarled hands together. "Looks like marriage has improved your cooking!"

"It comes frozen in a bag, Grandpa," Wendy admitted.

Rodd kissed her forehead. "But you opened the bag." They both sat down. "Harlan, will you say grace?"

Burke bowed his head.

Harlan began. "Dear Lord, thank you for Burke coming to help Rodd in his duties. And for Nick. Please keep both of them in good health and in your will. Bless this food, Lord, and the hands that prepared it . . . even if it came out of a bag. Amen."

Burke hadn't prayed for a long time except in church. Though feeling rusty, he added, "Lord, keep Nicky safe and out of trouble. I need your help. I'm getting—"

The phone rang.

Burke looked at it, hoping it wasn't dispatch with an emergency, and hoping that the emergency wouldn't be Nick wrecking Harlan's pickup.

Rodd groaned and walked to the phone. "Durand here."

The three of them waited at the table, watching Rodd's expression.

He hung up. "I'm sorry, Wendy. I've got to go to LaFollette."

"What's the problem, son?" Harlan asked.

"Dispatch got a call. Someone in LaFollette reported shooting near the high school."

CHAPTER THREE

TAKING SEPARATE VEHICLES, Burke and Rodd sped to LaFollette—using their sirens and lights all the way. Burke had only been on the school vandalism case for one day. Had some kid already progressed from digging holes in the football field to shooting near the school? Or was this more than one kid?

An unpleasant thought intruded. Last weekend he'd spent an afternoon of target practice with Nicky. Was Nicky's twenty-two home in Harlan's gun case or in the back of the pickup?

Burke exhaled. Imagining the worst never helped. And the 911 call to dispatch had been sketchy. The caller hadn't known if the school had been empty when the windows had been shot at. Rodd had called for the ambulance to meet them just in case. And what about Keely Turner?

He told himself that she'd be safely home by this time of night. But he knew he'd feel better when he saw for himself that the school had been unoccupied.

He and Rodd parked near the school doors and jumped out of their vehicles. Scanning the scene, Burke saw that several large windows had been shattered. Broken glass littered the grass and bushes near the building. A small crowd already milled around the school entrance. Little town, big city—crime attracted crowds.

Burke hung back and let Rodd approach the crowd. "I'm Sheriff Durand. Is there anyone inside the school?"

"I think the principal might be," a woman wearing a bright red blouse and shorts volunteered. "I saw her walking by with a sack from the café. She works late lots of nights."

"Her car's parked in back," a man offered.

At this, Burke moved to the door and tried the handle to the school entrance. "It's locked. Who would have a key?"

The same woman spoke up, "I called the police; then I called the school maintenance man."

A clattering pickup truck turned the corner on two wheels and zoomed into the parking lot. Brakes squealed, and a middle-aged man in khaki work clothes got out and hustled toward the group. "I've got the keys."

Rodd ordered, "Everyone stay out here. Deputy Sloan and I will go in and see if Ms. Turner's in the building—"

"I better come with you," the maintenance man interjected. "She usually locks the door to the outer office, too, when she's in here alone at night."

Rodd waved him inside. As they jogged to the principal's office, the sheriff used his cell phone to summon more deputies. Rodd and Burke exchanged looks. They both understood they needed crowd control. They had to examine the scene without interference. If they could identify the perp, that might nip this vandalism right now before anyone got more than a sprained ankle.

Burke's anxiety grew when he didn't see Keely. "Ms. Turner!" he called. "It's Sheriff Durand and Deputy Sloan!" As soon as the man unlocked the door, Burke pushed inside. "Ms. Turner?"

A moan answered him.

Burke darted behind the counter. Keely lay crumpled, facedown on the floor beside a step stool. His adrenaline surged at the sight. "She's down!"

Dropping to one knee, he checked her carotid pulse. Had she gotten hit? "She has a pulse." He bent his face down to feel her breath against his cheek. "She's breathing." Then he gently rolled her head to view the underside. "One small cut over her right eye." Relief rushed through him.

In spite of his concern, Burke continued the routine he knew so well. He ran his hands over Keely's form, looking for, feeling for, more blood.

Someone had fired at the school, probably not meaning to injure anyone. But bullets ricocheted and traveled farther than people expected. He found no sign of any other injury on Ms. Turner, and the tension inside him eased. She hadn't been seriously injured.

But the ugly gash marred the pale skin of her forehead, lending her a vulnerability that tugged at his sympathy. "She must have fallen and bumped her head. Ms. Turner, can you hear me?"

Her eyes fluttered open. She looked at him, then frowned. "Deputy?"

Thankful that she'd regained consciousness without medical aid, he asked the necessary question, "Do you remember hearing anything?"

"Yes." She started to rise. "Shots. Someone shot . . . the windows." She groaned.

"Take it easy," he cautioned, taking hold of her slender shoulders. *It was my duty to prevent something like this!* Knowing thoughts like this only clouded his judgment, he concentrated on Ms. Turner. "Can you feel your arms and legs?"

"Of course I can," she said in a grumpy tone.

He grinned. Her spirit hadn't been quenched—good!

"Then let me help you up." He assisted her to a sitting position on the avocado carpet.

"Who was . . . shooting?" she asked.

Her expression—clouded, uncertain—kept him close. Violence took a toll on a person. Burke sat on his heels at her side.

Rodd replied, "We don't know yet, Ms. Turner. But we'll find out—and fast. Can you tell us what happened?"

"I came out to find some data . . . and climbed on the step stool," she replied slowly as though thinking hurt her. "I heard . . . shots. I remember falling. . . ." Her words trailed off.

Her paleness worried Burke. He wanted to carry her to a lounge, somewhere she could lie down. Instead, he kept his hands clasped in front of him. She should be moved as little as possible till the EMTs checked her over. "You must have hit your head as you fell."

She nodded, pressing one hand to her temple.

"Hey!" a gruff voice from outside the broken window hailed them. "Is Ms. Turner all right? Did she get shot?"

Rising, Burke glanced out and saw the crowd had moved to outside the window. "Don't pick up or disturb anything. You could destroy evidence. Back up," Burke ordered.

Rodd stepped to the window. "Which of you saw something or someone at the time of the shooting?"

A few people raised their hands.

"You saw the shooting?" Rodd pressed them. "You didn't just hear the shooting?"

A few hands went down.

"Okay," Rodd said, "I'm coming out to take your statements. Please step away from the window."

"Burke, you take care of examining the crime scene. I'll do the questioning—"

The insistent wail of the arriving ambulance cut off the

exchange. The sound sent cool relief through Burke. Now the lady would be checked out and made more comfortable. He touched her shoulder. "Stay—"

"Ms. Turner," the maintenance man interrupted, "can I go ahead and call the glass company to board up these windows? Before we know it, moths will be all over every-thing, making a real mess."

Keely looked to Burke.

"Go ahead. Call them." Burke motioned to the EMTs entering with a stretcher. "Here she is." He glanced down. "I'll be right back. I have to get the camera from my Jeep. When I've taken pictures of everything inside and out and collected physical evidence, the windows can be boarded up from outside." He touched her shoulder again, reluctant to leave her even for a few minutes. "Will you be okay till I get back?"

She nodded.

Her forlorn expression reminded him of the shock he'd felt the first time someone had started shooting around him. He squeezed her shoulder. "Hang in there," he murmured.

Burke hustled outside into the warm August evening. He pushed his way through the growing crowd to his Jeep. Two more deputies had arrived. One stood by the school door to keep nonwitnesses out, and the other stood in front of the broken window area to keep people from tampering with the crime scene perimeter. Wanting to get back to Keely fast, Burke dug into the glove compartment and pulled out the compact digital camera case.

Just as he reached back to close his car door, his radio crackled and spat out, "Sloan, disturbance at the LF Café. Code three."

Burke unhooked the receiver. "I copy that. On my way." He shouted the information to the nearest deputy and took off in his Jeep.

Only blocks away, he pulled up in front of the café and looked inside the large front window. Walachek was there, shouting at a woman standing by the cash register. *Why am I not surprised it's him?*

"Walachek!"

The big man, obviously very drunk but unarmed, swung around. "You!" He charged Burke.

Near the door, Burke bodychecked Walachek, then dodged him. He turned back and landed a hard punch to Walachek's jaw. The man went down. Burke leaped out of the way, preventing Walachek from taking him down too. Bending, he handcuffed the breathless man on the floor, then hauled him up and out to the Jeep. He pushed him into the backseat and slammed the door after him.

The woman from the café ran outside. "Thank you! Thank you!" Her voice shook. "That man belongs behind bars!"

Burke nodded, reaching for his cell phone. "What was Walachek doing here? Do you know him?"

"I'm the sister of his late wife. I've got his daughter—"

That explained everything. "Was he threatening you about taking Carrie?"

"Yes."

Burke burned with aggravation. That injudicious judge would be faced with Walachek a second time in two days. Burke hoped he'd have enough sense to keep Walachek locked up this time. "Someone will be back to take down your statement. I've got to get back to the high school."

"What happened at school?" the woman asked. "I heard the sirens."

He gave her the bare facts and then drove off. He'd hand Walachek over to another deputy at the school, who could run him to the county jail. Burke had more important work to do, the physical investigation.

And though he would examine the crime scene thoroughly, now it didn't take a genius to guess who was responsible for shooting out the windows of Ms. Turner's office.

※ ※ ※

THE SOUND OF the crickets and cicadas surged in Keely's hearing. Half-asleep on the screened-in back porch of the Family Closet, she opened her eyes. She had the feeling someone was watching her.

"Ms. Turner? It's Deputy Sloan."

The deputy! She jerked up in the Adirondack chair, and all that happened hours before came flooding back. She pressed a hand to her forehead, where the swollen bruise reminded her of her fall. She felt a little sick, dizzy. Then she glanced through the moonlit shadows beyond the screen door.

Here he was—just the man she'd been thinking of before she drifted into semiconsciousness. Burke Sloan stood on the steps, moonlight glinting off the brass buttons and badges on his uniform. Awareness trickled through her, a tide awakening her senses. The cool breeze brushed over her skin, and moth wings whispered around the screens.

"Sorry to disturb you, ma'am."

Her heart beat double time—from surprise? Or from knowing the identity of the man who'd surprised her awake? Hoping this didn't show, she hastily lowered her bare feet from the matching footstool and swiveled in her seat. *Why did I slip off my sandals? Because you didn't expect* him *to appear here!* For some reason, having bare feet made her feel extra vulnerable. *And I feel fragile enough already.* Then a nasty thought startled her and she asked, "Did something else happen at the school!"

"No, ma'am. But we got a call that someone was lurking around the Family Closet."

"Don't call me ma'am. I can see we might as well get on a first-name basis, Burke." Rising, she unlatched the screen door, letting herself groan softly with irritation. "Let me guess. It was Veda McCracken." *Veda had to know it was me out here. I come here often enough, day and night. She just wanted to embarrass me if she could. The old snoop.* "The McCracken woman lives within binocular distance and watches this place like a hawk." *Hoping to make trouble for us.*

"I don't know who called it in." He mounted the steps and came in, shutting the door behind him quickly, keeping the mosquitoes out. "I just finished up the crime scene at your office and got the call from dispatch. I said I'd check it out on my way home."

"Sorry if I sounded grumpy." Her dry mouth tasted like a used dishrag, and she wanted to stall him, find out what he'd discovered at the crime scene—which after all, was her office. Also she didn't want to be alone right now. She'd come to this familiar place for comfort and had fallen asleep. Being startled awake put her on edge again. She took a deep breath. "Are you thirsty, Burke?"

He looked at her. "Sure. Water would be good . . . Keely."

His relaxed stance made her feel more scattered than she already did. "Have a seat." She motioned toward the matching Adirondack chair next to hers and entered the kitchen at the back of the store.

Returning with two glasses of ice water, she handed him one. He nodded his thanks and eased against the slanted chair back. She sat down, very aware of his large form just inches from her. Her pulse betrayed his effect on her. *Why am I reacting so foolishly? Is it because he's a new face? Get over it. I don't have time or energy for this now.* She closed her eyes, shutting out his disturbing presence, focusing on the night. Its sounds had died down again, now just the lulling song of crickets. Too soon, the cooler evenings would still the nocturnal chorus.

"Since I had to stop here," his voice intruded, "mind my asking why you're here and not home?"

"I volunteer here and have a key," she replied. *I have a question for you, too, Deputy.* Should she ask him the question that had troubled her since coming to on the floor at school? Would asking it be a good idea or a disastrous one? *Why do I have to deal with this, Lord? Why did my father have to put me in this situation?*

She repeated his question to herself. If he weren't a police officer, she'd have taken umbrage. But it was probably just part of his routine. He'd stopped, and it was his duty to ask why she was here when she should have been home in bed.

Bracing herself, she took a sip of the cool water and then held the glass against the aching bump on her forehead. Reluctance to reveal her reason for being here held her mute. But she'd seen him outside her door last night. He probably already had an inkling of why she was hiding out here! Why beat around the bush? "You came to my door last night, didn't you?"

After a brief hesitation, he reached into his pocket and pulled out her missing lipstick.

"That's where that went. Thanks." She took the silvery tube from him. His fingers brushed hers, and the hair on the back of her neck prickled. Banking this tingling sensation down, she gazed out the screen into the gray shapes of bushes and a clothesline in the yard. "Then you know why I'm not home tonight. When I called to tell my father about the window thing at school, he was still hip-deep in his ongoing war with Grady. I couldn't face it."

"That your brother's name?" He glanced at his watch and then undid the top button on his collar.

Had he checked the time to see if he was off duty before officially relaxing? The action fit him so well. Then she paused to watch his hand loosen his tie, a very male movement.

She looked away. "Yes . . . and I just didn't feel like witnessing the latest skirmish. Last night Grady was grounded for the millionth time. Sorry to be so blunt, but this is a small town and you'd hear about the latest Turner family war soon enough."

"I try not to listen to gossip."

"Then buy a good pair of earplugs." She gave a short unamused laugh. A Turner was always on display! She couldn't even sit silently in the dark all by herself without someone calling the sheriff.

She worried her lower lip. Should she go ahead and ask him if he'd found any evidence tonight? Her brother's track record of misbehavior made it impossible for her to overlook the possibility—even though a faint one—that he might be a suspect in tonight's shooting. A recently overheard argument about Grady's lack of skill at target practice played back in her mind. Her father wanted Grady to go hunting with him this deer season, and Grady was resisting as usual, probably due to his blanket principle of noncooperation.

Grady was grounded. He couldn't have been out tonight. But he'd snuck out before. She closed her eyes. When her father had started in on Grady about learning to handle a gun, she hadn't said anything. But had putting a rifle into her rebellious brother's hands been a wise idea?

And would it be wise to consult this officer about the possibility that Grady might have shot out the windows? Or would that only make matters worse? On the other hand, if this man had found evidence that might prove Grady was responsible, saying anything would be meaningless. She glanced at Burke sideways. Did he ever get restless?

Another worry flickered in her mind. One of the math teachers had sent her a note saying that he'd had to separate Grady and Burke's nephew earlier today. The two had been taunting each other in his class. It would be just like her brother to pick on a new kid, just to stir up trouble. A silent groan worked its way through her. But she wasn't about to burden Burke with that right now!

Her head ached more. She drew in breath. *Heavenly Father, I've prayed and prayed for Grady. Only you can change his heart. What's it going to take to get through to him? I don't know how much longer I can carry this burden. I'm sorry, but I want to get away from this endless wrangling. I just want to be free of it all!*

◈ ◈ ◈

BURKE TOOK A long swallow of the cold water and let its coolness flow downward. This woman had a way of putting him on edge, not an angry edge. She just made it harder to talk to her . . . without staring. She reclined in the Adirondack chair like a woman in a painting. Her every move was graceful. And her honesty was refreshing—to a cop. People lied to him so many times. . . .

Why had she come to a thrift shop this late? She should be at home by this time. And how did Turner's daughter fit in with a resale shop anyway? "Do you come here often late at night?"

She sighed that soft feminine sigh of hers that he'd found so intriguing last night. "I help run the Family Closet. It's a charity outreach. Since I don't have a place of my own, I come here when I want to be . . . by myself. Living at home is getting old . . . I'm just about to move into a new home over on Loon Lake. But there have been . . . delays." Her voice became grim in the last sentence.

"It's hard to live with family when you're used to being on your own." The truth of her statement tightened his throat. Boarding in Harlan's house and having Nick around threw Burke off, shook up his whole routine.

Every day he found himself wondering if he should be home for a meal or checking on where his nephew was. Worse, he found himself watching Nick, trying to figure out what the kid was thinking and if it was something Burke should be worrying about. After all, if Nick hadn't gotten into trouble in Milwaukee, he wouldn't be here finishing high school. Was it just a matter of time till . . . what? Nick tried to run away? started a fight at school? shot out some windows?

Worrying about someone else every day was working on him. His peace of mind was breaking up. He didn't feel like himself anymore. What if this started affecting his work? To be a good deputy, he had to remain cool, detached . . .

"I've lived at home," Keely's voice intruded, "since I came back with my bachelor's degree." She stretched out on the chair and propped her bare feet up on the stool. "Then right away, I started commuting nights to do my master's. I just didn't have time to keep house. But this year, I graduated and broke ground. My home should be done very soon."

So she had her master's and he had two years of law enforcement. She'd probably been one of those little girls who had an answer for every question the teacher asked. He'd not been the studious type himself. Recess had been his favorite subject.

He glanced at her sideways. Her pale feet fascinated him, and they looked so well cared for. He couldn't help noticing things that didn't add up. Her parents had a big house. Did that denote wealth or merely pretension? Keely Turner drove a brand-new SUV—worth what? Around forty thousand. And now she was building a home. Teachers must make good money in this county, or did her parents provide extra for her? Questions.

More importantly from his prospective though, he'd expected her to probe him about the crime scene. Why hadn't she?

She glanced at him. "So am I allowed to ask what you found tonight?"

He was relieved that she'd finally asked what any person would expect after tonight's events. Years of questioning had taught him to analyze not only what people told him but also what they chose not to say. Still, he had the feeling that she was holding back something. "You can ask," he deadpanned.

"And what would you reply?" Her hair had come undone and lay tumbled on her shoulders. The moonlight picked up the golden highlights, inviting him to reach over and rub strands of it between his fingers.

He forced this image out of his mind. "The investigation is proceeding through the normal routine," he said dryly.

"I am the principal, remember. I'll have to know what you find out because I'll have to take the matter to the board."

"My reply only signified that I'm just starting. If I find some hard evidence, I'll let you know."

"Okay, Deputy. Then we won't pursue that now. I checked your nephew's file today. I wasn't prying," she added quickly. "I wanted to see if the counselor had placed him in the right classes. Our one counselor does all the student scheduling and, at times, takes a somewhat . . . cavalier . . . attitude when we get a new student. He kind of dumps them in anywhere there's an open desk."

"I see." It irked him that she'd looked up Nick's file. Her reasoning sounded on target, but that didn't make him like it.

He tried not to stare at her long, slender arm resting on

the chair beside him. Why couldn't he ignore her? *I don't have time for this attraction right now. Stop noticing her!*

"Your nephew is quite bright, but . . ." She paused. "I noticed that there was a pronounced downward slide in his grades last year. Is there anything that I need to know in order to help him?"

That's a very good question. He didn't know her well enough to give her more information. He thought she would be fair, but perhaps he'd find that this woman was a stickler or prone to make snap judgments. Burke knew how kids could get branded as problems. That's one of the reasons he'd brought Nick with him.

But more than Nicky's grades had gone down the tube last year. Keely's words reminded him of how inept he felt in this situation. *How do I turn Nicky—this whole situation—around?* It would be nice to have someone who worked with teens on a regular basis to talk over what to do with him. But would that be prejudicial to Nicky's fresh start? And how could Burke ask for her help?

Then he was forced to wrestle with the unpleasant fact that she'd read his nephew's file. That must have included all the truancy, detentions, and suspensions Nicky had racked up in one year. No secrets left to protect.

"You don't know me," she conceded, "but I try to help my students."

Burke watched her lower the glass from her forehead and take a sip. The incongruity hit him again. What was this beautiful woman doing here on the back porch of a shabby thrift shop? She belonged on a magazine cover.

So far he'd heard only positives about Keely Turner—though a few people had made strange comments about her father, like the ones Wendy and her grandfather had made this evening. And what was with that arguing at her house last night?

He went over her behavior last night and tonight and made his decision. He'd go with his gut instinct—that this woman would care and give good advice. And he needed good advice.

"Nicky's parents divorced two years ago." He hesitated, recalling the bombshell this had caused in the family. His three brothers had itched to "deal" with their erring brother-in-law. "Then Nicky's dad got a new job in New York. Now he doesn't get back to Milwaukee much and couldn't have Nicky to New York last summer like he'd promised—"

"I get the picture," she cut in. "Unfortunately, it's a common one—adults with no time for their kids. It's good Nick has a caring uncle like you."

Her innocent words stabbed him like red-hot knives. *You were too busy for Nicky, too,* his conscience chided. *This all could have been avoided if you'd . . .*

Her cell phone rang in the stillness. She put down her glass and reached for her purse on the floor by the chair. "Hello, Father." Her voice sounded tight. Pause. "Yes, I'm planning on coming home tonight." Irritation crept into her tone. "I'm just discussing what happened tonight with the new deputy. Please go to bed. I may be a little longer. Okay. Good night."

She put the phone away and gave Burke a glance. "I guess I better get going. Usually he wouldn't worry like this."

"After what you've been through the past two nights, he wants to make sure you're safe."

She only nodded; then she slipped on her sandals and gathered up her things.

He rose with her. "I'll follow you most of the way home anyway. It's on my way." But the impression that she was holding out on him still nagged him. *I asked you my question, but what was it you wanted to ask me, Ms. Turner? And why didn't you ask me? What are you hiding?*

CHAPTER FOUR

ON THE SUNNY morning after the shooting at the school, Burke jogged down the steps of the county courthouse on Main Street in Steadfast. The investigation was moving along. He had the search warrant he needed to get the rest of the evidence from last night's crime. He halted and stared at the outstretched hand in front of him.

"You Sloan?" The man's powerful voice carried through the clear morning air, calling attention to itself. "I'm Turner, Franklin Turner."

Though annoyed at the interruption, Burke nodded, shook the hand, and then studied Keely's father, in daylight this time. Turner was a tall, distinguished-looking man. "Nice to meet—"

"Have you found out—" Turner's brows drew together—"who shot at my daughter last night?"

The question hit Burke wrong. So far everyone else had jumped to the conclusion that some kid had just driven by and shot out the windows as an act of aimless vandalism. And that's what Burke wanted everyone to go on thinking until he'd solved this case. He especially didn't want his suspicion that it was Walachek who had shot out the windows getting spread around. Why worry Keely with this nasty suspicion when it might turn out to be some vandal after all? He decided to use misdirection. "Since your daughter's car was parked behind the school, the assumption is that the shooter didn't realize she was in the building—"

"Humph! There's no reason for her to be at that school. There's no need for my daughter to work at all. But Keely's always been independent."

The man's peremptory tone and boasting made Burke bristle. So the Turners did have money—just as he'd suspected. Biting back his heated response to the man, Burke digested this information. It didn't sit well with him. But why? He'd recognized right off that Keely Turner was a step above him. Definitely a cut above.

And evidently Turner didn't require a reply to continue with his speech on the superiority of his family. "But if a Turner was going to waste her life at that blasted school, I told the school board chairman that since she'd do a better job than anyone else she might as well replace the retiring principal." He somehow combined a glare and a half smile.

Why are you telling me all this? If the man was trying to impress Burke, he'd failed—miserably. Another thought hit Burke. Was this bragger warning him to stay away from his daughter? *Save your breath, Turner. I already get the picture.* Steaming inside, Burke took a step away.

Then Turner leaned closer. "She knows how to run a taut ship. I taught her that much. Now if I could just whip her brother into shape." A frown drew the man's whole face downward.

Burke nodded noncommittally and distanced himself with another downward step. He wondered if Keely had any idea her father had pressured the school board into naming her principal and was going around bragging about it. He doubted it—she struck him as a straight arrow.

But it explained the mystery of how such a young woman filled that position—and at a school where her younger brother was a student. Not a good position to be in, he thought with sympathy. And her own father had engineered that awkward position for her. What a jerk.

Burke had met Keely only two days ago, but he already knew how embarrassed she'd be if she'd overheard her father's speech. And why did his thoughts keep returning to her? While working on a case, it wasn't like him to focus on a woman, let his feelings get involved. But Keely Turner wasn't like any woman he'd ever met.

Burke took another step down. "If you'll excuse me, I've got places I have to be."

"Right." Turner looked surprised as though he wasn't used to others ending conversations with him. "Don't waste any time wrapping up this investigation. I want whoever took potshots at my daughter caught ASAP."

We are in complete agreement there, Turner. But he repeated in a firm tone, "We are investigating all possibilities, but your assumption doesn't seem likely." Burke ended with a curt nod.

He headed for his Jeep, going over a second time what Keely's father had said and wondering why the man had taken the time to stop and talk to him. Maybe Turner was just an overprotective father. Was he checking him out?

Turner knew that Burke had been with Keely late last night, so was he laying down the groundwork to tell Burke that he wasn't good enough for his daughter? Burke had seen that at first glance. Then the memory of Keely's slender form reclining in the—

Burke's cell phone rang. It was Rodd. "We've received two anonymous phone calls about the shooting. One caller said that he'd seen Grady Turner in LaFollette last night about the time of the shooting."

Keely had said her brother was grounded last night. Had she said that on purpose? He didn't think so. "Why would he shoot at his sister's windows?"

"According to the caller, everyone knows that Grady has a chip on his shoulder about his sister and . . ."

"And?" Had this been on Keely's mind last night? She'd mentioned friction at home.

"And he has a twenty-two rifle. That's what you're looking to match, right?"

"Right. Did the second caller say the same or something different?"

Rodd paused before replying. "I didn't mention this before, but two people from the neighborhood whom I questioned said they saw Harlan's truck near the high school right before the shooting."

Burke's stomach clenched. That meant Nick had been in the vicinity of the shooting last night. Again, he heard Nick's lame excuse for not showing up for dinner: "I wasn't hungry. I just drove around and came home. What's the big deal?"

Was Nick capable of shooting out school windows? *God, forgive me, I don't know. How could I have been so blind?* A familiar quote taunted his memory: *"There are none so blind as those who will not see."* Even his recent target practice with Nick—something he'd thought would bring them together—now took on the appearance of further negligence on his part. *I never thought . . .*

If this accusation proved to be true, how would he explain this to his sister? Burke cleared his throat. "Do you want me to pursue these leads, get bullets from both kids' guns? Do you think Turner would make us get a search—"

"Hold up. This is a small town. I don't want to damage either kid's reputation by casting suspicion his way on the basis of anonymous calls. There's no rush. The judge is keeping Walachek in jail on charges so we have time. Before we ask for any more search warrants, let's check out the most obvious suspect. You still going to send Walachek's bullets to Hansen at MPD?"

"Yeah. Hansen still owes me a few favors, and the state lab could hold this up for weeks. I'm sending the evidence off right after I hang up—"

"Wait." Rodd stopped him. "You have to head straight to the high school first."

"Why? Did something else happen?" Burke's voice rose in disbelief.

"Keely Turner called. She needs to see you right away. Your nephew's sitting in her office."

A lead ball landed in Burke's gut. He'd known Nick would give him trouble, but this wasn't good timing. One thing on top of another and it was only the first full week of school! Another danger was that Keely might start classing Nick as a troublemaker right off the bat. He knew how a reputation could dog a kid. "Thanks, Rodd," he said dryly.

Within ten minutes, Burke walked into the principal's area at LaFollette High. He knew how to handle an investigation. He knew how to reassure the school board at a meeting. But how did he handle being the guardian of a kid in trouble at school? Especially when the principal was an attractive woman he couldn't get out of his mind?

He paused just inside the door. Keely had her long, slender back to him, leaning against the counter talking to a woman, probably her secretary, behind the counter.

Keely's hair was pulled up high again. Little wisps trailed at the back of her neck. She wore a suit—pale yellow linen, expensive. Again, everything about Keely's appearance belied her position here. She didn't look like she belonged in this shabby building.

Well, she didn't, according to her father. Why *was* she

here? Why had she stayed in LaFollette and taken on the job as principal at a small consolidated high school? Burke didn't think her father's opinion weighed much with her. What made her tick?

His mind snapped back to reality. Nick was depending on him. If Nick was guilty, Burke would make sure that he got a reasonable punishment. But if he wasn't guilty, he wasn't going to let Nick be the fall guy just because he was new.

Keely didn't strike him as unfair, but you never knew. He'd just met her father. Did the acorn fall far from the tree? He pulled himself together. *I'm here on business, unpleasant business. Stick to business.*

"Are you sure you feel well enough to be at school today?" the silver-haired secretary was asking, sounding motherly.

"I'm fine," Keely replied. "Really. I'm just a bit tired from not getting much sleep after all the excitement."

Would Keely's father let on to her about his suspicion in last night's incident? His sympathy stirred in spite of the situation. This lady didn't deserve having to deal with the idea that someone might have been shooting at *her,* not just her school.

They'd called each other by their first names last night, but in this setting, he reverted to formality. "Ms. Turner?"

She turned around. "Officer Sloan."

In the bright sunlight, the purple bruise on her forehead disturbed him. The secretary was right. Keely should be resting today, not here dealing with his nephew. His stomach smoldered. *Nicky, if you're guilty of some stunt, you're in for it.*

The secretary cleared her throat loudly. "So you're the new deputy." She looked him over and then held out her hand. "I'm Freda Loscher. Been secretary here since the dawn of time. Welcome to the county."

He stepped forward and shook her plump hand. He'd be happy when he'd gotten through all the introductions around here. "Nice to meet you," he said. Then he lifted an eyebrow at Keely, bracing himself for bad news. "You needed to see me, Ms. Turner?"

"Yes." She dipped her chin. "I'm afraid that your nephew got into trouble this morning." She nodded toward a small room off to the side. Through the open door, he glimpsed his nephew sitting with his head down. Nick didn't look up.

"He was a busy bee in the parking lot," Freda inserted in a chatty tone. "He let the air out of a whole row of tires. Mine included. What's his problem?"

"Freda," Keely said repressively, "I'll take the deputy into my office and discuss this." She motioned him toward her door.

Her prim tone did the trick. Freda hurried back to her desk. Franklin Turner was right about one thing: Keely knew how to run a taut ship. Nick could be in for it. Burke entered her office, across from the one where Nick sat, and waited for her to close the door behind them. Watching her take her place behind the desk distracted him. *Focus on business.* He sat. "Are you sure Nicky is the one responsible?"

She sighed, sounding fatigued. "Yes, he didn't even attempt to hide what he was doing. A teacher on the second floor looked out and watched him go from car to car, uncapping tire stems and unscrewing valves."

What did Nick hope to accomplish with this stunt? "Why didn't the teacher report it right away?" Burke complained. Lax discipline here wouldn't help him turn Nick around.

"The teacher did, but by the time a student got to me with the note, your nephew had finished one row of cars and started on the next. He was *supposed* to be in his first class." She sounded as if she were trying to give Nick the benefit of the doubt. But Nick had forced her hand.

His hand too. *Cocky kid. Wanted to be caught, I bet.* Had Nick done this just to embarrass Burke, the new deputy? Did a seventeen-year-old kid think like that? *Lord, I'm out of my league here.*

What had happened here last night rushed through him. Seeing Keely facedown on the floor had affected him more than seeing a victim he didn't know. He could see now that keeping the law in a small town would be different. He'd know more of the victims and perps as people.

"Burke?"

"So he was skipping class and vandalizing cars," Burke repeated.

"Yes, that's it unfortunately. But no property was destroyed and no one was hurt."

He nodded, frowning. Compared to the possibility that Nick could have shot out her windows last night, this wasn't as serious. But he couldn't let Nick get away with this because it looked so innocent by comparison. Considering the fact that both their relatives were suspects in a case made the whole situation . . . sticky. "What's the punishment for this type of prank?"

She raised her eyebrows at him. "A one-day suspension—after he gets an air pump and reinflates all the tires he flattened."

"Is that all?" He slid forward on his chair. "Sounds like—"

"Let the punishment fit the crime. I'll save the big guns for . . . well, *if* I need them in the future. But let's hope this will be enough to prevent a further incident."

"Okay." He moved to stand.

She stopped him with a raised hand. "Before you leave,

I'd like to ask—what do you think your nephew was trying to accomplish today? I need some hint if the staff and I are going to help him get settled in here."

Discussing how to handle Nick only emphasized how out in left field he felt. He hated to have to bare his nephew's problems to someone else—since his neglect had contributed to Nick's difficulties. Burke had put duty to the MPD before his family, and now Nick might pay the price. Burke gripped the wooden arms of the chair and then met her eyes. "I don't usually deal in rehabilitation. But I suppose you need to."

She smiled with sympathy and moved from behind her desk, settling herself on its edge. "Yes, I do because I'm in the business of helping teens mature so that *you* won't have to deal with them later."

Her nearness distracted him. He wished she'd stayed behind her desk. But he admired her for offering him help with Nick. Her whole handling of this prank impressed him. Though his nephew might not recognize it, he'd lucked out with this new principal. Still, this thought didn't ease Burke's shame.

"Okay," he started grudgingly, "my nephew didn't *want* to come with me to Steadfast. But my family—" *especially my father*—"thought Nicky needed a strong male influence."

"I see." She nodded. "Well, that helps me understand this better. I will say this. Nicky wasn't rude or disrespectful when caught—"

"Why should he be? He wanted you to catch him. He may think that if he acts up enough I'll send him home." *No way, Nick!*

"That fits teen logic." She grinned.

Her amusement loosened a tightness inside him. *That's right—he just let air out of some tires. No bloodshed.* "It also won't work. He's here for the year and I'll tell him so."

Burke stood up. "If that's all, I'll run him over to the garage and pick up an air pump."

"Good. I wish all guardians were as cooperative."

"I'll make sure Nick takes responsibility." He'd been on edge when he came in, ashamed. Dealing with Nick kept his emotions mixed up daily. Could this be why he was more susceptible to this appealing woman? Or was it just the lady herself?

I don't have time for attraction now. As a guardian of a teenager, I don't even rank as adequate yet. Lord, any one of my brothers would have been more help to Nicky than I am!

She accompanied him into the outer office. There, a kid of medium build and with spiked blond hair stood, propped against the counter. "Hey, Sis, I need a pen. Lost my last one."

So this was Keely's baby brother. Burke looked him over, recalling the anonymous call. So here was another suspect. Burke noted the resemblance to Turner, their father. More to the point though, he didn't like the insolent way the kid looked at his sister.

"The school store," she said, "will be open during lunch—"

"But I'll lose points for not having one in my next class," the kid complained.

"That's unfortunate—"

"This your brother, Grady?" Burke asked to cut off the wrangling, make the kid aware of him.

"Yes. Burke Sloan," she performed the introduction, "Grady Turner."

Burke offered his hand to the teen. "I hear you were in town last night."

"Couldn't have been me." The teen dropped Burke's hand. "I was grounded." He turned to his sister. "So you can't afford to give me a measly ten-cent pen?"

To Burke's experienced ear, Grady's too quick, too casual denial rang false.

"If this was the first time you'd asked . . ."

While Keely lowered the boom on her brother for his careless attitude, Burke watched Freda open the door to the small adjoining room and shoo Nicky out to him. Grady was blond. Nick was dark like his dad, and he had a cocky grin on his face, too.

Burke straightened. "Wipe that smirk off your face, Nicky—"

"Don't call me that," the teen snapped, "Uncle *Burke-ee.*"

Grady barked a laugh that sounded more like a sneer. "So the new kid's uncle's a cop?" Before anyone could respond, he left, slamming the door behind him.

Ignoring Grady's dramatic exit, Burke regretted the slip. Maybe Nick hadn't wanted anyone to know about their connection, but in a small town it wouldn't have taken long to get around. "Nick, apologize to Ms. Turner for behaving like a jerk this morning."

Nick glared at him.

"Do it—" Burke stiffened his tone—"or you won't be driving yourself to school tomorrow."

Nick flushed. "I apologize, Ms. Turner." The words sounded wrung from him.

She nodded and then turned to Burke. "One moment please. I heard that Walachek was arrested again last night. Why?"

Burke didn't like this line of questioning. It was too close to his real suspicion. "Walachek was harassing the cashier at the café in town here. I arrested him and turned him over to another deputy to run in."

"I see. It's over Carrie's custody, right?"

You're too smart, Keely. Don't go there. Hoping she wouldn't guess what could only upset her, he said, "Don't worry. Walachek isn't going to get out this time. No judge is going to let him put up bail a second time. The man has threatened two women two nights in a row. That can't be ignored."

She nodded again but with pursed lips.

"I'll call when I have anything on the shooting." With a hand at the back of Nick's neck to urge his nephew out the door, Burke walked out.

❖ ❖ ❖

KEELY HESITATED OUTSIDE the doorway of her office. Watching the deputy walk away through the sunlit main entrance held her in place.

His effect on her students was no less striking. The hallway as usual was clogged with noisy students rushing to their next classes. But Burke parted them like Moses parting the Red Sea.

She heard the students' voices: "That's the deputy. . ." "From Steadfast . . ." "What's he doing . . ." "Maybe they caught whoever shot . . ."

Memories rushed though her—Burke helping her up last night, his tender touch, his sympathy. And today his no-nonsense, right-to-the-point manner impressed her. What a nice change from most parents. Don't be too hard on your nephew, Burke. This was Nick's first trick, and no one was hurt. Would more follow?

Coming back to the present, she tried to tighten her control over herself. *I can't stand here gawking at Burke. Not with Freda watching.* Keely couldn't let anyone here even suspect that she'd noticed the man.

I should turn and walk into my office. But she couldn't bring herself to move or stop watching Burke until the outside door closed behind him. That finally broke their connection. She turned to find Freda right behind her.

"My, so that's the new deputy," Freda cooed.

Keely felt her cheeks warm. "Yes, he's very efficient—"

"I should say so. That was the first word that popped into my mind when I saw him." Freda patted her heart. "Oh my, if I were only thirty years younger."

Keely refused to give Freda any reaction. Matchmaking was a popular hobby around here, especially with ever-romantic Freda. Keely would have to be more careful how she behaved around Burke. She walked into her office.

Burke's question came back to her. Why had he asked Grady if he'd been in town last night? Did he think Grady might have been the culprit in the drive-by shooting? Had Grady snuck out again? But even if that were true, why would he shoot out the school windows?

Waves of worry washed through her. Had Grady known she was at school last night? If he had shot the windows, did he realize that a bullet might have gone astray and wounded someone, her? Or could he have shot at her—wanting to scare her, hurt her? Her nerves quivered with each wave. How had things gotten so bad between her and her brother that she could even entertain thoughts like these?

The unwelcome answer popped into her mind. Grady was capable of doing this just to pay her father back for insisting that Grady learn how to shoot and for refusing to send Grady away to that school in California where he'd wanted to finish high school. Over and over, she'd wanted to repeat that verse in Ephesians to her father: "Don't make your children angry by the way you treat them." She thought her father sometimes went out of his way to anger her brother.

The bump on her head started throbbing again. *Dear Lord, what's the answer? Who's responsible? Why did this shooting happen? Is there anything I should be doing? I'm at a loss.*

Nearly a week had passed and every day Burke's mind had drifted, against his will, to the lovely principal of the high school. It had been years since a woman had entered his mind and refused to leave. Why her?

He'd tried to figure this out so the solution would break the connection he felt to her. So far, he'd only come up with the fact that besides being good-looking, she was excellent at her job and had a quality of transparent honesty that he'd rarely seen.

Maybe this was all due to the disruption of his life—the move, dealing with Nick, attending church again weekly. . . . Last Sunday, he'd come home feeling like a peeled onion—layers of his protective covering had been stripped from him. Pastor Weaver had preached on the parable of the unfaithful servant.

Burke had realized that he was like the third servant who'd buried his talents, not even gaining interest with the master's talents. Burke's remorse over not "spending himself" in doing what he could to help Nick get through his parents' divorce had expanded inside him, making it hard to swallow.

And to make everything worse, Walachek's bullet hadn't been a match, so the bullet from the crime scene had yet to be identified. Now Burke had no choice but to pursue the two anonymous phone calls implicating Grady and Nick. He had to compare bullets from the crime scene with ones from both firearms. He'd had to ask Harlan for a spent bullet from his rifle. And now he might need a search warrant to get bullets from the Turners' guns. To avoid this, Rodd had suggested Burke talk to Keely first.

Burke didn't want to talk to Keely first. It made him feel like a high school kid again—being sent to the principal. He didn't need the distraction of her now. It was one of the first times Burke could recall not agreeing with Rodd on a case. But Rodd was the sheriff, Burke's boss.

Evidently, Rodd had to worry about playing hardball with the son of the richest man in the county. Burke thought the Turners shouldn't get "gloves on" treatment. He knew what his working-class father would have to say to Rodd about that! This situation only reinforced that Burke had no business thinking about Keely Turner!

And now, to top everything off, he'd had just about enough of his nephew's lip for the day and it was only ten in the morning. Fuming, Burke pulled up to the little bungalow a few miles out of Steadfast, The Family Closet. The shop was closed for Labor Day. But when he'd called the Turner home, Keely's mother told him that Grady and Keely were there sorting new donations. Looking through the open garage door, Burke glimpsed Grady rummaging through a box.

Keely must be in the shop. He studied it. He hadn't gotten a good look at it that midnight visit when he'd sat and talked to Keely on its back porch. *Why does everything keep pulling me back to this woman?* It didn't help his mood that he'd even thought once or twice this week about calling her—just to hear her low voice. *I have to shake this. I have all I can handle.*

Switching off the ignition, he turned to Nick on the seat beside him. "Behave yourself here."

Nick said something under his breath.

Burke didn't ask him to repeat it. He just climbed out of the Jeep, slammed the door, and stalked to the thrift shop. He knocked on the door.

Keely opened it for him. "Mother called. She said you would be stopping by."

Inside, he halted, looking around. He'd been in a few consignment shops years ago—when he and Sharon were furnishing their apartment. . . . He shut down that line of thought—fast. He concentrated on this shop—so completely different. It had style. Even the used clothing and housewares looked . . . "This isn't so bad. It doesn't look depressing."

"Hey, thanks." Keely chuckled. "I'll tell our interior designer." She motioned him to follow her to the rear. "Come in. What brings you here?"

Keely's laughter eased his tension and just being near her warmed him like walking out into sunshine. Her presence made him want to relax, forget business, and simply experience the day. Listening here and there as he patrolled the county, he knew now why Keely had stayed in LaFollette—to help. People who didn't know her well resented her wealth. But those who knew her spoke of her giving heart. None of this changed the fact that she outclassed him in education, wealth—everything.

On this summery afternoon, she was wearing jean shorts and a pale blue blouse. As she preceded him, he tried not to focus on her long legs and arms. And again, she looked out of place in this setting. "Have you found out who shot the windows?"

He realized the moment he'd hoped wouldn't come had arrived. "No, I've just found out who didn't."

⬛ ⬛ ⬛

IN THE THRIFT shop kitchen, Keely went straight to the ironing board, stacked with cotton shirts. Burke had shaken up the tranquility of her day. Suppressed temper layered his final sentence. Irritation showed in his expression and the way he moved. She looked into Burke's eyes and was caught by their intensity. *What's upset him, Lord?* Had he discovered evidence that implicated Grady or his nephew? The thought that it might be Grady made her queasy.

His tension was palpable. She wished she could find a way to help ease his frustration. She'd been doing what she could to relax. Listening to Mozart, letting her mind float along on the melody while ironing was a tension releaser for her. What was his? "I'm not following you. I thought you were trying to find—"

"I didn't tell you earlier, but I suspected Walachek had taken a potshot at the school that night." He looked at her—a grim twist to his mouth and chin.

That's what set you off? Did he actually think that some-one had tried to shoot at her? *I'd much rather it be Walachek than your nephew or my brother!* Ignoring his gaze, she picked up the iron. "Ah." She pressed it down on a shirtsleeve and steam puffed up, hissing. She looked at him. "That had crossed my mind too."

He appeared disconcerted, shifting his weight to lean back against the kitchen counter. "I didn't want to worry you."

"Walachek's still in custody?" She smoothed the iron over the cotton. His passionate reaction to her being a target gave her an unusual feeling. She wasn't used to having someone concerned about protecting her.

"Yes."

"Then I'm not worried. And I don't think I was the target anyway. It's just our vandal or vandals." Which was maybe Nick or Grady or who? She concentrated on the shirt collar for a few moments, trying to ignore how his presence filled up the small, cluttered kitchen. "So who do you suspect now? Is that what you came to tell me?"

He looked her over with a glum expression. "I'm afraid that two teens were reported driving near the school that night and both had access to guns."

She concentrated on rearranging the shirt on the padded board. *He doesn't want to tell me. So that's what is bothering him—the fact that he might upset me. Let's get this out into the open.* Ignoring bad news never made it go away. "Grady and Nick?"

He stared at her. "You guessed?"

She shrugged, frustrated. "I told you you'd need earplugs if you were going to avoid gossip around here. I heard that Grady was seen in town that night—even though he was grounded. And your nephew was seen driving through town in Harlan's truck with the gun on the rack in the rear window."

Burke sat down at the cluttered kitchen table. Placing his elbows on his knees, he propped his chin on the back of his hands. She gazed at him. It was such a masculine pose. "Well, so much for information security." His voice twisted sardonically.

"It's not your fault. I'm sure no one in the sheriff's office said anything." Very aware of how intensely he was watching her, she hung the shirt on a hanger and lifted another from the ironing board. His attention made her feel . . . like he was noticing *her*—not Turner's daughter. Not Ms. Turner. A shiver trickled through her. His gaze had power.

"It's just the way a small town works," she said as naturally as she could. What would her father's reaction to Grady's being a suspect be? Whatever it was, it wouldn't be good! "Everyone's always watching and then talking about what they see. You shouldn't look so surprised! Veda reported me for sitting on this back porch! Remember? What do you do next?"

He frowned. "I've already taken a spent bullet from Harlan's gun and my hunting rifle." He looked up. "Now I'll need one from your brother's twenty-two. Rodd wants to know if you'd talk to your father about voluntarily giving us spent bullets from all his rifles."

She stilled. So that's why he'd come. He wanted her to

help him get her father to cooperate. Did the sheriff think she had any real influence with her father? *He'll go ballistic! And I want to be a million miles away!* "I don't—"

Crash!

It came from the garage and caught them both by surprise. Keely turned off the iron and headed for the door. "Grady! What fell?" Burke stayed at her heels through the connecting breezeway to the garage. "Grady!" she shouted.

Her brother bounced up from a pile of empty paint cans that he'd fallen backwards onto. His face twisted, he picked up the nearest object, a baby car seat. He sent it flying at Burke's nephew.

Nick caught it.

"Nick!" At her elbow, Burke yelled, "Stop!"

Nick ignored his uncle and lobbed the car seat back— hard.

Grady grabbed it.

"Grady!" she scolded.

But this time, with a glare at Keely, he slammed the car seat as hard as he could to the cement floor. The plastic seat thudded and bounced twice before landing on its side. Between the two bounces, something small and golden flew out from under the thick padding and onto the floor.

Her gaze fixed on the object, Keely heard Burke breaking up the fight. She walked over and bent down to look at what the fight had dislodged. It was a heart-shaped pendant on a gold chain that had the look of a family heirloom.

Was this what she thought it might be—a clue? Could this possibly have been in the seat from the beginning, in January when the car had exploded? She stopped herself from touching it. There might be fingerprints. *I'm overreacting.*

Or could it simply be Penny's? But it didn't look like anything Penny would have handled around the baby, letting it slip under the padding of the car seat. She'd never seen Penny wearing anything like it. And her friend hadn't mentioned losing anything of value. "Burke," she called.

"What?"

"Call the sheriff . . . now." She stared at the pendant, trying to make out the elaborate but faint engraving on it.

"What . . . why?"

"There's something here—it fell from the car seat." She swallowed, trying to moisten her mouth. "Penny Weaver brought that car seat in." Keely's voice shook as she thought about how this might affect her friend. "The Weavers' foster daughter, the one your department has been trying to identify since January, was found in—"

Burke was at her side. "That's the car seat from the exploded car?"

"Yes," she said, still staring at the necklace. "Maybe we should just call the Weavers."

Burke snapped open his cell phone. "We need them and Rodd. Don't touch it."

CHAPTER FIVE

JUST OVER AN hour later, Penny and Bruce Weaver, Rodd, Burke, and Keely sat around the oblong table in the small kitchen of the thrift shop. Keely had folded up the ironing board and poured iced tea, which no one was drinking. The softly buzzing window fan over the sink blew fresh air into the room, the atmosphere already heavy with concern.

Keely felt it inside her, a dull heavy ache in her midsection. Burke and the sheriff had donned gloves and examined the car seat thoroughly. They had found a slit on the underside of the padding. The slit had obviously been cut and then glued shut so the pendant had been concealed on purpose. The tossing of the seat, and then Grady's slamming it to the floor had broken the seat, and the necklace had flown out.

Now the car seat sat in the middle of the table and beside it on an envelope lay the vintage golden pendant. The name *Maria* was engraved faintly on the heart.

Both Penny and her husband, an attractive couple in their early thirties, looked subdued. Their expressions belied the fact that they were dressed for a picnic, for fun. They held hands.

After Burke's call, Rodd had come straight from his farm. He looked grim. Keely's heart went out to him too. No doubt he was remembering the day in January when he'd lifted this car seat with the baby in it out of the car. And then as he carried the baby to safety, the car had exploded into flames.

Keely glanced across at Burke. His eyes had that shuttered look she'd begun to recognize. That look signaled that his mind was turning, turning, examining events and he didn't want to be disturbed.

Unhappy at having his fight with Nick overshadowed, Grady had driven off in a huff. What had Burke thought of her brother and his nephew fighting with each other and then worse—her brother's leaving so rudely like that? It could only hurt his opinion of her brother.

A muffled whistling came from the garage. Grady's departure had left Nick alone, whom Burke had then ordered to sort clothing as punishment for fighting with her brother. Keely hoped Nick wouldn't take a dislike to the Family Closet over this. It was the kind of place he needed to volunteer at, a place that could show him how much worse life could be if one didn't count the cost. But now, Nick's insouciant whistling contrasted sharply with the somber mood of the five around the table.

"The waiting," Penny, looking crushed, began, "has been the worst—"

"Don't jump to conclusions," Keely said. "You might end up keeping Rachel."

"Keely's right," Rodd agreed. "Just because—"

"But the pendant isn't mine." Penny brushed the sheen of tears from her eyes. "It must belong to Rachel, to her mother—"

"The car seat might have been borrowed," Burke cut in, "or Rachel's mother might have bought it at another thrift shop and never knew the necklace was there. This might lead us to your foster child's parents or it might be another dead end."

Burke's logic was irrefutable. This might not give them the answer. It might only add another question to the unsolved mystery of who baby Rachel belonged to. This lowered the mood around the table.

Keely longed to leave this serious scene. Just an hour ago, she'd looked forward to a quiet day here, peacefully sheltered in this, her second home. But now she wanted to escape. Sunshine pouring into the windows and the warm breezes beckoned her.

Keely looked at the grave faces around her. "What do we do now?"

"First, we have to find out if anyone around here recognizes this necklace." Rodd pointed to it. "It's distinctive, obviously old, and engraved with the name *Maria,* so it should be easily identified. And second, the fact is the car was in this county when the accident happened."

He looked around, his jawline jutting out as though he expected an argument. "This county isn't a destination anyone would just casually choose, especially in January— especially last January, the coldest and snowiest recorded in nearly fifty years. If the couple who died . . ." Rodd took a deep breath. "If little Rachel is connected with anyone around here, this could be the link we've been hoping for."

"The couple might have been driving through here on their way somewhere north or west," Bruce offered, lifting one hand in obvious frustration.

Rodd nodded. "That means I'll need to get this story out to the papers—first to Cram for the *Steadfast Times* but also as far north as Duluth, west to Minneapolis, east to Green Bay, and everywhere in between. I'll take a digital photo of it and fax it out. It's the kind of mystery most small-town papers like to run, and I'll ask for information about it. I won't mention the baby angle the first time around."

"You think it's best to see what pops up first?" Burke asked.

Rodd nodded again. "Right."

"You never know what something like this can stir up," Burke agreed. "We'll probably end up with a lot of false leads. But that's all we can do now."

"That's not all we can do now," Bruce said. "God brought us little Rachel and he knows where she belongs. Let's pray." He took his wife's hand and bowed his head.

Everyone followed his lead. Keely's hand itched to reach out and take Burke's. She remembered how his strong hand had felt when they met. She folded hers together in her lap. The desire to hold the deputy's hand caught her off guard. She rarely had these flashes of attraction to someone. But that shouldn't surprise her. She spent her life surrounded by adolescents.

"Dear Father," Bruce prayed, "you know how much we have loved having Rachel with us. We are willing to keep this sweet child the rest of our lives, if that's your will. But if she belongs with someone else, if someone else is grieving over losing her, let us find that person, that mother or father. God, we want what you want, the very best for Rachel."

Yes, Lord, Keely prayed, *we do. God, this isn't up to us alone. You are acting in this situation. Thank you!*

"Let word of this evidence find the person who needs it. In Christ's name, amen," Bruce finished.

Each of them looked up. The prayer should have eased Keely's tension, but she felt a restlessness, unusual for her. She saw this reflected on Burke's face as he looked back at her. Was it because he suspected her brother of shooting the windows? Whether Grady was guilty or not, he knew how to push all of her buttons and had done so today. *Lord, this is all too much for me and too much for Burke. He needs a break. I need a break.*

Rodd grinned, showing how his spirit had lightened. "Thanks, Bruce. With God, we can't go wrong."

Nick sauntered in, slouching to show he didn't care that he'd been forced to obey. "Hey," he grumbled, "I sorted that stuff and I need to go."

The aggrieved voice tightened Keely's neck muscles. *Lord, could I have one day off from teenagers?*

"Harlan wanted me to drive him to the VFW Labor Day picnic."

Rodd stood up. "I'll drop you at Harlan's. It's on my way to Cram's." Rodd looked at Burke. "I'll take the photo right away and get busy on the fax machine. But I don't want you working on this." He gave Burke a pointed look. "You're not the sheriff and this is your day off. You've worked enough overtime since you arrived in Steadfast to finally make even me feel guilty. Take this lady—" he nodded toward Keely— "out for a bite of lunch." Rodd retreated with Nick beside him.

Bewildered by the sheriff's announcement, Keely turned to Penny and hugged her close. "Penny, I'll be praying for you."

Looking close to tears again, Penny nodded. Bruce squeezed Keely's upper arm affectionately and the couple left.

The Weavers' sadness had communicated, spread to her. Keely was so tired of worrying. *I need to do something completely unexpected—something that would let me shed all this worry, tension.* But what? She closed her eyes and an image came to her. *Yes! That's exactly where I want to be!*

Now all alone in the little kitchen, Keely and Burke looked at each other.

The deputy looked tense, uneasy, ready to explode with

frustration. He looked like a man who wanted to be doing, not waiting. Why had Rodd suggested that Burke take her to lunch? Had he caught the matchmaking virus? He didn't seem the type for that. Maybe he just thought she'd keep Burke from spending his day off working on this case in spite of the sheriff's orders. He should know Burke better than anyone else. And it would be nice to . . .

She leaned back against the counter, trying to figure out how to let Burke know that she didn't want to spend this beautiful afternoon alone, but that she didn't consider this a date. Saying that was impossible. *Stop thinking and just ask him. I'll waste the whole day!* "I don't know about you but I can't be serious one more minute."

He studied her and then nodded.

When he made no move or further comment, she decided to take action. And there was only one place to go. If he bowed out, so be it. "Let's get out of here." Without waiting for a reply, she reached for her purse, locked the back door, and headed toward the front. She switched off lights and fans as she went. "Coming?"

"Where are you going?" Burke followed her outside.

She closed and locked the door behind them. "I need something to cheer me up." *And so do you.* "If you're coming, come on."

She jumped into her Tahoe. Burke hovered at the passenger door with a show of reluctance. "I know you'd rather take your vehicle," she said, "but I'm driving 'cause I know the way."

He seemed to consider this. "Okay."

In all their conversations, Burke Sloan had never said a word he didn't need—so unlike her father who liked to hear his own voice.

But Burke's terseness piqued her curiosity. What was always going on underneath Burke's deputy sheriff's hat?

Thoughts about Nick? And what else? The impulse to remove the lid, to get to know this man was suddenly irresistible. She eased back in her seat, revved her engine once, and took off, gravel flying!

Opening the windows and turning up the country-western station, she headed down the back roads she knew so well. Today had turned out the perfect Labor Day—sunny and warm. Everyone's picnics would be held without wearing raincoats and without anchoring everything down so it wouldn't blow away.

The wind tossed her hair around as they bounced over dirt roads. She felt herself grinning. Tomorrow she'd return to school and again face all its challenges. Today she'd planned to spend the day spiffing up the Family Closet, but plans . . . had changed for the better!

Out of the corner of her eye, she observed the handsome deputy, whom every single woman in LaFollette was buzzing about. He was studying her as though she'd suddenly gone crazy. She grinned wider. Confounding him made her feel even freer, more audacious. She tapped the steering wheel in time to the music. It felt so good to run away!

Finally, she turned down a rutted lane and skirted a familiar thick stand of pines. The sight before her instantly heightened her joy. She drove up to the building site and parked. After a moment of drinking in the view, she glanced at him. "This is . . . *will be* my home soon." She opened her door and jumped out. "Come on in!"

※ ※ ※

KEELY LEFT BURKE behind in her car. He gazed out the windshield. Why had she brought him here to a long ranch home covered in sandy brick and shades of gray fieldstone? Though it was obviously still in process, it fit the setting—which looked like it had been waiting for such a dwelling.

Keely bounded to the door and unlocked it. Uncertain over this sudden change of events, he got out, still studying the house. He'd recognized the symptoms of catharsis in her. He'd seen it before when he'd been working with someone and they just had to stop and blow off steam before they broke under the pressure. But why had she included him in her escape? What did it mean? How should he react?

He made his way over the deep ruts in the ungraded drive and stopped on the newly poured concrete walk to the front door. Ducks flew overhead, quacking. They were heading for the lake he'd seen beyond one corner behind the house. He pictured the modest cabin he'd thought of renting. The financial gap separating him and this woman stretched before him again, and it caught him up short. Never before had he been in this situation, an unpleasant one.

"Come on in!" Keely's voice floated to him.

His hands in his pockets, he went inside. So she had more money than he did. More education. But they weren't going to get involved, so what did it matter?

Inside, he found that the walls were being painted and the trim had been cut. A miter saw, various lengths of oak trim, and painting supplies littered the rooms and hall. First quality oak trim.

"Come here and see my view!"

Keely's voice drew him toward the lake side of the house. She sounded so happy. He didn't have the heart to let his own low spirits spoil her fun. The change of events, change of scenery, change in Keely—as she had sung along with the radio and driven with abandon over deserted, pine-lined roads—had begun to loosen his own stress.

Maybe he needed a short "vacation" too. He couldn't let on that he was less than thrilled she was willing to share this place, this holiday afternoon with him. At the least it would be rude. At the most, it would ruin her attempt at "breaking out" of her gloom.

Trying out a grin, he entered what must be the family room and stood getting the feel of the room with its oak beams and fieldstone fireplace. And the house was beginning to work on him. The expansive room with its view, worthy of a wildlife documentary, opened something deep inside him. It was like a cracking of ice.

Standing in front of a wall of windows and sliding glass doors, Keely smiled at him. Then she slid one of the doors open. The warm wind that blew in the door flowed through him, deep inside him. He felt his face ease into a grin, a real one.

"What do you think?" She motioned toward a porch overlooking the lake. "Doesn't it take your breath away?"

You take my breath away. He froze, not daring to venture farther or speak. Witnessing her expressions of joy—her smile and even the way she moved with a spring to her step—was thawing him, layer by layer. He had to stay rooted where he stood . . . or he would take her into his arms.

What's happening to me? I don't get it. Holding Keely Turner should be the last thing on my mind! This isn't like me.

"Is there something wrong?" She searched his face, her head cocked to one side.

"No," he covered up. He'd let himself come here with her, and now he couldn't stop staring at her. She'd been on his mind every day—whether he'd admitted it or not. Ever since he'd gone to that school board meeting, everywhere he turned this woman appeared right in front of him. He'd tried to ignore her—impossible.

What was so distinctive about her? What did she do? What did she have that made him forget that he was single and meant to remain single? The answer was easy. She was like no woman he'd known . . . in a very long time. And he hadn't been worthy of Sharon either. Events had proved that. But now, he couldn't leave Keely here alone.

"Then let me show you around," she offered.

"Okay," he finally managed to croak from a dry throat. Realizing he wanted to be here with her, couldn't resist being near her, wasn't easy to swallow.

"I'm sorry. Do you want to leave? I kind of dragged you here . . ." She paused in front of him.

"No." And it was deeply true. "No, this is great."

"Are you sure? It's just that there is so much going on inside you, and you let so little of it out."

Her words surprised him. She was curious about him too? He wasn't interesting. That's all she'd find out. And soon she'd realize that they had too little in common, stood too far apart to come together.

She pursed her lips. "Come outside." She led him out onto the unfinished porch and down the steps without a railing to the lake. Farther down the shore, a man stood on an old pier fishing. Across the lake, someone was canoeing alone. She turned to face him.

He couldn't help but nod. What was she getting at now?

"It's been one thing after another since you got here, right? That's what's tying you into knots," she said as though continuing to analyze him.

He grimaced with feeling. "You've got that right."

"So let's lighten up. I've been feeling glum too. Let's face facts—Grady or Nick might have shot out the windows at school." She shrugged. "But it might be neither of them." She leaned toward him.

Burke wished she'd keep her distance. His resistance was disintegrating. Her vibrancy, her lively appeal had broken through. He felt himself wanting to relax, to shed his shoes and socks and wade in the warm shallows beside her. Let the sun warm their faces.

"Now the case of the Weavers' foster baby may have opened up. But maybe not. We can't do anything more than we've done. And this is the last day of summer—are you going to waste it?" She slipped her arm through his.

Some of her sparkle flowed through her touch into him. He had to hold out against the way she was dissolving his defenses. He felt like an ice cube melting in July heat. The last piece of mortar in the wall he'd kept firmly around himself today disintegrated in a heated flash. "When—" he cleared his throat—"are you planning on moving in?"

"Let's take a walk along the shore and I'll tell you. I can tell you because—" she paused to beam at him—"you're not exactly a chatterbox." Not letting him comment, she went on. "Now if it weren't for my father, I would have been in this house over two months ago."

"Why the delay?"

She looked away from him, out across the lake. The canoeist paddled closer to them. "My father wanted to make sure everything was done . . . right," she replied with an edge to her voice.

Burke had only known this woman briefly, but he instantly got the underlying message. Her father had probably made trouble for the contractor and subcontractors. He drew her closer to him and began walking, suddenly wanting to cheer her. "Did you draw up the plans yourself?"

Turning back to him, she gave him another of her radiant grins, so spontaneous, so generous. It flashed through him, taking him back years. No one had looked at him like that for . . .

"Yes, I did," she replied. "I wanted something simple, something that would harmonize with this place. . . ."

He lost himself in the ardor of her low voice. No need to do more than listen, to do more than stay close. No need to think, remember.

�֍ ✷ ✷

"SHERIFF!" A SHORT, round, gray-haired woman burst through the sheriff's department door on Wednesday morning around eight. "Rodd Durand! It's me, Patsy Kainz!"

Hearing the urgency in the woman's voice, Burke sat up behind his desk. Behind the counter, the dispatcher took off her earphones and gawked at the excited woman.

Rodd stepped out of his office. "Patsy, what—?"

"That pendant . . ." The red-faced woman paused to catch her breath.

She worried Burke. She looked like his grandmother had just before her triple bypass. Burke stood up and rolled an office chair toward her. "Please sit down. You look . . . here sit down."

She plopped on the chair. "That pendant . . . in the paper. I think . . . I think it's . . . my grandmother's. Can I see it?"

Rodd nodded to Burke, and he in turn strode back to the evidence room, snatched the bagged necklace from the safe, and returned. His heartbeat sped up. Had they gotten lucky? The local paper had just been delivered this morning.

Receiving the sealed plastic bag from him, Rodd held it in front of the woman. "Don't take it out," he warned. Then he let her hold it and examine it through the plastic. She gazed at it, turned it in the light. Tears moistened her eyes. "Seeing the picture like that in the paper . . . shocked me. How did you find it? It's my grandmother's. It's Jayleen's."

"But the engraving says *Maria*," Rodd pointed out.

Burke watched the woman, gauging her replies. He couldn't think of an ulterior motive for her claiming the pendant. It wasn't valuable unless it truly belonged in her family. Rodd was acting like he deemed this woman a credible source. And he should know.

Patsy swallowed her tears and drew herself up, sitting straighter. "My grandmother wore this as a girl in Germany. Her name was Maria. She gave it to me and I gave it to Jayleen, my granddaughter. I didn't have any daughters. Just sons. Just like my grandmother. How did you get it, Sheriff? Jayleen's not here, is she?"

Burke and Rodd exchanged looks. Burke saw that Rodd was buying it, and he had to agree—the woman did sound believable.

"Come into my office, Patsy. You, too, Burke." Rodd turned to the dispatcher. "Unless there's murder or bank robbery, don't interrupt us."

Burke understood Rodd's desire to wrap this up. No one wanted a baby left unidentified, a fatal case unsolved. And this case was special to his friend.

Rodd urged Patsy into his office. Burke followed and closed the door behind them. Rodd settled Patsy into the chair in front of his desk while Burke sat to one side. "Patsy, you say your granddaughter's in Milwaukee?"

"Yes." Patsy primmed her lips. "That *woman*, her mother, divorced my son when he shoulda been the one to get rid of her. While he was working hard at the mill all day, she started hanging around Flanagan's. The drink got her. My boy'd come home and—" Patsy frowned with deep disapproval—"find the kids had been all alone after school, and no housework done, no supper cooked for a man—"

"When did this happen?" Rodd stemmed the flow of recrimination.

"Over three years ago," Patsy said. "Then one of her . . . men talked her into going to Milwaukee with him. She divorced my son, who was too good for her anyway. And she took the kids, Jayleen and her two younger brothers, with them." Patsy scowled. "In my day, a woman like that wouldn't have gotten custody. The kids should have stayed with their father. But she knew it would hurt him so she took the kids away. Besides, she wanted Jayleen along to do the work, and she wanted the child support—couldn't get that without the kids."

"How old is Jayleen?" Burke asked. The story was adding up, but who was the baby's mother? Rodd and he traded glances. Would the granddaughter be old enough to be a mother? Or did the baby belong to the girl's mother?

"Jayleen's fifteen, will be sixteen come Christmas." Patsy's lined face crinkled into concern. "Where did you find my necklace? How did you get it?"

Rodd leaned forward, his elbows on the desk. "You remember the car that blew up, the one—"

"The one with the baby in it?" Patsy sat forward in her chair. "The baby that the Weavers took in?"

Rodd nodded. "Yes, this necklace was found inside the padding of the car seat that the baby was in."

"What? How?" Patsy looked stunned. "When I rushed in here, I thought maybe Jayleen had come back on her own. Or maybe she'd lost the necklace before she went and had been afraid to tell me, and now someone had found it. I just didn't want to lose it. I know Jayleen wouldn't let go of it on purpose. I don't understand. What are you saying?"

Burke waited to hear how much Rodd would reveal.

Rodd frowned. "Does your son go down to see his kids often?"

"Once a month like clockwork. Gets a motel and spends the weekend in Milwaukee with them. I know he wants the kids back. Jayleen's old enough to make up her own mind, but she stays to take care of her two younger brothers. Least, that's what I think. I don't believe that woman has changed much since she left Steadfast."

"So he'd know if she had a baby?" Rodd asked.

"A baby?" Patsy looked aghast. "You mean you think the Weavers' foster baby belongs to that woman?"

"Could it belong to your granddaughter?" Burke asked in a quiet tone, nearly a whisper. Remembering last winter, he inquired further, "Did your son manage to get down to Milwaukee last winter? It was a bad one. State highways were closed more than once."

Patsy turned to look at him—wide-eyed. "You're right. He made it there in October, but he didn't get back till late February. Every time he'd be ready to go, another storm would blow in. He got halfway twice and was turned back by the state troopers, shutting the highways." She paused, her mouth working as though saying words to herself. "But he called every week to see how the kids were."

"And how were they?" Rodd asked.

Patsy frowned more deeply than she had before. "Jayleen was always out when he called. He thought she was mad at him because he kept promising to come and then couldn't make it. At least, that's what her mother hinted."

Burke considered this added information. The time frame fit. Jayleen could have had a baby last fall. Girls hid pregnancies all the time. Sometimes even from themselves. But who had driven the baby north last January? And why? Or the mother might have concealed it from the father for whatever reason. Maybe the mother hadn't even known someone had taken her child.

Then Patsy put the question they all had into words. "If the baby belongs to the mother or to Jayleen, how did the necklace and baby get here?"

"Maybe we should call the mother—," Rodd started, reaching for the phone.

"No," Patsy growled. "If you give her any warning, she'll have lies ready. I haven't seen my granddaughter for three years. That woman wouldn't let them come for a visit, and my son wouldn't go to court and complain about it. And I didn't go see them because I can't stand that . . ." She closed her mouth and tightened it up with maximum disapproval.

Rodd looked at the clock. "Then I think we need to go to Milwaukee. Can your son get off work if it's an emergency?"

"Sure. And I'm going too." Patsy took on a fighting expression. "If my Jayleen needs me, I'm going. I've waited too long to make my son do right. If I'm a great-grandmother, I want to know it!"

Rodd stood up. Frowning suddenly, he made a sound of disgust. "Burke, I've got that meeting with the DA today on pending cases; you'll have to handle this. Patsy, my deputy will do just what I would. I'm positive of that. You can trust him." Rodd turned to him. "Touch base with MPD if you have to, but find out whose baby we have and how it got here."

Looking Burke over, Patsy nodded. "I need to call my husband."

"Will do." Burke turned to Patsy. "I'll drive you to where your son works. Let's get going right now."

CHAPTER SIX

Burke usually avoided weddings. But here in Steadfast, he hadn't been able to duck out. His friend Rodd was the best man and his wife was the matron of honor for the older couple at the front. Burke had almost rented the cabin from the groom, so he was stuck. He'd resigned himself and now sat in the small crowded church about a week and a half since the unidentified baby case had been solved.

At the front of the church, the buxom bride in a pale lavender dress and the silver-haired groom in a navy suit held hands. Pastor Weaver, his sandy hair a halo in the bright sunshine, was reading from Ephesians chapter 5. " 'You husbands must love your wives with the same love Christ showed the church.' "

To Burke's left, farther forward, sat Keely Turner. Her blonde-streaked hair worn high drew him like a candle glowing in a darkened room. Images of her from the Labor Day they'd spent together bobbed to the surface of his mind often. He tried to keep his eyes on the bride and groom, but his gaze slipped back to Keely sitting so straight with her head held high. The carefree woman that he'd waded in Loon Lake with had disappeared. Ms. Turner had reappeared.

Pastor Weaver paused in his reading and gazed at the congregation. "I feel almost foolish to be speaking to these two fine seniors about making the commitment of marriage. Their first marriages both lasted longer than I have lived." He beamed at them. "But it has been a real treat to talk to them about their love for each other. Bruno and Lou have known each other for . . . forever."

The bride chuckled.

Bruno kissed her cheek and pulled her a few inches nearer him.

The pastor continued, "The groom told me that one day last year, he looked at Lou and he was 'surprised by love'! What a beautiful phrase! In this dark sinful world, all of us should wish to be so blessed."

"Dark, sinful world,"—the pastor has that right, Burke thought. Did anyone sitting here—apart from Rodd and him—know how evil lived and breathed right beside them and destroyed lives day by day? The dark story he'd unraveled in Milwaukee had left him feeling grimy.

No wonder he kept thinking about that stolen afternoon with Keely. But he'd only escaped his responsibilities for one afternoon. Burke felt drained from the weight he carried. He'd been the one who'd had to handle the brunt of the baby case.

What a case it had been—the speedy trip to Milwaukee last week, the dealing with all the anger and loud blaming between the Kainz family and the ex-wife. . . . What a tangled mess had unfolded when he and the Kainz family had begun to peel back the layers and layers of the ex-daughter-in-law's lies.

He rubbed his forehead as though wiping away these memories, especially memories of the girl's father—his anguish over what had happened to his daughter—when he hadn't been there to protect her. Burke had felt it as a growing concern for his nephew. *God, how can I keep Nick from getting into trouble!*

The pastor went on with the ceremony. "Paul begins his homily about marriage with 'You will submit to one another out of reverence for Christ.' It is a verse that many overlook. Many focus on another verse, the one that teaches about the submission of wives. Bruno taught *me* something in our counseling session. He said if more husbands concentrated on loving their wives, they wouldn't have to worry about their wives devoting themselves to their husbands. I loved his phrase 'devoting themselves'—what a wonderful understanding."

"He's a keeper all right," the bride spoke up, making the congregation in the packed church chuckle. "And I'm keeping him."

"Amen!" the groom asserted.

The congregation laughed and a few applauded.

Everyone's cheerfulness only made Burke feel more solitary, more separated from the joy that surrounded him. His gaze slid back to Keely. She turned to smile at the person beside her, and he glimpsed her cheek, soft and ivory. He could almost feel it under his fingertips. He wanted to cup its peach softness in his palm.

The last time they'd been alone together, she'd turned to smile at him like that. A phantom sensation—he felt again her arm in his. They'd walked the shore of the small lake by her house. How had he let down his guard like that? He should have spent that day with his nephew. That's where his duty lay. But Keely Turner had a way of easing past his defenses and the power to persuade him. On Labor Day, she'd coaxed him into taking off his shoes and socks and waded beside him in the shallow water. The sand, the water, the sun—luxuriating in the sensations of that unexpected, unrepeatable interlude.

His nephew fidgeted beside him. Burke tensed and glanced at Nick sideways. This ignited an unwelcome but familiar slow burn inside him. He'd been feeling this ever since . . . he dreaded having to talk to Keely about last night. The culprit of a mindless prank once again, Nick ought to look uncomfortable. He could have harmed property and people. Kids' stunts went bad every day of the week! He'd seen too many go that way in Milwaukee.

The smiling pastor looked back down at the black leather Bible he held and read, "As the Scriptures say, 'A man leaves his father and mother and is joined to his wife, and the two are united into one.'"

The pastor's words hit Burke as though he'd spoken directly to him. A decade ago, Burke and Sharon had made their vows. Within two years, Sharon was gone—dead and buried. The coldness of that reality had never left Burke. Now he realized that was when he'd disconnected from his family, from God. His family had tried to comfort him, but his overwhelming guilt had pushed them away. Only Nick's present need had brought Burke back—reconnected him with his family and made him call out to God for help.

Around him, the church grew silent as the bride and groom exchanged their vows, a most solemn moment. It fell over Burke, too, lifting his mind toward the bigger picture, Nick's future. He felt like this plain sanctuary, adorned with golden fall leaves and butterscotch mums, was filled with the presence of God.

He swallowed. *God, help me get hold of Nick before he does something stupid, something he hasn't thought through. I don't want him to end up injuring himself and maybe some innocent person. I'm sorry for turning a blind eye for the last two years . . . for the past ten years. I won't bail on him like his dad.* Guilt crowded him. *If I'd stepped in earlier like my dad said . . .*

The pastor concluded the Scripture reading: "'This is a great mystery, but it is an illustration of the way Christ and the church are one.' In another translation, this passage begins with what is to me chapter five's main point, 'Since you are God's dear children, you must try to be like him. Your life must be controlled by love, just as Christ loved us and gave his life for us as a sweet-smelling offering and sacrifice that pleases God.'"

I want to be controlled by your love, God. I need it for Nick. Tell me what to do! Just tell me! I'll do it.

His gaze returned to Keely as if on autopilot. He took a deep breath. Though he wanted to avoid her, Keely was the one he needed to talk to. When he talked to her, things made sense. He didn't feel like reaching Nick was hopeless. But . . .

Keely, I just need help turning Nick around, but I don't want to mislead you. I've been alone too many years. I'm not looking for love. I'm no good at it.

❈ ❈ ❈

LATER, AT THE VFW hall in Steadfast, Keely watched the crowd of smiling people wearing their best clothing for the wedding reception. Shane, her former student whom Keely had hired as DJ, was manning an old stereo and a stack of vintage 45 and 33⅓ records, playing in the background the best swing music of the forties and early fifties before rock and roll had taken over. Even Shane looked like he was enjoying it.

Patsy Kainz, in a bright green dress, walked in with Jayleen—a tall, very slender girl with long chestnut hair—tucked close by her side. Across the room, Penny sat with Jayleen's baby in her lap. For Penny, not knowing who her baby belonged to had been torture—but now, knowing had only made matters worse—much worse.

Ever since Burke had called Keely before he'd driven Patsy and her husband and son to Milwaukee, the Steadfast-LaFollette gossip mill had raged like a grass fire in a high wind. By now everyone knew that the Weavers' foster baby Rachel was Jayleen Kainz's baby, born out of wedlock last fall. The story of how the baby had actually ended up in Steadfast in that ill-fated car hadn't been clear. Too much talk and speculation and not enough truth. *I need to ask Burke.*

So far, the baby remained with Penny, but when would that change? Keely's heart broke for her friend who might soon lose the baby she'd cared for for nearly a year now.

Penny assumed it was only a matter of time before Jayleen would reclaim her child, and she was trying to prepare herself for the painful break. Keely had comforted Penny as best she could. But who could see the future? What was best for the baby?

Keely watched the way Jayleen avoided looking toward Penny and the baby. What must she be feeling? Was seeing her baby joy and torture at the same time? *My heart breaks for Jayleen! God, your heart must be breaking too.*

In the midst of this convivial scene, Keely felt surrounded by troubled lives. *Oh, Lord, this is supposed to be a happy occasion. I'm glad for Ma and Bruno, but there're so many in this room who need your healing.*

With the weight of all this unexpressed pain pressing down on her, Keely glanced around once more looking for Burke. She'd seen him at church during the wedding. Though she didn't want to spark gossip, she had to find a moment alone with him. She needed information about Jayleen, who sometime soon would be back in school, her school.

I need all the information I can get so I'll be able to help the girl. And what Nick had pulled last night at the football game must have upset Burke again, too. It had just been a childish stunt, setting off firecrackers in the stands during the game. *God, help me lighten Burke's load. He's taking all this too seriously.*

Taking matters seriously—she tried not to think about Grady and the unsolved shooting out of the school windows. Why had her father meddled in that? Nick had been ruled out of that by evidence. That left Grady and who else?

Then the bride appeared at Keely's side, interrupting her thoughts. Ma, who'd "mothered" half the county, gave her a bear hug. "I'm so glad you came, honey."

Keely hugged Ma back. Remembering Ma's visits and her hugs brought tears to Keely's eyes. Ma had taught her some of her first lessons in loving and doing for others. Keely couldn't let worry over others spoil Ma's special day. How beautiful that Ma had been given love and marriage a second time. *Ma deserves it, Lord. More than I ever will.* "I wouldn't have missed it, Ma," she murmured close to the older woman's ear. "I'm so happy for you."

Ma's lavender cologne and soft plump arms brought nostalgia pouring through Keely. Ma had come often to sit for Keely as a child and later cooked for special occasions at the Turner household. "I wish you and your new husband all the best!"

Ma beamed as she released Keely. "How's your mother?"

"The same as always." Keely sighed. Her mother was still in California, and Grady grew more outrageous every day.

"I miss cooking for those fancy teas she used to give," Ma said. "Gave me a chance to get my cookbook out and try something different—"

"And delicious," Keely finished for her. A few years ago, her mother had tired of entertaining and Ma had stopped coming to Keely's house. "I still think you should have started your own tearoom like mother suggested."

Ma snorted. "Wouldn't that be something! A tearoom in this county!"

"Well, now you'll be busy with your new husband," Keely whispered as Bruno came up behind Ma. Putting his arm around Ma's ample shoulder, he welcomed Keely warmly.

"I'll let you two greet your other guests." Keely kissed Ma's soft, crinkled cheek and turned to find Burke right behind her. His nearness went through her like a shock wave. He wore a well-cut dark suit and looked too handsome for *her* own good. But did he even notice the appreciative glances that were being sent his way? She doubted it. He had that focused, intense look on his face.

"Can we talk?"

His blunt question was so Burke Sloan, it almost made her smile. She had no doubt what the topic would be—Nick and his fandango with firecrackers last night. "I have a better offer. Let's go through the buffet together." She took his arm.

"But I—"

"You did plan to eat, right?" She stared into his eyes. Realizing she'd pay for this in more gossip, she lifted her head high. She led him over to the potluck buffet that the ladies of the church had organized and were serving. She had to get him to relax or at least appear relaxed.

If he looked worried, it would only make matters worse, like Nick had done something even more reckless than lighting a string of firecrackers. Or people could use his preoccupation to spark further speculation about Jayleen. She had to wake him up about this. He wasn't an anonymous face in a big city anymore!

He looked down at the array of dishes. "Can we talk about Nick later?"

She chuckled. "Yes, we can. Later." His single-mindedness didn't surprise her. But she realized she was guilty of letting the pain of those around her lower her mood, too.

Not only for her sake, but for Nick's and Burke's, she had to work him out of this moodiness. It wasn't good for either of them to get so wrapped up in the troubles of others. If nothing else, she needed to show him how to lighten up.

After filling their plates, Keely and Burke sat down at a long white-paper-covered table across from a familiar gentleman who rose when he saw her. She gave him a smile.

"You know Harlan Carey, don't you?" Burke asked her.

"Mr. Carey has been involved with the Family Closet since its beginning," Keely replied, opening her paper napkin. "How are you this evening?"

"I'm fine, Ms. Turner, and let me say that you look more than lovely this evening." Harlan beamed at her.

Nick sat down beside Harlan and plopped a plate on the table in front of him. Without a word of greeting, the teen bent low over his food, ignoring everyone.

Harlan glanced his way. "Young man, I think you forgot to greet your principal, Ms. Turner." The voice was gentle, but it scolded without compromise.

Nick looked across at her, his chin still down. "Hello, Ms. Turner."

"Good evening, Nick." Without skipping a beat, she went on. "That trick last night—setting off firecrackers during the game—better be your last. That's all I'm going to say about it—tonight or in the future. Now when are you going to come over and finish the job at the Family Closet you were doing on Labor Day?"

Her one-two punch, a technique she'd perfected in the classroom, left Nick openmouthed.

"I think Nick and I will have time to mosey over Monday after school," Harlan said. "That sound right to you, son?"

Looking cornered, Nick glanced at them all in turn. *"Fine."*

Keely felt Burke lean forward as though preparing to deliver a lecture. She laid her hand on his arm, urging him not to press the matter now. Nick just needed some TLC. Jayleen, sitting a few tables away, needed more, so much more. Didn't anyone else feel the tension between the two mothers and the one baby?

Burke gave Keely a sideways glance. Would he take her hint? He picked up his fork and began eating. She relaxed.

Then she heard a change in the rumble of conversation and looked around. Veda McCracken had just walked in. She had come dressed for raking leaves, not a wedding reception. No doubt Veda had a twisted reason for attending. Keely closed her eyes. *Not her tonight, Lord. Please don't let her stir up trouble, hurt anyone, especially the Kainz girl.*

"I was hoping she wouldn't come tonight," Harlan said softly.

"Who?" Nick asked.

No one answered.

"Who?" Nick insisted.

"My sister-in-law, Veda McCracken," Harlan replied at last and nodded toward Veda.

Burke looked over at her as though trying to take the woman's measure from a distance.

"She's related to you?" Nick asked in disbelief.

Keely wasn't surprised at Nick's reaction.

"She is the only sister of my late wife," Harlan explained. "And, Nick, she is a very troubled woman. My advice, stay clear of her."

Harlan had such a tender heart that Keely knew it must have pained the old saint to say that much. He went on drawing Nick into a discussion of fly-fishing.

Out of the corner of her eye, Keely tracked Veda as she made her way to the buffet table, filling two plates with food. People made way for her as if she were Steadfast's

Typhoid Mary. Did that bother Veda? Or did she get perverse pleasure from the negative attention as some of Keely's students did?

It reminded her of Grady. Sometimes her heart broke for him, too. *If only I could have taken him with me when I left for college.* But that had been impossible, of course. There had been no way that she could shield him from their own parents. Now Grady was being forced to stay at home to finish high school when he'd thought he'd graduate out East. *Lord, Grady needs you so much.*

Her father was making matters worse. Insulted or fearful, he had refused to volunteer any spent bullets from their hunting rifles. She was sure he'd pressure another judge to refuse a search warrant. Didn't her father realize that it would be better for Grady to turn over the spent bullets? They might have proved him innocent!

"You done with that plate of food, young man?" Harlan asked at last.

"Yes, sir." Nick leaned back in his chair.

Keely was glad to see that Harlan's efforts influenced Nick. She wished he'd done the same for Burke.

"Then I'm going to take you over and introduce you to Jayleen Kainz." Harlan rose. "From what Patsy, her grandmother, told me at the church, Jayleen's going to be starting high school here on Monday. She's just come back from Milwaukee. Maybe you two will have something in common." Harlan and Nick left together, clearing away their dishware.

Keely's heart warmed. She'd thought she was the only one concerned about Jayleen besides Jayleen's family. But she'd been mistaken. *Bless you, Harlan Carey. Please, Lord, help Harlan help Nick and Jayleen.*

Burke turned to her and frowned. "Do you think that's a good idea?" he asked in a low voice.

Keely leaned closer to him and shrugged. "I trust Harlan's instincts."

He gazed at her. "I can't argue with that statement." He nodded toward the far side of the room. "Is Harlan's sister-in-law the one that called the police on you that night—"

"Yes, that was Veda." Keely couldn't keep her low opinion of Veda out of her voice.

"She looks like a few bag ladies I used to see downtown in Milwaukee."

Keely pursed her lips.

"I need to talk to you about Nick," Burke started.

Then Shane called out, "Let's start off with the 'Bunny Hop'!" The lilting traditional tune with its marked rhythm ricocheted off the cement-block walls. Keely uttered a thank-you under her breath.

Keely saw Harlan nudging Nick and Jayleen into the bunny hop line, a large irregular circle that snaked around the room. Toddlers to grandmothers—practically everyone in the room—joined the dance. She began singing the cheery and silly lyrics along with everyone else.

Nick shook his head but stayed by Jayleen. Keely watched the girl react, as uncomfortable as Nick. Keely turned to Burke. "Last night was no big deal. I'll handle it."

"Nick could have started a fire. He could have burned himself or someone else—"

"So the rich man's daughter from LaFollette shows up to the peons' wedding in Steadfast." A strident voice came from behind Keely. "That's big of you."

Keely stood up, acting as if she hadn't heard the woman. She felt Burke rise and stand near her.

"So someone took a shot at you?" Veda persisted, giving a nasty, gloating twist to each word.

Keely half turned from the woman. Nick and Jayleen were coming toward her.

"So the Weavers got your kid," Veda jeered at Jayleen.

"Veda!" Ma snapped, coming up fast behind her. "You've had your free meal. It's time you left."

Burke moved closer to Keely as though ready to protect her.

Veda took a menacing step toward Ma. "Think you're the cat's meow now that you hooked an old fool. How did you trick Bruno into marrying you? You couldn't have gotten pregnant like you did the first—"

"I said it's time you left," Ma repeated, "or do I have to have you put out?"

Ma and Veda glared at each other.

Harlan Carey joined the unhappy group. "Veda, do you need a ride home?" he asked. "I'll be glad to run you—"

"I can get myself home!" Veda swung away and headed toward the cloakroom by the front entrance.

"Thanks, Harlan," Ma murmured. "You'd think after all these years that woman would grow some sense."

"She needs more than sense," Harlan replied.

CHAPTER SEVEN

AFTER VEDA STOMPED out of the VFW, Burke let Keely draw him away toward the other exit at the rear. He needed to talk to her, but being alone with her wasn't a good move. Caught in this crosscurrent, he hesitated. "Where are we headed?"

Passing through the door, which had been propped open, she motioned him to follow her. Without a word, she crossed the parking lot to a large grassy area at the rear of the deep lot.

He followed her, wanting to voice his doubts about the wisdom of their talking out here—being private in such a public place. Being alone with her at the lake had been different. Couldn't they have talked inside? Wouldn't that have been less noticed?

She finally stopped and bent down to pick up a stack of four rusty horseshoes lying around a rugged metal stake. Dressed elegantly for a wedding but holding these rough objects, a study in contrasts, seemed to sum up the puzzle that was this lady. Why was she in this little town, trying to help teens? His mind supplied the answer from Scripture: *"Anyone who loves is born of God and knows God."*

"You want to play horseshoes?" he asked, disbelieving.

She sighed. "Not really. I just needed to talk to you without a hundred people looking on. These—" she held them up—"give us a reason to be outside together." She walked over to a worn-bare spot in the grass and began swinging her arm back and forth, aiming her first shoe.

Burke found himself captivated by the sight of Keely, dressed in a stylish rose pink dress, swaying in the twilight. The dress was made of a soft fabric that flowed over the length of her, molding to her slender curves, ending by hugging her calves. She tossed the shoe. It missed. "I'm out of practice."

Watching her casually toss the horseshoes eased the tension he'd been feeling. She hadn't sounded that upset about Nick's stunt with the firecrackers. Maybe he'd been overreacting.

She glanced at him over her shoulder, worry creasing her forehead. "From what I've heard, Jayleen got herself mixed up with a bad bunch in Milwaukee."

He snorted, trying to react to her words, not her. But he couldn't take his eyes off her. "The worst."

"I'll be her principal and I need to know the girl's story." Bending at the waist, she began swinging her second horse-shoe. "Please tell me the bare-bones facts of what happened to Jayleen and how the baby got here." She tossed the shoe. *Clang.* It hit the stake and bounced away. She straightened and shrugged, giving him a leisurely smile.

She was right. As the girl's principal, she'd need to know what had happened to the girl. "Jayleen got mixed up with an older guy in his twenties, very smooth. She told us she didn't know that he was in a gang, a drug dealer—but who knows?" He went on, speaking fast, "Anyway, he got her pregnant, and she ran away from her mother last fall right after school started and moved in with him. Said he was going to marry her."

A burst of laughter from the reception came to them carried by the breeze. Keely began swinging her third shoe, pointedly judging the distance. "But that changed after the baby was born?"

Her facing away from him let him speak more easily. "He had a bad temper and started using heavy. She said she tried to go home, but he wouldn't let her. I got the feeling he thought she'd inform on him." He watched Keely swaying. As always, her every move was graceful, intriguing, distracting. He pressed on, "Anyway, she felt unsafe, so she entrusted her baby to her girlfriend—who then stole a car with her boyfriend and headed north to give the baby to Jayleen's grandmother."

"Why did she hide the necklace?" Keely asked.

"She didn't trust her friend not to steal it." Burke shrugged. "And she wanted it with the baby so her grandmother would know it was really Jayleen's baby. Her friend had a sealed letter to give Patsy with the baby; it explained everything and asked for help for Jayleen."

Keely tossed the third shoe. It hit fast and spun around the stake, making a metallic ring. "But the letter and baby never got to Patsy. And her father couldn't get to Milwaukee because of the bad winter last year. Why didn't her mother report her missing to the police?"

"She wanted the child support, and she probably didn't want social services nosing around her." He hoped Keely never had to confront that woman. She'd been a piece of work.

"Poor Jayleen. She must have been terrified." Frowning, Keely shook her head, looking grieved. "How did she get away from the drug dealer?"

He wasn't surprised by Keely's quick sympathy. Jayleen was lucky to be getting Keely Turner as her principal. "When the baby disappeared, he beat the girl up and made her tell him where the baby was. Then he took advantage of the child's disappearance. He acted like he'd gotten the baby away from her friends and she was with his family. He let Jayleen go home then but told her if she gave evidence against him, he'd make sure she never saw the baby alive again."

"Oh," Keely moaned, sounding as though the word had been twisted from her.

The sound roused his compassion. His unexpected reaction startled him. He'd learned to be detached from the cases he worked on. But this lady's empathy had opened the door to feeling. The stirring inside him took him all the way back to when he'd been in the thick of the confrontation—in the midst of the shouting and crying, dragging the truth out of the mother and helping the girl tag the drug dealer. He hadn't let himself think . . . or react then.

But now it overwhelmed him. The girl wasn't even as old as Nick! And she'd been sick with worry about a baby she'd tried to protect but lost. The torture she'd suffered flooded him. He looked to Keely and for the moment, he saw that they shared sympathy for Jayleen.

Then Keely turned away. As though consciously breaking the mood, Keely swung her arm back and forth, aiming the final shoe. Finally, she let it go. It went wide. She groaned—such a commonplace sound—and started walking to retrieve the shoes.

"You've been wanting to talk about Nick's prank last night." She tossed the charged words at him—almost casually.

Over the uneven ground, he moved to catch up to her. "I can't seem to connect with him."

"Stop trying then." She gathered up the shoes.

"What?" *Stop trying! That's what I'm already guilty of—not trying!*

"You can't push yourself on a teen." She didn't turn to look at him. "From what you told me, you haven't been a frequent part of his life in the past, especially the immediate past." She sighed. "So you can't make up for that by getting in his face all the time."

Was that what he was doing—getting in Nick's face? "There's no way I can reach him then?"

Turning, she gave him an easy smile. "I didn't say that. It's just that with teens you have to be gentle as a dove and wise as a serpent."

"I don't get it."

Looking up at him, she placed the coarse, heavy horse-shoes in his hands. "You decided not to move out of Harlan's, right?"

He nodded. How did she always know things? "I decided we should stay. Nick's happy there."

"Wise move. You're learning to be sensitive. Let Harlan get through to Nick. And it's good to have someone else living with the two of you. Don't you realize that Nick would give you more trouble if Harlan weren't around?"

So he'd made one right decision about Nick—at last. "I hadn't thought of that." He looked away, enjoying the unex-pected relief.

She motioned for him to try his luck with the horse-shoes. "You just have to hang around Nick and watch for openings to be there when he needs you."

"Whatever you say." He didn't feel like playing horse-shoes. But they were throwing off the gossips. He sighted the stake. "I sometimes think it will never be right between Nick and me again."

She touched his arm. "A time will come when he turns to you for help. Just be there and do what you can to help him. That's what will build the bridge. If you try to force it now, he'll just put it down as too little too late. He's wounded and wants to hurt you and every other adult he thinks has let him down. But he'll get beyond that."

He absorbed her touch, taking it deep inside. "Can you guarantee that?" He let the shoe sail toward the stake.

"Yes." She nodded. "Nick isn't bad. Good runs straight through him."

She sounded so confident that he started to feel it. She stood only inches from him. The pull to draw her closer, hold her against him flamed its way through him. The attraction he felt toward this special lady just wouldn't go away. Did she feel it too?

Turning her head, she brushed away a mosquito near her ear. Her long slender nape beckoned him. His lips anticipated . . . what it would feel like if he pressed them to the white skin just behind her ear.

"I think," she murmured, "we should let him be Jayleen's hero."

"What?" Her words broke his mood.

"You noticed Harlan taking Nick over to meet Jayleen? A good idea."

"I don't want Nick hanging around with her." He gripped the horseshoes tighter.

"Let him who is without sin cast the first stone." She frowned at him. "Just because Jayleen's father made a poor choice in the mother of his children doesn't mean that Jayleen will be a bad influence on Nick. In fact, I think helping her will take Nick's mind off his own problems."

Turning over in his mind what she was saying, he aimed and tossed another and then another shoe. Each one clanged and spun around the stake.

"Impressive," she complimented him. "We both know that Nick's doing pranks in the vain hope that you'll get disgusted with him and send him back to Milwaukee. But if he's interested in Jayleen, trying to help her, it could stop this."

Her convincing explanation left him speechless. Keely,

with her gentle voice and concerned expression, had the power to make matters clear . . . and the power to make him want to draw near her and open up—a dangerous combination.

"One thing though," she said. "The baby's father is in custody?"

"Yes, statutory rape—Jayleen was under sixteen and he was over twenty-one. As soon as Jayleen knew her baby was safe in Steadfast, she informed against him. The MPD caught him right in the middle of a drug deal. They'd been after him for months."

"So that proves my point. As soon as she could, she did the right thing, didn't she?"

He couldn't find any flaw in her logic. But experience had taught him that girls who got mixed up with drug dealers rarely had happy endings. He decided not to point this out. Maybe here with family around her, Jayleen could get off to a better start. He tossed the final horseshoe, another point.

His gaze lingered on Keely. She was a risky woman for him to be around. He'd gotten a hint of that the first night they'd met. And today, she'd managed to pierce his detachment with the rich compassion that flowed from her.

"We'd better go in." She helped him collect his stray horseshoes and deposit them all around the iron stake.

"So soon?" Suddenly he didn't want to go back into the loud, crowded hall. He wanted to stay out here—with her. No matter the consequences.

"Yes, unless we want this horseshoe game to be Monday morning's gossip." She folded her hands and looked up at him with a wry expression.

"I'll never get used to small-town gossip," he said. He recalled that he had intended to steer clear of being alone with Keely. But he resented others thinking that he wasn't good enough to be associated with her. He wasn't being consistent; he knew it and it made him cross. "Don't people have anything better to do around here?"

"Let's go back in and mingle." She led him to the rear entrance. A thick line of fir trees ran along the lot line near it. A group of men had come outside to smoke and were shielded by the trees.

"Did you see how that new deputy's headed straight for Turner's daughter?" one anonymous voice asked in a sly tone.

Someone chuckled dryly. "He's not letting any grass grow under his feet. That's for sure. Maybe he came up here because he was tired of being a cop. Being a rich son-in-law might suit him better."

Burke took a step toward the voices.

Keely stopped him with a hand on his sleeve. She said nothing, just shook her head and walked inside.

Burke squelched the urge to walk over and shove the slimy words down the throat they'd come from.

❈ ❈ ❈

"HELLO, MS. TURNER."

Keely was kneeling on the floor of the Family Closet a week after Ma's wedding. She was in the midst of refolding a stack of crib sheets that customers had left rumpled. Keely looked up. "Hello, Patsy. Hello, Jayleen."

"Give us those sheets," Patsy ordered. "I'll refold them. Jayleen needs some clothes and won't let me spend much on her." Patsy sounded grumpy and proud at the same time. "Says secondhand will do."

Keely had been hoping Patsy would bring Jayleen by. She relinquished the stack of sheets to Patsy, knowing that the older woman was always pleased to help. Also this would make Jayleen's first visit here go easier, seeing that her family was already a part of the Family Closet team.

"We have some like-new things," Keely said. "What do you need, Jayleen?"

"School clothes mostly." Jayleen didn't lift her gaze from the floor. "Just jeans and a winter jacket."

"No!" Patsy objected. "That will be new. I seen a down-filled one in a JCPenney catalog that will suit you to a T. And no arguing. Now let Ms. Turner help you pick out a few things. She knows the stock here." Patsy ambled over to the counter, turned her back, and began carefully refolding the small bundle of sheets.

"Our jeans are over here." Keely led her to a long shelf of folded denims. "Let's see, this stack should be your size. Oh, here, these still have the original tags on them. Why don't you try these on first? The fitting room is—"

Nick walked in from the garage. "Someone's here with another donation," he announced, sounding put out by this imposition.

"Good, Nick." Keely noted that his eyes sought Jayleen and lingered. "You know where the charitable receipt pad is. Just fill one out and sign it for them."

Nick rummaged behind the counter. "Hey, Jayleen!" he called out in a completely different tone. "Thought that was you I saw come in."

"Hi, Nick," Jayleen replied without turning to look at him.

But Keely noted a change in Jayleen's voice. Evidently, Nick had made an impression on her. *Yes!*

"Did you take notes in history yesterday?" he asked in a studied nonchalant tone.

"Yes." Jayleen looked down.

"Can I come over and check mine with yours later?" Nick asked on the way out. "See if I missed anything?"

"I don't—," the girl began.

"You come right over," Patsy chimed in. "I baked chocolate chip cookies today. Jayleen's friends are always welcome."

Jayleen hung her head, her cheeks pink.

Nick mumbled an okay and escaped to the garage.

Though Jayleen might be embarrassed by her grandmother's offer, Keely thought Patsy's welcoming attitude and cookies would only help. At least, Patsy was behaving just like herself.

"Keely?" Penny Weaver walked in the front door. "I just found the match to that sock I brought in—" At the sight of Jayleen, Penny, with baby Rachel in her arms, froze just inside the front door. "Oh."

Keely couldn't think of a thing to say.

There was an awkward silent moment; then Jayleen speed-walked into the fitting room and shut the door firmly behind her.

Penny looked crestfallen, as though caught doing something wrong. Complaining loudly, Rachel twisted in her arms, trying to get down.

Patsy broke the awkwardness. "Oh, let me hold her." She hurried forward, arms open in welcome.

Keely felt Penny's distress as her own. Forcing a smile, Penny let the eager great-grandmother take Rachel, and then she walked over to give Keely the sock. "I didn't know," she said. "I didn't think."

"That's okay," Patsy said loudly. "No use trying to avoid each other. Everyone knows you're taking care of Jayleen's baby. It's best to keep things plain and honest," Patsy went on. "And this little sweetheart looks like she's as happy as a clam. Though how a person knows when a clam is happy— who knows?" The woman grinned.

Keely tried to think of something to say to help lessen Penny's discomfort. What was going to happen to the baby? Would Jayleen reclaim her child or not?

Penny walked over and held out her arms. "Sorry, Patsy. Can't stay. I'm on my way to pick Zak up from a play date."

Patsy gave Rachel a hearty kiss and returned her to the pastor's wife. Tears moistened the older woman's eyes.

Penny made her getaway. Nick walked back in. Looking unhappy, Carrie Walachek trailed in after him. Where had she come from? Was she here to sign up for their pre-motherhood classes? Keely hadn't spoken directly to the girl since the night at her trailer. She sighed, feeling over-whelmed.

Nick put the receipts back into the drawer behind the counter. *I need backup.* Keely called to the other volunteer, who was in the kitchen making iced tea, to come out.

Then unexpectedly, Grady slouched in the front door—looking sullen. He carried a large cardboard box.

Keely frowned. How had the small thrift shop suddenly become Grand Central Station? "Grady?"

"Mom told me to drop this off." Dramatically, Grady dropped the box on the floor and turned.

"Hold it!" Keely ordered.

Jayleen stepped out of the fitting room and paused to look at herself in the long mirror on the fitting-room door.

In unison, both young male heads swiveled to view the pretty girl.

Grady wolf-whistled. "You're hot, babe!"

Patsy launched herself at him. "I don't care if you are Franklin Turner's son! You keep a civil tongue in your head. Now pick up that box and take it into the garage where donations belong!"

Keely was taken aback by Patsy's tirade.

So was Grady—but only for a moment. He cursed Patsy. Then he turned on his heel and left, slamming the door.

"Jerk," Nick pronounced. He went over and picked up the box and headed for the garage.

Mortified, Keely glanced at Jayleen, who had frozen in front of the mirror. "Those look good on you," Keely said, making her voice as normal as possible in spite of her shame. "I apologize," she murmured.

"Not your fault." Patsy slapped wide a sheet and began folding it.

The other volunteer came out and approached Carrie, who wore a peevish expression.

Embarrassment over Grady's behavior warmed Keely's cheeks. But all the troubled currents swirling around her—here, at school, at home—threatened to throw her off balance. Not for the first time, she felt the strain. Maybe she was trying to do too much, spreading herself too thin. Being principal was much different than being a teacher—especially with Grady as a student.

She took a deep breath. *Lord, I love my job. I love the ministry of working here at the thrift shop. But I'm running out of patience with my family, especially Grady. Am I trying to help someone who won't be helped?*

The image of Burke in his suit, tossing horseshoes at the reception, came back to her. He'd been responding to her, not just as a confidant but as a man noticing a woman. And she'd felt the same sensation. His every move, every expression had taken its toll on her heart, her peace. *Lord, I can't handle all this at once! This isn't the right time!*

※ ※ ※

LESS THAN A week later, Keely's urgent voice repeated in Burke's ear—"Come quick. There's a fire on the athletic field." Passing yellow school buses, he zoomed into the high school parking lot—siren blaring. He headed straight toward the entrance-ticket-booth area of the football stands. The fire engines still flashed the red and white lights. A fire. What next?

He jumped out of his Jeep. Bullhorn in hand, Burke shoved his way through a thick cordon of kids gawking at the fire engines. "Fall back," he demanded as he shouldered his way through them. Most looked surprised, some resentful, but they all moved away from him. He glimpsed Keely's blonde-streaked topknot and headed for her. He reached her side. Stirred by the frenetic activity of the volunteer firefighters, he demanded, "What happened? Was anyone hurt?"

Keely whirled around. "They don't think so. Someone set the bleachers on fire."

"Probably his flaky nephew," a student shouted above the hubbub.

The comment hit home. The kid had put Burke's worry into words. His jaw worked.

Frowning, Keely looked over Burke's shoulder. "You students go home," she ordered.

"No!" Burke stopped her. "All of you report to the gym. I'll need to question you."

"School's out!" a few answered. "We don't have to stay!"

"If you leave, that may be construed as an admission of guilt," he shot back. "Now head to the gym."

"But other kids left!" a girl whined.

"That can't be helped. Report to the gym now!" He stared them down.

The mass of students turned—grumbling loudly—and headed back toward the school. He and Keely kept an eye on them until they had all funneled into the school entrance across the parking lot. He looked for Grady and Nick—in vain. "Most of your students already left?"

"The buses were already leaving when the fire was reported. My first duty is the safety of my students. I let the buses leave."

Her distress was clear. He understood her reasoning, but he couldn't help being unhappy that this might have let the culprit leave with physical evidence of fire-setting on him. Burke snapped open his cell phone and called for backup. He turned back to Keely. "How did it happen?"

A soot-faced firefighter approached before Keely could reply. "It's out. We've checked all around and that should be it. Since it was reported right away and we were able to respond immediately, the damage was kept to a minimum."

"What caused the fire?" Burke asked.

The firefighter looked him up and down. "You're the new deputy, right?"

Burke nodded and shook hands with the man.

"Come on in. I'll show you the scene of the fire. The school custodian called in the alarm and he's still here. I've asked him a few questions, but you'll want to talk to him yourself."

Burke and the firefighter and Keely walked side by side through the arched entrance to the athletic field, surrounded by wooden bleachers. The gritty smell of smoke hung over the field. One section of bleachers, the one closest to the school building, was blackened and charred. Most of the wood would have to be replaced. A depressing sight. The school year had started with small holes dug in this field and had advanced from there. In August, Burke had thought being assigned to the high school would be a breeze. *How wrong I was.*

Keely hailed a man dressed in khaki work clothes who was standing to one side staring at the destruction.

The man turned to her. "Oh, Ms. Turner, I hate this. Just look at this mess. We have another game here on Saturday night! How am I supposed—"

"Did you see who set the fire?" Burke interrupted.

"I was here," the man started, "giving this last section of bleachers another coat of paint. I didn't get it finished before the season started, had other things to do."

"You were using an oil-based enamel, right?" the fire-fighter asked for clarification, looking pointedly at Burke.

He got the message. An open flammable container had been left unattended. "Do you smoke?"

"No." The man looked confused. "Sometimes kids sneak a smoke out here, but I didn't see anyone this afternoon. I use oil-based enamel because it protects the wood over winter. I always use—"

"But you were called away when we had the toilet over-flow in the boys' bathroom?" Keely prompted.

Burke wondered if two kids had been working together or if this was the work of one smart one. . . .

"That's right," the man said eagerly. "I expected I'd just be gone a minute. I hadn't seen any kids around so I left my stuff right here. I didn't cap the paint. I only laid the lid on the can to keep bugs out."

"Are you sure you didn't see any kids around?" Burke asked. *Like my nephew?*

"No." The custodian shook his head. "And I was only gone for about ten minutes. The toilet didn't take long—just needed to be plunged. And I was right back here. I smelled the smoke before I saw it. I ran in to make sure, and then I headed right for the office. The fire engine got here within eleven minutes, which I think is pretty good." The man beamed at the firefighter.

"What time did you leave the bleachers to go inside to fix the toilet?"

"Just a little after three."

Keely glanced at her watch. "It sounds like it was timed to happen right at the end of school."

"No, it sounds like a crime of opportunity to me," Burke said, looking over the field, trying to figure out where some kid—probably skipping class to smoke—could have been lurking, watching the custodian paint.

"I'll go get the attendance cards for the last period," Keely said. "Let's see who wasn't where he or she was supposed to be. I realize now—" she frowned—"that I should have kept the student body here—"

Burke stopped her recriminations with a touch on her sleeve. He wished to save her worry. Would this be a mark against her in her first year as principal? "You did what you thought was best—"

The welcome sound of another police siren cut him off. "That's my backup."

Keely gazed at him for a moment and then turned away. "I'll get those records ready for you and have a few teachers monitor those students till you can question them."

He wished they could talk freely, but now he could only nod. He had to secure the crime scene and speak to the remaining students. "I'll be in to talk to you when I've finished my examination."

The custodian offered his help. Burke refused it and asked him to go back to the entrance to the field and keep out any stray kids. The firefighter told Burke his company was only volunteers and had to get the engine back to the station. Most had jobs to get back to.

Finally, Burke stood alone. One last glance at the scorched bleachers and he turned back to get the yellow crime-scene tape out of his Jeep. Rodd would be here any minute. The fire felt like a crime of opportunity. Who could have predicted the custodian would paint today? Some kid sneaking a smoke saw the man leave the paint. A dropped cigarette and a lot of excitement. That was all that had happened—if they were lucky.

CHAPTER EIGHT

TWO HOURS LATER Burke walked into Keely's office, a sinking feeling inside him. The school was quiet. He'd sent the kids home after examining the hands of each one and taking swabs from their fingertips. The other deputies had left, too. He and Keely were the only ones remaining in the school.

She looked up from her desk. "Did you find out anything?"

"Very little." He dropped into the chair across from her. "I don't know anything more now than I did after the custodian gave his information."

"None of the students saw anyone around there?"

He shook his head. "No. Do you have the attendance cards?"

She handed him a list of eleven names. "These are the kids who weren't where they were supposed to be when the fire started."

When he read the list, that lump of cold dread landed in his stomach. Nick's name was on the list. He stared at it. But this time Burke didn't blame him immediately. *I don't think Nick would do this.* This came from deep inside him.

Was he getting to know his nephew or was he just deluding himself? Then he realized that Grady's name was also on the list. He looked at Keely.

Consternation creased her forehead. "Yes, unfortunately both Grady and Nick are unaccounted for at just the wrong time."

He studied her face. The suspicion that clung to both Grady and Nick hung between them—as both an obstacle and an obligation. He hoped he wouldn't be forced to arrest her brother, and she probably hoped she wouldn't be forced to put his nephew before the school board for an expulsion hearing.

"So where do we go from here?" Keely exhaled, giving sound to her frustration.

"Not very far. I still think it's a crime of opportunity, and anyone might have done it." Still, it was impossible to sweep arson under the rug. Digging a few holes, shooting out windows of an empty school—all had the possibility of damaging consequences. But fire kicked the chance of causing harm to a whole new level of danger since it could injure more people than a single bullet. But were these incidents all by one perp? "We have no way of even connecting this to the cheerleader prank or the shooting." He shrugged.

Earlier, Rodd had been troubled by not being able to identify the baby he'd rescued in January. Now, Burke couldn't get a break on keeping the peace at the high school. His face twisted in irritation.

"Are we trying to find a pattern where there isn't one? Some nasty student dug those holes. Walachek threatened me and Carrie's aunt but never headed toward school, so someone else shot out the windows." Keely's voice faltered.

That thought doubtless took her into a touchy area—her father's obstruction of Burke's search warrant. Was she thinking of her brother and her father's interference?

In a stronger voice, she went on. "Nick let air out of the tires and set off firecrackers at that game. Just because all of these incidents happened this year doesn't mean that they are connected. I have hundreds of students. We shouldn't focus only on Grady and Nick as culprits. We're more concerned about them. That's what keeps bringing them to mind."

He considered her words. As usual, she made a lot of sense. But that didn't help him stop some kid or kids from damaging more property and perhaps endangering themselves and others. Someone here needed help—as much as or more than Nick.

"It could have been anyone on that list of skippers," she pointed out. "Look, Carrie Walachek's on there too. This may be the last time you get called to school this year for an incident."

He shrugged again.

"By the way, Nick's looking after Jayleen, and he's begun making friends," Keely said. "Harlan's trying to sign him up to volunteer again at the Family Closet."

Burke kept a lid on the hope that this might make a difference in Nick. It was too soon for that. Nothing in the past weeks had led him to be that optimistic. "But now we have a fire," he said in a quelling tone.

He stood up. "Well, I guess that's about it for now." As he moved toward the door reluctantly, he almost asked her if she would like to go out for a bite to eat. Just talking to her now—even discussing this prickly topic—eased his tension. *I enjoy talking to her. And that leads me to want to be with her.*

But he couldn't mislead her. He had no time or talent for romance. And the nasty words about him chasing her for her money that they'd overheard outside the VFW hall had come back to taunt him over and over.

❈ ❈ ❈

KEELY WATCHED BURKE wave good-bye and leave. She knew he'd overheard that nasty remark outside the VFW hall. It was only what she'd expected people to say, but it had to have bothered him.

Still, she wished she could have thought of some excuse to make him linger here. When he was with her, she forgot her father's continued efforts to prevent her from moving out. He'd managed to find several construction errors that he insisted she have fixed before taking possession. But she knew her father had discussed this with her builder and gave him conflicting instructions that had delayed everything while she changed them back. Keely took a deep breath. She had to let Burke go.

Her plate was full to overflowing. At night as soon as she lay down, she passed out with fatigue. *Lord, just take this attraction away. Or could you put it on hold? I'm just . . . I need a lull in the rush-rush of life now—more than anything else!*

She pictured her new house. It would be a haven of tranquility. But a vague disquiet niggled inside her. Would her father, Grady, and her mother ever let her have that peace?

❈ ❈ ❈

THE NEXT SATURDAY morning, the first Saturday in October, Keely simmered with anticipation. With Burke, Harlan, and Nick standing behind her, she unlocked the door of her finally finished home, the snug ranch with its large back porch overlooking Loon Lake—the spot where she'd always wanted to live. Over the past months, she'd stopped here often to watch its progress from a foundation to a real home. Looking at it now gave her a fresh thrill. Her furniture would be delivered today. *My home. Tonight I'll sleep in my own home.*

Harlan had enlisted Burke and Nick to help her move in. She'd had other offers but hadn't wanted to put anyone out. So she'd tried to hire a few movers. Unfortunately, her father must have let it be known that he was unhappy about her move. So in the end, when Harlan had spoken to her at the thrift shop again, she'd accepted the help he offered. But what did Burke think about this? He wouldn't even meet her gaze. Did he feel cornered by Harlan?

Edgy over this, she wiped her feet on the thick indoor welcome mat in the quarry-tiled entryway. Then she stepped onto the sculptured berber carpet in the living room, which was stacked with overflowing boxes, bags, and laundry baskets. She'd been bringing boxes of clothing and personal items over for the past week. Burke and Nick would help her arrange her new furniture when it arrived and carry the bags to the right rooms. It shouldn't take long. Then she'd spend the weekend she'd reserved for herself, getting things settled.

The scent of newness permeated the house—a mix of cut wood, latex paint, new carpet, and linseed oil. She breathed it in like an expensive perfume.

"What time's your furniture going to be delivered?" Burke asked.

Trailing in behind them, Nick scanned the rooms visible from the foyer, looking hesitant to step on her new carpeting. Nick's expression made her remember all the times in her childhood when her mother had shooed her off furniture and carpet that had been purchased primarily for show, not for use.

"Come on in, Nick." With an encouraging smile, she waved to him. "This house was built to be lived in—not just to be looked at! The delivery truck should be on its way. I'll call the store and see when it left."

Fizzing inside with excitement, she pulled out her cell

phone and dialed the furniture store. Her simple inquiry brought several transfers to one person or another. *What is wrong? It's just a simple delivery.* Finally in exasperation, she asked for the owner of the store.

The owner said in an apologetic tone, "I'm sorry but your furniture didn't go out on today's truck."

"Why not?" This didn't make sense. Inside her, warning bells began pealing. "I purchased those pieces over a month ago, and I scheduled their delivery then. And I called to reconfirm this week. What's the difficulty?"

A brief silence greeted her question. "All I can say, Ms. Turner, is that the furniture wasn't loaded on the truck going out today."

Suddenly Keely recalled her father's face this morning. He hadn't said much about her move, but she'd sensed that he was feeling some kind of satisfaction. She had put it down to her parents' sudden plans for a California getaway. But was that the real reason? Had her father gone one step further in expressing his resentment at her leaving home?

In that instant Keely realized why her furniture hadn't gone out on the truck today. Both the store owner and her father sat on the country club board, and her mother redecorated one room every year and ordered everything from his store. Had her father pressured this man to delay delivery and inconvenience her? Would her father do something like that? The question was ludicrous. Of course, he would.

For one second she thought she might be ill. How could he do something like this? Outrage sizzled through her. *I won't be manipulated!* She grappled with inner flames. *I'd better let it be known right now exactly what will happen from now on if anyone else "cooperates" with my father like this!* What if she needed repairs or something else in the future?

She gripped the receiver tighter. "I've changed my mind

about the furniture," she said coolly. "Please send me back my check—"

"Ms. Turner—"

"I will expect my deposit to be returned this week—"

The man tried to interrupt again.

"Or you'll be hearing from my attorney." She hung up, her insides roiling. The unfairness hurt the most. She'd tried so hard to be a good daughter. But what her father really wanted was a perfect daughter and a perfect son who would be his puppets, not people.

Brushing aside hot, angry tears, she stalked to the window. She stared outside at her view, wrestling with her resentment and hurt. She'd chosen this setting because it held all she loved about the north woods—a thick pine forest, a silver blue lake—altogether a rugged natural canvas for God's art.

Today, fall leaves were turning amber, russet, and crimson, fluttering on branches and then floating down onto the still lake. The view was dazzling. She took a deep cleansing breath.

She heard Burke come up behind her. "What's wrong?" he asked.

She pulled herself together. "My furniture isn't going to come today." She kept looking out the window. "I cancelled the order. I don't think I should have to put up with such bad service." Her voice shook though she tried to hide it.

"Don't let him win," Harlan said behind her.

Keely tensed, knowing that Harlan had somehow guessed that her father was the one responsible for this delay.

"Come on, Nick," Harlan said. "We'll go outside and look around. I want to see if they assembled her dock right."

Then only she and Burke stood looking out the window—so near and yet so separated. For a second she imagined herself turning and resting her head against Burke's chest. She could almost feel the brushed cotton of his plaid shirt under her cheek. What would it feel like to have someone to turn to?

"Don't let anything spoil today—this moment . . ." His voice was rough and low. What was he struggling with? "Your first home, your first day in it."

His words were just the right ones. She moved her shoulder muscles, making herself loosen up. She inhaled again, regaining control. Then she turned around and, with an effort, smiled up at him. "Well, let's go over to my parents' home. We can pick up my bedroom set. It belongs to me, and I'll at least have something to sleep on."

"Do you think that's a good idea?" Burke looked skeptical.

"My parents won't be there. They flew out to California for a week. My mother was thrilled to finally get my father out there." And her father had made it sound like it was her responsibility to see that her brother didn't get into trouble while they were gone. Though she'd keep an eye on Grady, she refused to go along with the guilt trip. Grady was seventeen and ought to be able to take care of himself for one week. It had been another bid from her father, trying to torpedo her efforts to have an easy move.

"Okay, let's go." Burke gestured for her to lead the way.

Harlan and Nick were waiting for them out in Harlan's truck. Keely led Burke to her SUV, but this time she gave him the keys. She just wanted to sit back and relax.

When they pulled up to Keely's parents' house, she got out and walked to the door. Her key, the one she'd had since she was sixteen, didn't fit. She stood staring at the door stupidly, bewildered. She'd left just over an hour ago to pick up a few things and meet Harlan at her house. Her father must have had the locksmith out right after she left! She seethed. *Petty* was the word that came to her mind.

Didn't her father realize that the locksmith would let

this story get out? Didn't he care what people thought of him? Recalling that he was still blocking the search warrant made her realize that her father didn't care what people thought—as long as he was in control. *Why am I surprised?* She turned back to the truck. *I should have expected this.*

⬥ ⬥ ⬥

NOT IN THE least surprised at seeing Keely unable to unlock her parents' door, Burke eyed Keely's discontented expression. "He changed the locks?"

"Yes." Her one-word answer was laden with a mixture of frustration and resignation. She got in next to him. Harlan stood by Burke's door, and Nick came over and leaned his wrists on her open window.

"Why'd they do that?" Nick spoke for the first time. "You can't get your furniture then."

"Exactly." Keely looked straight ahead.

Burke hadn't liked Franklin Turner when he'd met him that day on the courthouse steps. Now he had a few heated words he'd like to say to the man face-to-face. But further discussion of her father would only wound Keely. He stretched his arms forward, hooking his wrists on the top of the wheel, and changed tacks. "Isn't there any other place around here to buy furniture?"

"We could drive to Duluth or a few other towns, but I wanted to move in today—not shop for furniture." Keely's voice cracked with annoyance. "Usually the stores have to order the furniture. No one around here has a large local warehouse—"

"What about the auction?" Nick spoke up, an underlying gripe in his tone.

"What auction?" Keely glanced at him.

Burke asked the same question silently. How did his nephew know about a local auction?

"Shane asked me if I wanted to work the auction with him," Nick explained as though he expected an argument. "He carries heavy stuff to cars for people, and sometimes he delivers it home for them if it's big and they don't have a truck. He says he can make a hundred bucks in tips at an auction—easy. Usually more."

Nick's trace of enthusiasm was the first Burke had witnessed in the weeks his nephew had lived with him. "Why didn't you tell me Shane asked you?"

Nick shrugged. "You said you needed help moving Ms. Turner into her new house."

"*Next time*—" Burke emphasized the first two words—"let me know if you get a better offer. I have the whole day off. Ms. Turner and I would have accommodated your work schedule."

"Can we go then?" Nick watched them with wary eyes.

"When did it start?" Harlan asked.

Nick glanced at his watch. "It won't start till noon. We got more than an hour to get there and look around."

Burke looked to Keely. What would she think of secondhand furniture? On the upside—the auction might get her mind off her parents. "Up for it?"

She nodded slowly. "Why not? Let's go. If I can get a bed and a table and chairs, I'll be able to manage until I have time to shop again."

From his back pocket, Nick pulled out the classified ad from the *Steadfast Times* for "Another Colonel Rene Bouchard Auction" and read aloud the address of the farm where it would take place.

Soon Burke and Keely took off down the road in Keely's SUV, guided by her clear directions. Harlan and Nick, driving Harlan's truck, followed.

Over the past two years, Burke's sister had "guilted" him into going to a couple of auctions—one of her passions—

with her and Nick, so he wasn't surprised that Nick would feel comfortable around one. In fact, it would bring a familiar facet of his life in Milwaukee back to him.

The farm and its white frame house were flanked by a ragged line of parked trucks and cars up and down the country road. A crowd dressed in autumn colors and denim milled inside the barn and around the yard. Feeling an unexpected spurt of anticipation, Burke parked in a weedy wedge between two pickups and got out. Nick jumped out the driver's side of Harlan's truck while Burke helped Keely out of the SUV.

"This must be the Armbruster estate sale," she said, looking around. "She died about six weeks ago without any close relatives. The out-of-state heirs must want to sell everything off."

"Yes, and she never threw a thing away." Harlan chuckled. "No wonder they're having a tag sale and auction. Bet she left three generations of stuff."

"Looks interesting." Burke led Keely over the grassy verge, then took her arm to help her up the rutted drive. The day was bright. The cloudless blue sky had made it a crisp morning, but the sunshine was warming up the day.

Burke's spirits lifted, but he hid it. Here in the public eye, he had to make sure he didn't let his guard down and show how he enjoyed being in Keely's company.

"Hey!" Nick, who'd kept up with them, shouted and waved. "Shane!" From about thirty feet away, a grinning Shane motioned for Nick to join him near the barn.

Burke urged his nephew away. "Go on; help Shane out while we look everything over. We'll get together after the auction."

Without a backward glance, Nick galloped off.

"Well, I see they have a tent set up with coffee and doughnuts," Harlan said. "Now that sounds like just what I need. I do like a full-service auction." He grinned. "Happy shopping, you two. See you later." The older man waved at someone and took off, heading for a small tent with tables and chairs set up under it.

"I've noticed that Shane and Nick have been hanging out together this week," Keely commented as she took a small jump over a deep rut.

Burke appreciated her sympathetic tone, but he only nodded. Watching her every move tested him. He longed to reach out and pull her closer by his side.

"What do you want to look at first?" He had to choke back different words, words about how much he enjoyed walking beside her, how just being near her made him feel . . . different.

"Well . . ." A smile lifted her face.

The sight caught Burke and he couldn't look away. Her expression competed with the sunshine. *What's happening to me, Lord? Why can't I shut off these feelings? They aren't appropriate and I know it.*

"Why don't we see what Mrs. Armbruster had in the way of furniture?" she suggested.

With a courtly nod, he gestured for her to precede him toward the farmhouse. The furniture had been moved outside into the yard. The shaggy grass looked as if it hadn't been mowed all summer and fall. Burke and Keely strolled around the house, examining the antiques and old furniture scattered among the high grass, weeds, and dried wildflowers, the pieces looking abandoned or shipwrecked in the bright autumn sunshine.

"See anything you like?" Burke asked, trying to sound natural.

"Well, I hadn't thought about furnishing with antiques."

Keely studied the old iron bed frame in front of her. "But there are several good pieces here."

Burke noticed the people around Keely stopping to drink in Keely's words. He motioned her toward the front of the house and whispered in her ear wryly, "Don't say stuff like that. You'll drive up the prices."

He smoothed the collar of her red, green, and blue plaid shirt, really wanting to touch the pale skin of her slender neck. The wind was playing with tendrils of her hair that had come loose from her casual Saturday topknot—enticing.

At the bottom of the front steps, a woman sat behind a folding table with a cash box on it. She smiled automatically and handed them a long printed sheet. "Here's the list of the items to be auctioned. This is a combination tag sale and auction."

The woman continued in a singsong voice. "The big items—furniture and large pieces like floor lamps and farm equipment, many of them antique—are outside and will be auctioned. Inside, the smaller household wares and linens, etc. are all marked for sale. Enter at the rear and exit here by me. I'll tally and mark your items and receive payment."

Aware of how many times this poor woman had had to repeat this, Burke found himself smiling at her.

At first confused, the woman stared at him and then grinned back. "Did she drag you to this?"

"No, I brought her," Burke replied.

The woman chuckled. "Lucky her."

Keely glanced back and forth between them. Then she grinned too.

Burke felt himself loosening, relaxing. He tried to tighten up his self-control. *Keep it cool. Just stick to the program.* "Let's get started."

He led Keely around to the back door. The porch contained a huddle of garden implements and old clay pots.

Pausing, Keely picked up a rusty tin watering can and examined it as though it were a prize goblet.

"Uh, Keely," Burke cautioned, "I don't think that will hold water—"

"I know." She smiled at him. "But I think it would look pretty with dried flowers in it."

He shrugged. "You're the boss." He took it from her and waved her on.

Up three steps, the kitchen looked to Burke like it had already been picked over pretty well. But Keely took her time inspecting the variety of kitchen gadgets. "I don't really cook," she confessed to Burke. "I don't know what I'd need."

"Well, you'd need dishes and silverware," he said.

"Those sets will be auctioned later," a plump woman in a denim jumper, standing in the doorway, said.

"Thanks," Burke said. He let Keely precede him into the dining room with its faded carpet and curtainless windows. Yellowed linens in open boxes lined the walls. Keely knelt and began picking through the starched tablecloths and napkins. Burke stood behind her, observing her intense concentration on these everyday items.

Burke could see how much Keely was enjoying this tag sale and auction. It had obviously taken her mind off her father's unkindness. He thought about his own father. Burke hadn't appreciated his dad's pressuring him to take Nick with him. He hadn't liked facing up to his own sin of neglecting his family, but his father had been right, he realized now.

Franklin Turner had been wrong. But then Turner had been wrong about the shooting case too. His not handing over the bullets and blocking the search warrant had only cast more guilt over his son, not less. *You're not as smart as you think you are, Turner.*

"I wonder if they have sheets and pillowcases," Keely asked, looking around.

"Some are on the opposite wall. More upstairs." The same woman motioned to more boxes. "Here's a bag you can fill up."

Burke accepted the paper shopping bag from the local grocery, and Keely filled it with an embroidered tablecloth, matching napkins, and several embroidered hand towels. Then she went to the other side of the room and picked out sheets and pillowcases edged in hand-tatted lace.

"I see this all the time," the woman who'd helped them said. "People save the best they have and for what? For strangers to buy after they're dead. All this beautiful hand-work kept in tissue in drawers—I bet she never let herself enjoy it." The woman shook her head.

"Don't worry," Keely promised. "I intend to use it and enjoy it."

Enjoy it. His mind repeated those words, and he realized that he was taking pleasure in today, something he hadn't done in a long, long time. Keely merited days like this more often. She deserved a man who could give her this and more.

Burke deserved to be alone. A bitter taste came into his mouth. Memories, failure always came back to haunt him. He led Keely toward the staircase in the hall.

"Thank you." She gave him one of her dazzling, stagger-ing smiles.

Like a child opening a special gift, good feelings filled him. He couldn't help himself. He drew her a few inches closer and took her arm as they walked up to the second-floor landing. She smiled at him again. He tried to stem the warm and unusual tide this unleashed but failed. It carried him along, and each time she smiled it crested higher.

By the time Burke walked down the front steps to the woman at the folding table, he carried paper and plastic grocery bags filled with linens, knickknacks, books, some samplers, and old framed photographs and prints. After setting down the large box she carried, Keely beamed at the woman and paid the modest sum tallied for the items.

Though careful not to let it show, Burke relished Keely's happy mood.

As they walked back from stashing her finds inside her SUV, Keely enthused, "I've never been to a sale like this. Only to antique shops and they aren't fun like this. It's a treasure hunt!"

Burke chuckled dryly. "Watch it. Tag sales and auctions can be addicting! My sister and sometimes my mom go out once a week—rain, snow, or shine."

"Really?"

"Time for the auction!" a voice yelled.

Keely and Burke hurried back to the area in front of the barn. A distinguished-looking gentleman with white hair whom Burke assumed to be Colonel Bouchard stood on a platform there and explained the rules of the auction and the instructions about payment.

Burke settled himself, leaning against the open barn door. He was all too aware of people looking at them—and their glances said exactly what Burke felt. She was too good for him. Unaware, Keely, looking keyed up, stood just in front of him. Then with a tap of the colonel's gavel, the auction began.

After losing out on several bids, Keely won one of the antique, painted-iron double bedsteads. Next, she bargained doggedly for a bird's-eye maple dresser and matching vanity with its trifold mirrors and a matching chair. The other bidders glared at her.

Burke stood beside her, drawn irresistibly in by her animation and intensity. The items were coming fast and furious now—an antique hurricane lamp, a copper bed warmer, and ornate sterling silver tableware, then china— and the bidding was getting hotter. Colonel Bouchard rattled off, "One hundred—make it a hundred and fifty—make it two. Hep. Hep."

The oak dining-room set with a round table, leaf, and six chairs was brought forward by Shane and Nick, who had somehow become part of the auction process. The bidding started at two hundred and fifty dollars, but was soon up to twice that. Keely hung on until she won it.

"Sold for nine hundred dollars! To the lovely lady in the plaid shirt!"

Flushed with the thrill of success, she beamed at Burke.

From behind them came an envious voice laced with resentment. "That's Turner's kid. Showing off. Spending her dad's money."

Keely froze.

Red-hot anger scorched Burke inside; he pulled her closer beside him. For two cents, he'd have punched the guy. But he felt Keely relax and nod against him, her fine hair against his cheek. It was bad enough that he'd overheard the slam. This kind of talk hurt her. Surely she knew that she was highly regarded, that this was just spiteful envy talking.

He gave her a squeeze of assurance and then released her. She didn't need to hear any more snide comments about how he was chasing her for her money either. He turned to give everyone behind him a warning look. Few were able to meet his gaze. Why did people think they could say things like that about Keely?

Burke had yet to hear anyone say anything good about Franklin Turner. Was this a result of the resentment people felt toward Turner but were unable to express? Keely gave of herself to the county constantly. They ought to be ashamed of taking hard feelings toward her father out on her.

The rest of the auction went by quickly. Keely ended with enough to fill up three trucks. While Nick helped Shane lift heavy items and load them into cars and trucks for others, Keely and Burke inspected the items she'd bought—the bedroom furniture, the dining-room set, the Arts and Crafts floor lamp, the painted hurricane lamp, a pie safe, a primitive bench, and bookshelves. She'd done well for herself. He watched her admiring her purchases and was glad her father and the spiteful tongues hadn't stopped her. *We showed you, Turner. You didn't win today.*

Finally, Nick was done helping Shane. He and Burke lifted the first batch of Keely's heavy antiques onto Harlan's truck. "They sure made this stuff to last," Burke gasped with a grin as they hefted the iron bed frame up the final foot into the truck bed. Then Burke and Nick helped lift more of Keely's items into Shane's truck.

By then, the crowd had thinned to very few. Colonel Bouchard came over and shook Keely's hand. He gave her his card and said he'd let her know when he was called to the county to do another auction. Burke listened with dry amusement as the colonel also told her that he'd load the rest of her items on his own truck and deliver them as soon as he'd settled the take with the attorney. Burke smiled after the colonel went into the house.

Keely turned to him. "Let's go home! I can't wait to see all this in my new home!"

※ ※ ※

NIGHT WAS GENTLY dimming day's light. Burke stood beside Keely as they gazed out her windows overlooking the lake. Nick had driven Harlan home over an hour ago. Keely and Burke stood alone watching the lavender smudges and tawny gold darken into autumn evening. A day with Keely had lowered his resistance even more. He wanted to put his arm around her shoulders, pull her close and . . . he stuck his hands safely in his jeans pockets.

"I can't believe this is mine," she whispered. "I can't

believe that I'll be able to come to this quiet place every evening and watch the sun set each night."

Her voice set off a longing inside him. He'd spent the day with her, and everything about her had opened new doors to feelings he'd long forgotten.

"I guess I better be going." His voice sounded rough to his own ears. He turned.

She followed him to the door. "I can't thank you and Nick and Harlan enough for your help today."

"Don't mention it." He dragged on his denim jacket and paused at the open door. So much wanted to simmer up from inside him—*Thank you for a wonderful day. I wouldn't have missed it for the world.* "Okay," he mumbled.

Without warning, Keely leaned over and kissed him on the cheek. "Thanks! A million times—thanks! You made today special!"

In a rush, his resistance gave way. He tangled his hand into the back of her hair and pressed his lips to hers. He drew her closer and deepened his kiss, losing himself in the smoothness of her skin, the silky softness of her hair.

She sighed against him.

The sound snapped him back to reality. With reluctance, he released her. He touched her cheek and then stepped outside her door. Cursing himself, he jogged to his Jeep.

In his rearview mirror, he glimpsed her standing in the doorway, her arms wrapped around herself—watching him go.

What was she thinking?

❈ ❈ ❈

WHEN BURKE'S JEEP disappeared around her stand of pines, Keely finally closed the door. Waves of shock, sensation swirled through her. *He kissed me.*

Ring. The sound of her phone brought her back.

She hurried to her purse and pulled her cell phone out. "Hello."

"I'm sorry," Burke's voice apologized gruffly. "I had no right. Forgive me . . . it won't happen again."

"Burke—"

He broke the connection.

She pressed her fingers to her lips and then her palm to her jawline. She still felt Burke's roughened cheek where it had grazed hers. The truth glimmered, and she spoke into the silence. "But I wanted your kiss all day, Burke."

CHAPTER NINE

ON THE FOLLOWING Saturday night, sundown hugged the sky, trailing magenta. Keely sat beside Burke on a hardwood bleacher on the home-team side of the crowded LaFollette-Steadfast football field. But they might as well have been on opposite sides of the county.

He'd greeted her formally and said that the sheriff thought he should sit with her at the games from now on so everyone would be aware that she and the sheriff's department were working together. A daunting speech. That, after he kissed her, apologized, and then didn't call her all week.

Only feet away, the charred bleachers were still roped off—unusable. This didn't look good for her school in front of the competing team and fans, but what could she do?

And what should she make of this man's kissing her and then distancing himself from her? It was hard not to take it personally. In fact, impossible.

Out of the corner of her eye, she noted her brother moving through the stands. Why? She was sitting halfway up so she couldn't see what was going on behind her or too far to either side. Evidently, Grady realized this. What was her brother up to now? *Grady, just sit down and watch the game!*

Too aware of Burke, she tried to read his expression. But he had put the shutters up again. She stopped herself before she touched her lips. She'd found herself doing this once or twice before this week. Why? *I've been kissed before. Why is Burke's kiss affecting me like this?*

The fall breeze cooled her bare ankles. *I should have worn socks tonight, and I should act like this game is of some interest to me.* In spite of all her efforts, football remained an enigma to her. A glance at the scoreboard told her that the teams were tied and that the game was in its third quarter. The scent of hot buttered popcorn filled the air. She put a smile on her face.

Far below to her left, she glimpsed Grady's fair head. He was changing places in the stands—again.

Her parents had finally come home from California. Grady had managed to stay out of trouble while they were gone—that is, if he hadn't started the fire in the bleachers last week. Anyway, her parents were lauding this stretch of good behavior as proof that their decision to have him finish high school in LaFollette was working. Now her mother was busy filling out applications to colleges with low enough standards to admit Grady but with high enough tuition to please her.

"Hey, Turner!" the McCracken woman yelled. "Guess your brother must not be much of a man. He never made the team! At least your dad liked to break heads when he was in high school!"

Veda McCracken had parked herself high in the bleachers behind Keely and Burke as though she didn't want them to miss any of her "performance." Keely didn't even bother to look over her shoulder.

The unpleasant woman had turned up more grimy and disheveled tonight than she had been at Ma and Bruno's reception. Why did she make it a point to attend each home game?

"Can't you run any faster than that, Blackfeather?" Veda bellowed as Shane, the LaFollette quarterback, was tackled and stopped.

"Shut up, you old biddy!" Shane's grandfather shouted back at Veda, putting into words all the angry glances cast toward the woman.

"Hey, hotshot deputy, how come your nephew isn't on the team?" Veda countered.

Keely gritted her teeth, forcing herself to keep her eyes focused on the field. She wondered why Veda had brought this up when farther down and to their left, Nick sat on the team bench for the first time.

The coach had mentioned in passing yesterday that though Nick had come too late to make the team, he'd decided to let him practice with the team for the remainder of the year. She didn't doubt that Shane had talked to the coach on Nick's behalf.

She turned to Burke and whispered into his ear, "Did Nick play ball in Milwaukee?"

Burke looked at her as if he'd just realized that he was sitting beside her.

But she knew that wasn't true, couldn't be—not after that kiss last Saturday night. There had been no mistaking the kind of kiss it had been—the kind of kiss intended to melt her knees.

Suddenly, she wanted to shake Burke Sloan. He'd kissed her and apologized. She'd forgiven him. Why was he acting like this? Maybe he couldn't forget it either. *We need to talk about this, clear the air, get it over with.*

"Nick made the team the first three years," Burke replied at last, "but sat on the bench a lot last year because of poor attitude."

She nodded, biting back the question uppermost in her mind: *Tell me why you kissed me.*

Jayleen appeared in Keely's line of sight, walking hurriedly down from the vicinity where Keely had just seen Grady. Was he bothering her again? Keely looked down at the bench and noticed that Nick was no longer sitting there. What was he doing?

Earlier this week, a teacher had sent Grady out of the cafeteria to the office for "paying unwelcome attention to a female student." Keely had warned Grady that this school, like so many others, had zero tolerance of sexual harassment.

If it happened again, he'd be suspended. A third offense would put him in front of the board in an expulsion hearing. She'd also mentioned that it wasn't a charge he'd want on his record if he intended to get into college. As usual, she doubted he'd listened to any of her words.

On top of everything else, Walachek was here watching the game. She'd seen the big man lumber up into the stands, but he hadn't talked to her or come near her. Still, it made her uneasy.

Keely pressed her temples. *Lord, help me get through this night, this school year. Next year, Grady will be away at school. I'll have a year's experience as principal under my belt, and I'll have gotten used to Burke's disturbing presence. The kiss will be ancient history.*

She tried to keep her mind on the game—the teams were tied once more. Then she saw Grady heading toward Jayleen again, and she uttered a barely audible groan. Why did he want to force her to reprimand him in front of his whole school, strangers from out of town, and most of the county? Did he think that he didn't have to behave here since he was a Turner?

A voice nearby, spoken just loud enough for her to hear said, "Everybody knows Turner bought his daughter her job—probably did it so his kid could graduate from somewhere."

Tears nipped at the back of her eyes. She'd known some people had been saying that behind her back. She'd known her father's influence had swayed some of the board members. But she'd taken the job, believing that no stranger could love her alma mater more than she did. *Lord, I need backup here. Maybe I shouldn't have taken this job.*

Behind them, Veda started yelling obscenities. Keely tried to block out the words. Then Burke moved closer to her. A silent show of support? Keely wiped her moist eyes with her fingertips.

Both teams bumped up the intensity of play. The mood of the audience became more focused, more in concert with the teams.

The scores inched up in lockstep. The large clock ticked time away—two minutes remaining. When Shane fumbled a pass, an opponent claimed the ball and charged toward his team's goal. A LaFollette player tackled him. The stands roared.

Suddenly Keely's secretary, Freda—her face flushed and angry—appeared right beside Burke. "Ms. Turner, that brother of yours has been dogging the Kainz girl all night. Well, now he's got his arm around her. You can't see it, can you?"

Bone tired, Keely shook her head. *But I anticipated it.* How could she be simultaneously irritated at her brother and yet feel her concern for him increasing? *Lord, I know he's doing this to get back at our father. But I can't change him. Help me. Help Grady.*

She stood up. "Excuse me, Burke. I have to go take action against this."

He rose also. "I'll come with you."

Keely felt the knot at the base of her skull that announced a coming headache. She had read the story of the Prodigal Son in her morning devotions. Thoughts of

Grady had rushed into her mind. Had the prodigal's older brother ever tried to reach his brother before he'd taken his inheritance and left? Had he ever felt as powerless as she did?

Grady, haven't you spent one second thinking how this makes you look? Forget our father. You're acting like some lame character out of a teen movie. You have to be doing this on purpose. You aren't really interested in Jayleen or anyone else. You just want to behave badly. And get everyone's attention. He was also doing this to make her look bad and to cause their parents to pressure her into letting him get away with it. *But I won't! Don't you know that? Do you care?*

Nick got to Grady before she and Burke did.

Just as Keely reached Grady's side, Nick slammed his fist into Grady's nose. Blood spurted.

"Fight!" Veda shrieked with glee over the commotion of the game. "Fight!"

Burke shoved past Keely and grabbed his nephew before he could land a second punch. Seeing a chance, Grady rammed his head into Nick's abdomen. Burke threw Grady backward against the bleachers. He stumbled, landed, but did not get up—the wind knocked out of him.

On the field the game went on. The stands seethed and roiled with people shifting to get a look at the excitement. Shouts came from all around. "He knocked Grady down!" "The new kid broke Turner's nose!"

Keely felt faint at the sudden violence. The blood. Some had spattered on her arm. She put her hand to her forehead.

Burke let go of Nick and grasped her shoulders. "Put your head down. You're not used to seeing blood like this."

She obeyed and the light-headedness receded immediately. Ashamed of her moment of weakness, she looked up, trying to decide how to get everyone to sit down. The crowd had pushed forward to see the action, and she felt mobbed. She looked to Burke.

"Get back!" he ordered. "Everyone, back to your seats! Or I'll start picking people up for public disturbance. Back!"

His final word—a roar—turned the throng back. Teens and adults alike gave way before his stern face and forbidding tone. Keely stayed at his side, pulling herself together to confront Nick and her brother.

"Fire! Fire!" Shouts came from out of nowhere. "Fires in the parking lot!"

Shock ripped through Keely. She glanced at Burke and read her own shock in his eyes. What next?

※ ※ ※

BURKE STOOD IN the now-quiet parking lot, watching the fire crew wrap things up. They'd put out the fires. The crowd had dispersed, but the smell of smoke still hung in the cool, dark night.

Burke looked around him at the nearly empty parking lot. After all the tension and chaos of this evening, he was restless and edgy. He was waiting to consult with Keely. And the topic wasn't going to be a pleasant one—the second fire in two weeks on school property.

Keely had gone into her office to get her purse. The main entrance door opened. He was aware the second she caught sight of him waiting for her. Her glance sent an electrical charge through him.

He'd stayed away all week. Tonight he'd dreaded sitting beside her; he'd exulted in being around her again.

She halted, gazing at him intently. "Is there anything else wrong?" She moved forward quickly.

The sight of her hesitance wrung his heart. *She didn't deserve what happened tonight, God. She's a good principal, and she's too good for me.* He stood straighter, though the weight he carried dragged at him. "Nothing's wrong . . . nothing new," he amended. "We need to talk."

When she reached him, he felt that unexplainable pull toward her. Who wouldn't be drawn to such a gutsy woman? How did she keep it all together and do such a great job? And with her brother making so much of the trouble?

"Do you have time to talk?" he asked, trying not to let her see how he wanted to drink in the sight of her. The stillness around them swelled in his ears. The fall night had cooled and the crickets were silent.

She wouldn't meet his eyes. "Of course. What . . . where do you want to go?" She fumbled in her bag for her keys.

He'd already given that some thought. He needed someplace where he and she could talk without alerting the gossip grapevine—that much he'd learned. "I thought we'd have a snack at the truck stop out on 27. You wouldn't have far to drive home then." The thought of eating didn't appeal to him. But he knew he needed hot food to make it through the final hours of his night shift.

She still hesitated.

Then it hit him. He'd asked this classy lady to go with him to a truck stop of all places! *What was I thinking?*

"All right," she said, her teeth crimping her lower lip. "It's really the only place open this late."

He gave her an apologetic nod. "See you there."

Burke waited for Keely beside his car door under the glaring lights of the busy truck stop. His eyes adjusted to the brightly lit oasis in the clear October darkness.

Exhausted but keyed up, he wanted to sleep, put an end to the long day, but he needed to prepare Keely for an unpleasant development.

"I know," Burke apologized as she approached him, "this isn't the country club, but—"

"This is fine. I've eaten here before."

They were bombarded by the scent of fried chicken as Burke led her inside toward a padded booth in the rear of the restaurant. All eyes turned to them. He'd miscalculated. They weren't the only ones ending the evening here.

As they walked down a gauntlet of parallel booths, he caught a few whispered comments: "his nephew . . . fire-crackers . . ." ". . . Turner's kid . . . jerk . . ." ". . . didn't need a kid from Milwaukee causing trouble . . ." So the next wave of talk about Grady and Nick had taken off. The fight and fires would be served up as the latest gossip all over the county for breakfast tomorrow.

They sat down facing each other. After a greeting, a harried waitress wiped their cleared table and brought them water and menus.

Burke wished he could think of something to say, something that would lighten the gloom on Keely's lovely face. Instead, he stared at the green vinyl menu. Sudden hunger attacked him. "What do you recommend?"

"I usually have," she replied from behind her menu, "burgers and fries, and please no comments about my cholesterol level." A trace of her characteristic wry humor sounded in her voice.

It eased his tension a notch.

The white-aproned waitress rejoined them. Keely and he ordered, and the waitress left them, promising to return with freshly brewed decaf coffee and cream.

Burke concentrated on looking calm. He'd learned over the years that this made it easier to deal with any problem. If only he could keep his attraction to this pretty lady under wraps, he could carry this off. "We have to discuss the fires." He kept his voice and manner businesslike.

Keely looked down at the table. "I have a hard time believing everything that happened tonight really happened."

He nodded, listening to the raucous country-and-western ballad playing in the background, a counterpoint to the somber pall that hung over their booth. "I'm afraid we may have a fire-setter on our hands."

She looked up, her brows lifted. "What do you mean?"

"I could be wrong, but I was afraid that the first fire might spark this kind of behavior."

"I'm not following you, Burke."

He sucked in air. "Sorry. I guess I'm tired. Hard to marshal my facts. My shift ends in an hour, and I think my brain is shutting down." *And being alone with you . . .*

"Take your time."

"Okay." Making himself concentrate on the facts and not on the way her hair was slipping out of her topknot, he tightened his mouth. "That first fire was a crime of opportunity. Couldn't have been planned unless the custodian was in on it, and we know he wasn't."

"Yes."

"But there's always a chance—" his jaw clenched—"when a kid who has problems sets a fire for revenge or just to cause trouble, it can trigger . . . excitement, a thrill. A fire gets them more attention—and that's what they wanted in the first place. And it can become an addiction." He lifted one palm as though to say, *See?*

She gazed at him. "That's not good to hear."

Being so near her all evening was lowering his resistance to her, more and more. "Not good at all." He shook his head. "And that's an understatement."

"Did you get any evidence?" Her hair slipped farther. Then the topknot gave way, and her hair flowed down onto one shoulder.

"I think so."

"Well?" she prompted, reaching up and releasing the derelict clips that had failed her. "Sorry," she murmured and ran her fingers through her hair.

Fighting the urge to reach over and touch the spun gold in her hair, he pulled a short, blackened metal wire from his uniform jacket and handed it to her.

She took it, turned it over, peering at it in the garish lighting of the truck stop. "What is it?"

"We think it was a sparkler." He swallowed to moisten his dry mouth.

"What?"

"One of the firefighters recognized it. It's what's left of a sparkler." Farther forward in the restaurant, a couple slid out of their booth. Both tried to get a good look at Keely and Burke but hide it at the same time. Their expression stripped him of assurance, making him more uncomfortable. *Yes, I know I'm not good enough for her.*

"Like a Fourth of July sparkler?" she asked, disbelief coloring her tone.

He nodded. He'd had trouble believing it at first too.

"Is this evidence? Should I be touching it?"

"No fingerprints possible."

She let out a grumbling sigh. "Did anyone see someone burning sparklers before the game?"

He heard the continued skepticism in her voice. "No, the firefighter told me he's seen this before. Kids drop sparklers they think are burned out into the trash, and hours later the trash bin explodes into flames. That's why you're supposed to dispose of sparklers in a can. They get so hot that they hold enough heat to ignite paper if the conditions are right."

She frowned. "You know I think I've heard of something like that before."

Intruding, the waitress brought their bowls of soup.

After a cautious sip of his hot, salty soup, Burke forced himself to return to the topic at hand. But looking up, he watched Keely slide her hair behind one ear. The sight melted his resistance.

Being with Keely again was making him forget his life as it had been and must stay. He couldn't let himself fall under Keely's spell of honesty and compassion. A gap, one of his inability to show love, stretched between them. *Why did I kiss her? She must think I'm an idiot.*

"So you found this, but does that mean we have a fire-setter? Is that what you call it?"

"We found several of those shoved down into waste bins in the parking lot and around the outside of the school. But you're correct. I'm just hoping I'm wrong. But it feels right to me." He shrugged.

"When do you think it was done?"

"Anytime before or during the game. Could have been hours before anyone arrived. An imperfect plan. Not every sparkler could be expected to ignite." He took refuge in the facts. "But even a few would have been enough to create the desired effect."

She lowered her forehead into her hand. "It could have been anyone, right?"

He nodded. The high-pitched grind of an eighteen-wheeler starting up interrupted.

"But it might not be a fire-setter," Keely continued. "It could just be someone who wanted to cause a ruckus at the game tonight. It could even have been someone from the school we played tonight. Schools often play pranks on each other."

He nodded again, watching her push her abundant hair back from her face.

"But you don't think so," she added.

His inability to ignore his attraction to her ate at him; he put down his spoon. "I don't know what to think. Maybe I'm just jumping to a conclusion quickly because I'm so disgusted that I haven't been able to find out who's causing all this trouble and stop them."

He didn't want to think it, but his gut was telling him that this might be the beginning of a series of fires. A serial fire-setter—that's all they needed.

An hour later Burke walked Keely to her car. "I'll let you know the minute I get any information."

"Please do." She stood looking at him.

He found he couldn't break the invisible connection.

She looked at him a long time—as though wanting to say something more. But finally, she opened her car door and got inside. With a wave, she started her SUV and drove out of the lot.

He watched her go, words he'd longed to say to her clotted in his throat. Then he jogged over to his Jeep and drove out to the highway, heading home. The stars glittered in the black cloudless sky. The fall chill made him turn on the defroster. His cell phone rang.

"Burke, this is Harlan."

"Harlan? I thought you'd be asleep by now."

"Having trouble sleeping tonight and got to thinking . . ."

"Yes?"

"Is the A&W on 27 on your way home?"

"Sure. I'm on my way now and will pass right by it."

"Pick me up a black cow, okay?"

Burke chuckled. "Well, that will keep you up all night."

"Yep."

"Okay. Home soon."

Burke drove down the deserted highway. It was nearing midnight. Fatigue was setting in. Keely's face as it had looked tonight came and went in his mind.

He pulled in at the A&W. The parking lot was crowded. The under-twenty-one crowd must gather here after games. He walked inside and up to the counter, the scent of fried onion rings filling his head. Pop music was playing, and the buzz of voices was loud—laughter, a girlish squeal.

Then a shout and a shriek.

Burke spun around. His stomach sank.

Surrounded by kids, Grady and Nick were sparring in the middle of the aisle of booths.

"Police!" Burke bellowed. He plowed his way to the two kids. "Break it up! Now!" He brandished his nightstick.

Nick fell back in front of Burke with hands held high. "I didn't start it!"

Grady swung around to confront Burke. Breathing hard, the teen bunched up his shoulder as if he were about to throw a punch.

Burke stared him down. Silence blanketed the room, only the rock music intruding.

Grady slowly lowered his fists, a sneer spreading over his face. "It's good you came—you saved Nick from getting his rear kicked—good. He caught me by surprise at the game."

Ignoring this, Burke said, "Let's go, both of you."

Both teens' mouths flew open. "What!"

He collared both of them and dragged them toward the door.

Shane stepped out of the crowd. "Hey!"

"Shane," Burke barked over his shoulder, "buy Harlan Carey a black cow and take it over to him. I'm going to be busy down at the station."

CHAPTER TEN

EARLY THE NEXT afternoon, Keely walked out of the pizza parlor in Steadfast. The twin fragrances of garlic and oregano hung in the doorway. The Weavers, with little Rachel and five-year-old son, Zak, had invited her along with Harlan, Nick, and Burke to go for lunch after church. They needed to discuss the Family Closet workday this weekend. Before winter, the shop needed re-roofing, and several men had volunteered to supply the labor—Harlan, Burke, and Nick among them.

Keely had noted that these three had been quieter than usual, almost somber during the meal. In fact, Nick hadn't said one word, but fresh anger flamed in his eyes. She'd hoped sitting with the team last night would help. But the fight with Grady may have undone any benefit from that. Had Burke given Nick a hard time about the fight last night at home?

Burke's shuttered look moved her. She longed to touch his arm, draw him away to comfort him. She blocked that line of thought.

Last night after the game, she'd ordered both Nick and Grady to report to her office the first thing on Monday morning. She shook her head. This fighting between Grady and Nick only heightened the awkward position her father had put her in. Why hadn't her father realized that by insisting Grady be one of her students he was jeopardizing her relationship with her brother for the rest of their lives?

Oh, Lord, give me the wisdom of Solomon. I'm going to need it to get through to Grady. Sorry. I forgot that's your job. Help me, Lord; I don't know what to do.

The glaring sunshine made her squint after the darker interior of the pizza place. A squirrel chattered from above in a red-and-yellow maple across the street. She turned to say good-bye to the Weavers.

The sound of squealing brakes made them all whirl toward the street.

"You! Sloan!" Franklin Turner's voice boomed across Main Street. "I saw your Jeep!" Leaving his car still running, he jumped out and ran across to them.

Seeing the outraged expression on her father's face, Keely prepared for the worst. *But why here? Why now?*

Burke merely waited for her father. But Nick's face took on a deeper truculence, and Harlan frowned darkly.

In his black suit Burke looked more than her father's equal. In fact, her father looked like the child—Burke the man.

"What do you mean arresting my son last night?" Turner thundered into Burke's face.

Keely's breath caught in her throat. Arrest? Why hadn't anyone told her about this?

"He was fighting in public." Burke's voice was cool.

"Who do you think you are? Grady is a Turner! You should have called me!"

"He was breaking the law," Burke replied evenly.

"Well, I'm instructing my attorney to file a false arrest suit against you—"

"Hold up there, Franklin," Harlan said, raising a hand.

Heedless, her father went on. "I'll tie you up with litigation—"

"I said," Harlan interrupted again, *"hold up!"*

Burke shifted his attention to the older gentleman. This action made Keely proud of Burke and more ashamed of her father. She took a step forward, ready to nudge him.

Finally, Turner glanced at Harlan. "This matter doesn't concern you, Carey."

"It does. It concerns everyone in this town." Harlan moved right in front of Turner. "Now your father isn't here, so I guess it's up to me to set you straight."

"Set *me* straight?" Turner twisted his voice with sarcasm.

The older man's pluck impressed Keely. Not many stood up to her father.

Harlan ignored Turner's disrespectful tone. "Your father was a hard man, but he was honest. I can't approve of the way you've lived so self-centered, but you have still kept the mill open here and that's something."

Turner sputtered.

Harlan cut him off. "I've watched your daughter since she was a child trying to make up for your not doing what you should. You've been given much, and you've given very little back to your community. It's time you rolled up your sleeves and helped your daughter—"

Her father tried to interrupt, but Harlan went on in an even voice. "Your boy is in trouble. Doesn't it concern you that he was bothering a young woman and started two fights last night?"

Her father glowered at the older man. "My son didn't start anything. It's that punk." He pointed to Nick. "If he'd stayed in Milwaukee where he belongs, my boy wouldn't—"

"He started it!" Nick flared. "And he better leave Jay—"

"It takes two to make a fight," Harlan insisted. "I was at

the game last night, Turner, and you weren't. Your boy picked the fight. Not Nick."

Keely knew no one but Harlan Carey could have gotten away with this or would have had the nerve to even try to stand up to her father.

"This is none of your business," her father snapped. He looked as though he was restraining himself from shoving Harlan out of his way.

"I live in Steadfast," Harlan continued. "How your son turns out is the business of everyone here."

"What . . . is . . . your . . . point?" her father asked acidly.

"No one in this county wants the next owner of the mill to be the kind of person your son is heading toward. Do something about it before it's too late."

Keely nearly gasped. Harlan had put her hidden fear into words. How could anyone trust Grady to be the main employer in the county?

Turner clenched and reclenched his fists. "Are you finished?"

Not looking the least intimidated, Harlan nodded and stepped back.

"My son is none of your business, Carey. He's my son to raise, and I'm doing just fine." He jerked his head toward Burke. "I'm not done with you, Sloan. You leave my son alone—"

"If he obeys the law, I'll have nothing to do with him." Burke stared back at Turner, showing no fear.

Keely held her breath. Her father had been crossed twice in public. That had never happened in her experience.

Her father's face turned livid. He glared at her, and then he looked back at Burke. "Stay away from my daughter. I'll disinherit her before I'd let her marry an opportunist like you." Turning on his heel, he marched back to his car and sped away.

Trembling, Keely felt her face flame with embarrassment. This wasn't the first time her father had humiliated her in public, but this was the worst yet.

A self-conscious silence made them all mute. Keely noticed that a small crowd had gathered a few yards up the street. *Great. Another public performance by a Turner. More tongue-clicking and gossip.* Her pulse raced. She took a calming breath. Her father's insinuation that Burke was interested in her but unacceptable left her feeling . . . somehow degraded.

Bitterness welled inside her. *That's right, Father. No man would be interested in just me. He would have to be after your money.* No wonder so few men here had ever tried to date her. Who'd want Franklin Turner as a father-in-law?

"So what happened last night?" she asked Harlan, forcing herself to break the uncomfortable silence.

"I think that Burke should explain that to you," Harlan said, suddenly looking tired, old. Standing up to her father would sap anyone's strength. "Nick, let's go home. You need to study and I need a nap." The older man touched Nick's shoulder.

Nick sent his uncle an ugly, resentful glance. This took Keely by surprise—why was Nick mad at his uncle? Was it still over the fight at the game?

The teen gave Harlan his arm and then walked with him toward the truck parked on the street.

The Weavers said a discreet good-bye and left Burke and Keely side by side on Main Street.

❖ ❖ ❖

BURKE FACED KEELY. Her face downcast, she'd lowered her chin. Her golden eyelashes fanned her flushed cheeks. Now he had more sympathy for Nick squaring off with Grady twice in one night. He only wished he could have landed a punch on Franklin Turner's face. How could a grown man make such a fool of himself in public? And worse yet, talk to his daughter like that?

Burke took a step closer and stopped. He'd kept his distance through church and through lunch and now here they were—forced back together because of her brother and his nephew. He couldn't just walk away now—even though that might be the best thing he could do for her in the long run.

"Well, are you going to tell me?" She folded her arms in front of her.

The sight of her trying to bounce back left him without words. *What a lady. She's worth ten of you, Turner.* They needed some place they could talk in private. He glanced around. Shame-faced, the eavesdropping onlookers had dispersed. Fortunately, downtown was thin of people—most everyone had gone home after church—only the café and pizza place were open at this end of town.

Across the street, the silent courthouse stood among vivid autumn oaks and maples. He knew of a quiet bench in the rear where they could be alone. "Walk with me," he invited.

She nodded.

Pulling together his thoughts, he took her slender elbow and steered her toward the courthouse. Walking this close to her was an indulgence. He breathed in her spicy cinnamon fragrance. He felt a sinking sensation in his stomach over having to tell her about Grady's finale last night.

"Don't keep me in suspense," she said when they'd crossed the street. "How bad was the fight?"

She deserved a life unsullied by others. Why didn't she just move ten thousand miles away from her family? *Because she doesn't turn tail and run when the going gets rough like you,* his conscience replied. *She sticks with her family.* The words stung but were too true. Keely was willing to pour herself out for others. Keely was even acting as her thankless brother's keeper. But Burke didn't think that her love would make the difference.

Wishing he could take her far away from here, somewhere she could enjoy this late October day, he instead led her to the dark green glossy bench. She sat down. He joined her, but he didn't face her. It hurt him to have to tell her about Grady.

Bending over, he rested his elbows on his thighs and knotted his hands together. "I'm sorry I didn't call you last night. But it was late, and I thought you'd been through enough. I tried to get here early this morning so I could have a moment to tell you privately, but that didn't happen either."

He looked up. "This is it. After I left you last night, Harlan called and asked me to pick him up a black cow at the A&W. I went in and—"

"Caught Nick and Grady fighting again." Her voice sounded exhausted.

He nodded, hating the truth. "If it's any consolation, Nick had disobeyed me too. I'd told him to go straight home after the fight at the game. Except for church, school, driving Harlan, and volunteering at the Family Closet, he's grounded for the rest of the month."

She sighed and pressed her hands to her face. "And you took both of them in and charged them with disturbing the peace."

He nodded again. Her voice didn't show any censure, any personal reaction, so different from her father's bias. Keely Turner was some lady.

Early this morning, Rodd had sent Burke home *before* Turner had come in to get his kid. Rodd probably had gotten an earful from the man too. "I did it because I thought both kids needed to be taught a lesson."

"If I'd known this was going to go on and on," she said finally, "I would never have taken the job as principal."

He ached to tell her none of this was her fault. But he only looked at her. "I don't . . . no one could blame you for all that's happened." *I'm not making any progress with Nick either.*

How would it have been different between Keely and him if Nick had stayed in Milwaukee and Grady out East? As it stood now, every time he and Kelly got together it was because of trouble. And their two relatives were right in the middle of it.

The wind gusted suddenly, and red-tipped yellow leaves cascaded from the maple next to them, rushing over the lawn and pavement. It reminded Burke that time was passing and he was no closer to finding out who was responsible for the pranks, which had progressed from digging holes to shooting out windows to setting fires.

"People have gotten the wrong idea about your nephew. I'm sure you overheard—" her voice became gritty—"what people were saying about him at the game last night and at the truck stop."

He recalled all too well Veda's nastiness and all the snide comments people had made, not just about Nick but about Keely. But none of it mattered the longer he stayed near her. *How much longer can I hold back from touching her, kissing her again?*

"I'm not deaf," he answered at last.

She closed her eyes.

He nearly reached for her. But what if someone saw them together?

She opened her eyes. "My brother's reputation was bad enough when he only spent time home from school on vacations." She sighed. "I know why he's doing what he's doing, but why can't I get him to see that it will end badly for him, not just for my father?"

"Maybe he doesn't care—even about himself. I've seen

that. Some kids have no boundaries inside them. At least, that's how I see it. No sense of a future."

She turned to look at him. "Harlan is right, you know. People might well be afraid of Grady taking over the mill someday." She leaned back against the bench. "So it's natural for folks around here to want your nephew to be the culprit, to be the one who's causing the fights—"

"And setting the fires?" Her understanding glance warmed him. Her honesty drew him even as he fought its currents. *Everything between us is too mixed up.*

She nodded. "If it's Grady, it's worse for Steadfast and LaFollette. Your nephew has no influence here, and he'll probably finish school and leave. But my brother will inherit the mill and the rest of my parents' property. I've seen the will. I get heirlooms, stock, and money. My brother, the male heir, gets everything else."

Her voice was raw, but he could change nothing—not even for her sake. How did she handle all the talk? He had the urge to shove words down a few throats. But he had trouble to deal with now. *I think your brother is setting the fires, Keely. But I don't know how to prove it. I can't imagine the pain that it will cause you if I do. And I have no way to shield you from any of this.* He knew if he proved Grady guilty, she'd take it personally—not like her father had demonstrated today. But in her own way, as if she should have done more for her brother.

But his sympathy for her didn't make an ounce of difference. If he found evidence that would convict her brother, he'd proceed with it. He'd have no choice. Experience had taught him that a kid like Grady was headed for big trouble. Keely couldn't stop Grady, and her father wouldn't even try.

An unwelcome thought intruded—the guilty party might not be Grady. Maybe he was focusing on Grady because he couldn't deal with it being his own nephew.

Nick, after all, had set off the firecrackers during the game. And Burke knew that last year Nick had been accused of setting a fire in a waste bin outside his school in Milwaukee. Nick had staunchly denied it, but it had cost him a week's suspension. *Maybe I'm just fooling myself, Lord. Am I as blind as Turner?*

"I hoped Nick," he muttered, "was doing better when I saw him sitting with the team." His chest constricted. The thought came that he might have failed Nick—doing too little too late. On the other hand, what would it cost Keely to see her brother go the length of his rebellion? He bent his forehead to his hands, grappling with these fears. Fear for Nick. Fear for Keely. Fear for himself.

"I know you think Grady set those fires last night, and I don't doubt that he could have." Keely's voice intruded—soft, earnest. "But Nick is still smoldering with anger and not all of it is aimed at you. He's angry at Grady and at the school. And Walachek was also there last night. He didn't talk to me, but that doesn't mean he wouldn't like to make me look bad my first year as principal. It might still be someone we don't even suspect. Grady and Nick haven't cornered the market on rebellion."

Her words only upped Burke's pain a notch. *She's right. I haven't made any progress in solving this case. I don't even know if there is only one perp.*

※ ※ ※

ON SATURDAY BY the time the morning fog lifted, the volunteers had already stripped shingles off the roof of the Family Closet that was closed for the day. Surging electric saws cut out the spongy wood that had to be replaced and recovered.

Walachek—silent and sullen—had come to work off some of his community service hours, part of his sentence. Nick and Harlan had also arrived early. Now Harlan was giving advice, and Nick was on the roof as carpenter's helper. Shading her eyes with her hand, Keely tilted her head back and watched the men on the roof. *Thank you, Lord. Please help them get this done before the next rain. And keep everyone safe.*

She realized she had unconsciously been searching for Burke's face. *Lord, I haven't had a moment with Burke since my move that isn't ruled by everything going on around us. Help me forget his kiss. He's obviously forgotten it. This isn't the season for love. I'm just exhausted, given out.*

Trying to shed her uneasiness about having Walachek around, she walked back inside, where Jayleen and Carrie were waiting to help her. Both girls had signed up to be included in the Family Closet Outreach. *Lord, help me focus on these two young women today. Help us help them mature and draw closer to you.*

"Okay, girls." She forced herself to sound cheery over the general racket outside and the pounding overhead. "Let's get started. We aren't going to sort donations today. We're going to do something fun—decorate for fall. First, let's get the boxes of decorations down from the attic."

The next few minutes were spent locating the ladder, having Jayleen crawl up and hand down the boxes to Carrie and Keely. Then Keely had the girls spread the boxes around the tops of shelves and counters. "Here, Carrie, stick up these tiny suction clips all around the main window and then put up these strings of little pumpkin lights."

"Oh, cute." Carrie took the smaller box from Keely.

Keely turned to Jayleen. "Would you unpack all our ceramic pumpkins and make sure they have the 'Not for sale' stickers on their bottoms? People try to buy them every year." She grinned.

Jayleen nodded. Then Keely heard her name being called from outside. "I'll be right back, girls." She left.

She was given the bad news that another section of the roof under the shingles was ruined and needed to be replaced. "It can't be helped. Who can drive over to the mill for more plywood? Just put it on our account."

Nick and Harlan left in Harlan's truck and Keely walked around to the back entrance. She needed to check if Ma and Mabel Franz had dropped off enough sandwiches for the workers or if she'd need to make more.

From the front room, the girls' voices drifted to her.

". . . two guys like you. You're really lucky," Carrie said.

"Lucky? Me?" Jayleen's voice was softer.

"Grady Turner has it big time for you."

Keely's stomach turned. Grady had been sullen and sarcastic all week. She'd had to suspend him another day this week for skipping and starting another fight, this time with Shane Blackfeather. Two suspensions in one week. Her father had retaliated with an angry phone call, and her mother had wept on the phone—was Keely trying to destroy Grady's chances of getting into college?

"Me?" Jayleen barked something like an ugly-sounding laugh. "He just wants to use me."

"But he's got money, and I'd give anything to ride in that car of his."

Keely could only shake her head. *Carrie, you're heading for a fall. Don't. Please.*

A pause. "Then tell him." Jayleen's voice cut the heavy silence with an edge of sarcasm.

Carrie made an unhappy noise. "He wouldn't have anything to do with me. I'm not pretty enough."

"What about your baby's father?"

"Oh, he's all right. But *he's* such a baby. Grady's been around. He's hasn't had to spend his life in this Podunk county," Carrie complained. "You even got to go to Milwaukee. I've never been anywhere."

"I'm happy to be back here with my family." Keely heard the pain in Jayleen's voice. "You ought to be glad you're with your aunt now, and you'll have family to help you."

"Having a baby isn't such a big deal. My cousin's having her second. She gets money from the government, and she's going to be able to live in Eau Claire and go to school. She's going to be a beautician."

Keely had heard this kind of faulty reasoning before—unfortunately.

"Having a baby is the biggest deal there is," Jayleen stated. "You're a baby if you think—"

"I'm not a baby," Carrie snapped back.

"You are if you think going out with Grady because he's got money and a cool car is more important than doing right by your baby."

"*You've* got a lot of room to talk. I didn't run around with a bunch of druggies!" A door slammed. Silence. Had Carrie left?

Breathing a silent prayer, Keely walked into the main room. "I didn't mean to eavesdrop, but I came in the back way . . ."

Jayleen kept her back to Keely. "Carrie left."

Keely nodded, reading the distress in Jayleen's voice and the stiff way she held her shoulders. *Lord, give me the words.* "Jayleen, you've been through a lot. And I told you I won't let Grady bother you anymore."

Jayleen made a sound of dismissal, a sniff. "Your brother is a jerk, but he's nothing compared to . . ."

Keely took her heart in her hands and asked, "Your baby's father?"

Turning to Keely, Jayleen nodded, a shadow moving over her expression. Tears welled up. "How am I ever going to make it up to my baby Rachel?" Tears slipped down Jayleen's high cheekbones.

Keely went to her and folded her in her arms. "It all depends on you—what you do from this day forward."

Trembling against Keely, Jayleen wept, gasping for breath. "How can I ever make it right?"

"You don't have to. God will make it right—if you'll let him."

"I can't face God. Not after all I've done." Jayleen fought for composure, gulping air.

Keely combed her mind, seeking God's words of comfort. "Jayleen, if you read the Bible, you'll find out that Jesus only got angry at one kind of person when he was on earth."

"People like me," Jayleen choked out.

"No. He only got angry with religious people who put themselves above sinners. The holier-than-thou crowd. He had no patience with them. Jayleen, Jesus loved people. That's what drew people to him. His love."

"How can he love me? I don't love me. I hate me."

Keely tightened her hold on the girl. "God loves you. Jesus loves you. When he was on earth, he loved people so much that the religious people called him 'the friend of sinners.' They meant it as a put-down. But it was what he wanted to be, what he came to be! Sinners weren't afraid to tell him what they'd done—because he didn't judge them. He loved them."

"But how can you say what I've done is right?" Jayleen wiped her tears with the backs of her hands.

"You didn't do right. Jesus didn't tell sinners that they'd done what God wanted. He accepted their confessions, and then he'd tell them, 'Go and sin no more.' "

Jayleen relaxed against her. "I don't ever want to do what I did again."

"Then tell Jesus so. He can forgive you, and he will send his love flowing through you and change you forever. Let him help you change your life, and your baby will thank you when she gets older." Keely cupped Jayleen's chin with her hand. "That's why the Family Closet is here—to let people feel God's love in a way that they need right now."

Jayleen tugged her face away. "I still don't understand how he can love me."

"His love is beyond our understanding. His love changed me. I don't want to think what my life would have been without him."

Though drawing away, Jayleen looked up at her. "What did you do that he had to forgive you?"

Keely shook her head. "A person doesn't have to *do* anything we think of as evil to need God. Sin is sin. My mother sent me to Sunday school and I learned about Jesus when I was very small. I realized then that I needed him. I don't understand how—except that I felt his love and I wanted it in my life."

She shrugged. "I don't know how to explain it. But it's real, Jayleen. And it's yours for the asking. Do you want Jesus to wipe away your sin and become a new child in him?"

Jayleen frowned. "I don't know . . ."

Keely read by the girl's expression that Jayleen expected . . . what? For Keely to pressure her, reject her? She chose her next words with care. "Pray about it, Jayleen. If you ask God what he wants you to do, he'll answer."

Jayleen stared at her and then turned back to the orange ceramic pumpkins of all sizes.

Keely went over to the window to finish up what Carrie had left undone, her heart thanking God for giving her such an opening.

But she grieved for Carrie. *How can I reach her, Lord?*

※ ※ ※

IN THE COOL midnight air, he shut off his car. He got out and slammed the door. He didn't have to be quiet. He didn't feel like being quiet. No one lived near enough to hear anything, see anything. He unlocked his trunk and took out the full gas can. He felt in his pocket for the matches. This would get them all crazy again. Tomorrow was Halloween. He was just celebrating a day early.

Besides, he'd had enough. *I'm not taking their garbage anymore. They're going to be sorry. And this will get me out of this town.*

CHAPTER ELEVEN

THE LOOK ON Keely's face in the hellish light from the raging yellow-gold flames had been dreadful to witness. Burke had stood beside her, helpless to stop either her pain or the flames.

But now the firefighters had pumped enough water onto the blazing Family Closet to quench the inferno. Mud around charred remains and the lingering acrid smell of smoke and gasoline were all that was left.

Rodd walked over to them. "It's out. As soon as the firefighters clear out, we'll cordon off the site. I'm going to leave two deputies here on guard. I don't want anyone tampering with possible evidence."

Burke nodded, his anger over this latest tragedy still blazing inside him. Thank God, no one had been inside.

"Ms. Turner," Rodd said, "I'm so sorry about this. I know how hard you've worked to make the Family Closet something good for this community. I won't stop till I find out who did this. For the county, this fire's worse than criminal."

Burke agreed with every word his friend uttered. *Lord, why don't you help me and Rodd find out who's setting these fires? Is it one person or several? I can't seem to get anywhere. Where are you?*

"Burke, why don't you drive Ms. Turner home," Rodd suggested.

"No, I . . . my car . . . ," Keely mumbled. Her hair hung over her smoke-smudged face; her shoulders were bowed.

"I'll have one of the deputies drive it home for you when his night shift ends at 7 A.M. You aren't in any shape to be driving anywhere by yourself. No argument. Take her home, Burke."

Burke nodded again. "I'll come right—"

"Your shift ended at eleven. Go home. You'll be more use to me if you're well rested. At daylight, I'll want you to go over everything with me, step by step, so we don't miss anything."

"Okay." Burke was relieved. Rodd had only told him to do what he'd have insisted on himself. "I'll be back at seven." Burke took Keely's elbow and directed her toward his Jeep. She looked stunned, destroyed. Her eyes held the look of disbelief. She was taking this personally. Of course, that would be her natural reaction.

Worry dragging at his insides, he got her settled into her seat and then drove them off into the chilly night. He turned the heater on high and hoped the car would warm up quickly.

Driving the empty county roads to her house, he tried to think of words to say to the silent woman beside him, but he was at a loss. He'd seen Keely take one hit after another this fall, but this one had taken her down for the count. *Lord, you know I'm no good at comforting. But I'm here and she needs—deserves—comfort. Help me.* But no words came.

Finally he turned up her lane and drove around the pines to her house. Without waiting for an invitation, he went inside with her. Keely stood in the center of the entry-way, looking like a lost child.

Maybe if he got her talking she could release her grief and anger. "The place was insured?"

She didn't respond.

"Keely? It was insured, wasn't it?" *Speak to me!*

"Yes, but that won't help us now." She looked to him. "Don't you see—" her voice cracked—"it's not just losing the building that's the problem. We can't replace what was inside—in time! The single parents we work with are counting on being able to buy or work for winter clothing for their kids and Christmas presents. After the back-to-school rush, the holiday season is our busiest."

Her distress washed over him, taking his mood down with hers. "I didn't think about that."

"We had boxes and boxes of jackets, boots, hats, and mittens to distribute and sell. And Christmas presents—the garage was lined with boxes full of washed and repaired and even donated new toys and books!" She began crying. "Why did I keep everything there? I should have made sure that donations were kept at different—"

Of course, she'd tear at herself. "Keely—" he took her cold hands in his—"you couldn't have guessed that this would happen."

She looked away but let him keep holding her hands. "It's the fire-setter, isn't it?"

"It might or might not be." He gripped her hands, trying to communicate what he felt through his touch. *Please, Keely, ease up.* "We haven't examined the evidence."

"I should have expected—"

"You couldn't have predicted this," he reiterated, rasping over each word, his throat raw from the smoke he'd inhaled.

"But I'm the one in charge. I should have done something! I can't bear it!"

How could Burke ease this burden? Did he stand a chance? Words still failed him. He reached for her and pulled her into his arms. She trembled against him but didn't resist. He stroked her hair—feeling its silk between his fingers at last, making himself ignore how much he longed to draw her even closer.

He hadn't held anyone like this within recent memory, not since Sharon had been ill. He pushed this out of his mind and concentrated on the woman here and now. Was she crying for the loss she'd described or for something even more hurtful? Did she suspect that her brother might have set the fire? He couldn't ask that question.

He'd wait for daybreak to see what the fire told him. And when he got home, he'd check the odometer on Harlan's truck. He'd started checking it each morning and evening to see that Nick didn't abuse the privilege of using the vehicle and to make sure he was only driving as far as should be expected. How many miles between Harlan's and the thrift shop? Had Nick resented having to volunteer at the Family Closet enough to start the fire?

He'd also check Harlan's gas can again. It had been full the last time he'd checked it—knowing how teens often drove on gas fumes. He didn't even think of asking for a search warrant to check out Grady's trunk and gas tank for evidence. They hadn't received the bullets yet.

No wonder he understood what Keely might be feeling. But he had no comfort to give her. She wept against his shoulder. He pulled her closer and murmured soft words, trying to ignore how much he wanted to kiss her soft lips, so near his own. *Lord, I'm not worthy of this caring woman. Send her someone who is. Then let me go far from here and forget her.* . . .

※ ※ ※

VOICES. BURKE OPENED his eyes, then closed them. The bright October sunlight streamed from the windows across from him in Harlan's living room. The sunshine blinded his sleep-filled eyes. He must have fallen asleep on the couch when he'd come in last night. Sitting down here was the last thing he remembered. He groaned as he recalled how crushed Keely had looked.

"This seems to be the problem," a quiet voice said from the kitchen. Harlan? What time was it? He glanced at his watch. Nearly 7 A.M. He'd have to get up soon, but he couldn't move—too fatigued after dealing with the third fire, the most destructive yet.

"Why don't we just call a plumber?" Nick's muted voice sounded from the kitchen.

"I don't need a plumber," Harlan objected. "Who do you think put the modern plumbing in this house?"

"You?" Nick sounded impressed.

"Yes, and this is a good opportunity for you to learn something. Now you get down here and watch me. There may come a time when you can't get me or a plumber. And, Nick, it's better to know how to do stuff like this for yourself. Hand me that wrench and I'll show you what to do."

Burke knew he should get up and offer to help, but an unusual lassitude had him in its clutches. Keely's face came to mind—her forcing back tears last night. Who had wanted the Family Closet shut down, destroyed? And why?

Stiff and feeling every lump in the old sofa, Burke thought of Grady as well as his nephew. Nick had been home in bed, hadn't he? The truck's odometer had registered more miles than the previous morning, but he hadn't calculated if there was a major discrepancy. He'd have to talk to Harlan about any errands he and Nick had run. *I need to get up and get to the crime scene.* But he still couldn't move.

"Nick, hand me some of that Teflon tape to seal this connection." There followed a brief exchange about plumbing.

Burke stared at the ceiling. Every time he closed his eyes,

he saw white smoke billowing against a night sky, orange-gold flames engulfing the back porch where he and Keely had sat the night after they'd first met. Who'd wanted to destroy what Keely, Penny, and so many others had worked so hard to bring about? It couldn't be Nick. It couldn't.

"How about when we're done, we go to the Black Bear Café and have one of their huge lumberjack breakfasts?" Harlan suggested.

"I'm in." Another pause while tools clanged against old metal pipes.

Had someone acquired a taste for the excitement arson created, or was someone with a grudge using the school fires as a smoke screen? After last night, Burke wondered now if they had a fire-setter on their hands or a copycat.

Also, Carrie Walachek had been frequenting the Family Closet. Her father had been forced to help shingle the roof. Had Walachek realized how much pain destroying the thrift shop would cause Keely? But what if more than one perp was involved? How would they ever unravel this?

Lord, help us stop this before someone gets hurt! Maybe I'm fooling myself, but I don't think it's my nephew. I'm not taking any credit. If anyone's done him good, it's been Harlan Carey and you know it. I'm no good at relationships. You know what I did when Sharon got sick.

He pushed this aside. He wished there wasn't a fire-setter, and he didn't want it to be Nick. But he didn't want it to be Grady either—for Keely's sake.

"How's Jayleen Kainz doing?" Harlan asked in a casual tone.

Suddenly alert, Burke listened for Nick's comment. Was Nick interested in Jayleen? Competition over Jayleen had sparked the conflict between Grady and his nephew. Nick had been sentenced to one month probation for fighting at the A&W. So had Grady.

Evidently, someone—maybe his lawyer—had talked Turner out of pressing a charge of false arrest against Burke or the sheriff's department. It would have been hard to win with all the witnesses to the fight.

"Jayleen's still really messed up. She can't decide whether to try to get her baby back or to let the Weavers adopt her."

"I see." Harlan began discussing pipe threads.

So Nick and Jayleen were getting close enough to discuss important issues. He closed his eyes. He and Keely never discussed anything but problems. Why couldn't they ever have a peaceful moment alone? Where had that thought come from?

He couldn't stand the thought that he might have to tell Keely that her brother was responsible. How much would that wound her? As much as it would hurt to find out that his own nephew was guilty? Burke's temples throbbed.

"Getting back to Jayleen," Harlan said, "I'm glad I never had to make a decision like that."

"You didn't have to because—" Nick's voice became belligerent—"you cared about your kid, didn't you?"

"Yes, I loved Daniel. When he was killed in Vietnam, it devastated me. But you realize that Jayleen never intended to hurt her baby."

"Yeah, I know. She got hooked up with the wrong guy." Nick sounded convinced of Harlan's sincerity. "Not all parents are like you." Nick's words came out in a savage rush. "Some fathers don't care about their kids."

The resentment, the bottled-up rage in Nick's voice chilled Burke. How much fury did his nephew have stored up against his father, against him? Was it enough to spur Nick to set fires and gain the worst kind of attention in order to punish his father and his uncle for their neglect?

God, forgive me! Please don't let my mistake, my lack, hurt

Nick. A verse from the past Sunday's sermon repeated in Burke's mind: *"The Lord is close to the brokenhearted; he rescues those who are crushed in spirit."*

I am brokenhearted, Lord. Rescue me. Rescue Nick from my neglect!

"Do you mean your father?" Harlan asked point-blank.

Burke drew in a sharp breath. He'd never had the nerve to ask his nephew this.

"He cheated on my mom! He divorced her and then moved away. Bailed on us completely. I hate him." Nick's every word dripped with bitterness.

Oh, Lord, his father and I have sowed the wind. Will we reap the whirlwind? I know his father doesn't really care now. And I let myself be cut off from family. But I care now! I didn't see this coming, didn't see past myself—

"I don't blame you," Harlan declared with a tartness in his voice Burke had rarely heard. "If I met your dad, I'd have a hard time not blistering his ears. What did he mean by leaving you and your mom?"

"Everybody tells me—" Nick sounded affected by Harlan's passion, hurt overcoming anger in his voice—"these things happen—"

"They happen because of the hard hearts of men and women." Then Harlan said with a challenge in his voice, "Nick?"

"Yeah?"

"Don't ever do that to your own son."

A pause. "I won't."

"It won't be easy. What's happened to you will affect you a long way down the road. The only way you can keep from repeating your father's mistake is to think before you act and keep in touch with God. Look at Jayleen. Her mother's sins led Jayleen to do something she never thought she would do. Look at how she's suffering now. You have to *think*. Because everything you do will make a difference not only in your life but in your children's." Then Harlan grunted as though he was tightening something.

Humbled by Harlan's courage in bringing up Nick's father's sin and giving Nick direction, Burke waited to hear his nephew's answer.

"Mr. Carey, could I ask you something else?"

"Sure."

Burke went on alert. What did Nick want to ask?

"Do you think my uncle is in love with Ms. Turner?"

The question nearly bolted Burke upright on the couch, shock rippling through him.

"What makes you think he might have feelings for Keely Turner?" Harlan asked, sounding like he was sliding out from under the sink.

"Did you know my uncle lost his wife like you did?"

"He did?" Harlan groaned as if he was getting up. "She must have died pretty young then."

Burke shifted on the sofa. Nick—talking about Sharon! He'd only been in kindergarten when she'd passed away. *I didn't think Nick even remembered Sharon*. An image came to Burke, Sharon pulling Nicky, a pudgy three-year-old, in a wagon. They'd been baby-sitting him. A twinge crimped around Burke's heart.

"Yeah, she was just out of college. My mom tries to fix my uncle up with friends of hers, but nothing ever happens."

"It's very rare when matchmaking like that works out," Harlan agreed. "Your uncle should be the one to decide when he's ready to start dating again."

"Yeah. Did you date after your wife died?"

Harlan must have paused to test the faucets. Burke listened to each being turned on and off while he struggled to release the guilt he always felt when he thought of Sharon.

"No, I just didn't have the heart to date anyone," Harlan replied.

"But Bruno and Ma did. They got married."

"I don't think either of them had plans to fall in love again," Harlan said in a quiet voice.

"Then what happened?"

"God blessed them a second time. If you don't remember anything else I've said today, Nick, remember this. Love is a gift from God. Don't waste love."

Harlan's words rocked Burke's heart, sending shock waves through him. *"Don't waste love." I love Keely.* This truth glistened inside him. *I love Keely even though I have no right to.* How could he even attempt love again when he'd failed Sharon so? *I let her down first, Lord, and then I let everyone else in my family down after I buried her.* How could he ever release his guilt?

"Love's much too precious in this wicked world," Harlan continued. "Never be afraid to tell someone that you love them. That's wasting God's greatest gift."

The older man's words stripped away Burke's ambivalence, his lack of clarity about his feelings. *Have you brought Keely into my life, Lord? Have you blessed me a second time— even though I don't deserve it? Have I been wasting love again?* He felt a groan go through him. Old pain still scoured out flesh.

"Yeah." His nephew paused. "Yeah."

The phone rang. Nick picked it up. "Uncle Burke! Wake up! It's the sheriff for you!"

Burke got up and walked to the kitchen, stretching the kinks out of his back. Trying not to show how out of control his emotions were, he kept his head down and took the phone. "Hello."

"Burke," Rodd said, "we just had someone come in to inform on our fire-setter."

Burke came wide awake. "Who?"

"Veda McCracken."

"She set the fire?"

"No." Rodd sounded dubious. "She says Grady Turner did it. She saw him."

※ ※ ※

THE FOLLOWING THURSDAY evening, Keely stilled her nerves. Her very first dinner party had turned out better than she had anticipated. She was still waking up with nightmares seeing the Family Closet burn again, but she wasn't about to let that keep her from what needed to be done. So she ignored the tension at the base of her skull and offered her guests after-dinner decaf coffee with the dessert.

The fund-raiser committee, comprised of Gus Feeney, Freda Loscher, Shane, Old Doc Erickson, and Burke, subbing tonight for Rodd, sat around the late Mrs. Armbruster's round oak dining table. Soon they'd begin discussing the Christmas fund-raiser in LaFollette. But Keely was having a hard time concentrating. Burke's presence distracted her. The way he'd held her in his arms the night of the fire was never far below her conscious thoughts and popped up at will. Worry and attraction took turns tugging at her like impatient children tonight.

"A lovely dinner, my dear." Old Doc, with his bushy white eyebrows, beamed at her.

"Will you give us a tour of your home after our meeting?" Freda asked, glancing around the dining area off the kitchen.

"I'd be happy to." Keely's voice quivered, and she hoped no one noticed. *What's wrong with me? Why can't I shake this sadness?* She steadied herself. "But I really haven't finished decorating."

"It's a cool house," Shane added.

"Thanks." Keely gave him a smile. Shane had volunteered to take the lead on the student committee for this year's "new doctor" fund-raiser. He'd come so far in the past four years. *At least I didn't fail him.*

"Now we can get down to business," Gus said, accepting a cup of coffee from Keely.

She nodded and handed a cup of coffee to Burke. Though she tried mentally to keep him at arm's length, he'd managed to snag her attention all evening. What was the reason she couldn't put this man out of her mind? One crisis after another had dogged them since the first night they'd met. They should hate the sight of each other!

Now, taking the cup, Burke's fingertips touched hers; Keely's disloyal pulse raced. She took her seat again at the head of the table.

"What has yet to be finalized?" Freda asked.

"First, could someone explain what all this fund-raising for a doctor means?" Burke asked. "Rodd just called and told me to get over here tonight. He didn't have time to explain."

Keely tried to rein in her sensitivity to this man's voice, but she felt herself leaning toward him.

"Well, young man," Old Doc started, "I'm way past retirement. Have been for twenty years. Though we have a couple of other doctors and one dentist in this poor county, I need to retire and we need a new doctor. Trouble is, no one around here grew up wanting to be a doctor."

"Except for Dr. Doug," Shane put in, raising his hand as if he were in class.

Keely settled herself against the back of her chair and hazarded a sip of coffee.

"That's right. Except for my grandson. My son was a doctor, too, but we lost him early. God rest his soul. So it's really just me and Doug keeping the clinic open. Without this clinic, people around here would have to drive an hour or more to get to an emergency room."

"We don't want the clinic to close!" Gus insisted. "We'll never keep our young people or attract new people without adequate health care—"

Burke held up a hand. "You don't have to sell me the idea. I just want to know how raising funds can bring a doctor here."

"Well," Old Doc went on, "I finally decided that the only way we'd ever get a new doctor is if we got a medical student who needed money bad enough to agree to come here to practice medicine after residency. It took time, but we finally got one to sign a contract with us. We've been paying half her expenses every year for the past six years. When she finishes up, she'll come here and practice medicine for six years. Then she'll be free to stay on or leave."

"But of course we hope she'll stay," Freda crowed. "Dr. Doug needs a wife, too."

Keely groaned silently. The poor doctor. Just look at all the pointless gossip that surrounded her and Burke.

Old Doc shook his head. "Freda, you're a hopeless romantic. The doctor who's coming here has other plans for her life, bigger plans. But we've got her for six years. We just need one more big fund-raiser to finish our part of the contract."

Burke nodded. "Sounds like a good plan."

"I don't see why she shouldn't want to marry Dr. Doug," Freda corrected. "Any woman would be lucky to get him." She turned to Burke. "Deputy, you came up here. You're planning on staying, aren't you?" Then with an expectant look, she glanced back and forth between Burke and Keely.

Keely spilled her coffee. *Freda, no!*

Burke glanced at Keely. "I'm staying here."

Pressing her napkin to the spilled coffee on her antique

tablecloth, Keely tried to ignore the warmth that flooded her face.

"Well, I'm glad you came, Deputy, and I'm glad the new doctor is coming," Gus said. "Now maybe we could find somewhere to ship old Veda McCracken. She's lost her mind. . . ."

Not surprisingly, no one in the county had believed Veda's story that Grady had set the fire at the Family Closet, though the discontented woman still maintained—loudly—that she'd seen him do it. Keely's father had threatened to sue Veda for slander, but she held to her story. No one listened to Veda. Who could believe anything she said?

But every once in a while, Keely recalled all the times Veda had spied on the thrift shop with her binoculars. *Lord, what if it was Grady? Could he really heap hardship on those who need help, try to hurt me so much?* Her heart ached with the possibility. *Lord, help me. Help my brother!*

Clearing his throat, Old Doc asked for everyone's reports on his or her part of the Day on the Town, the fund-raiser that would take place the Saturday before Christmas.

Freda started. "All the merchants in LaFollette are participating again. Ten percent of all sales will go to the new-doctor fund."

"I talked to the student council," Shane reported, "and we decided that we'd go ahead and do our same Paint the Town part of the fund-raiser. Kids will get pledges and then paint store windows in town with Christmas scenes before the Saturday night fund-raiser. Everyone who comes downtown will get a ballot and can vote for their favorite windows just like last year. There will be prizes in several categories." Shane shrugged. "That's it. Everyone has a job and will do it."

"The student council did an excellent job last year," Keely spoke up. She found herself studying the way Burke sat so relaxed. It must be nice to be so detached. *But I can't ignore you. I've tried.* "The local churches are also planning," she proceeded doggedly, "to go caroling through the streets during the day, adding to the festive spirit." Her mind juxtaposed that snowy holiday scene from last December with the blackened thrift shop.

Ever since the fire, both Grady and Nick had been sullen. No trouble, but no peace for her or Burke. Had the two teens decided to just get through the rest of the school year and then leave? Or had one of them frightened himself by setting such a destructive fire? Could she stop worrying now or should she worry even more? What would either of them or some unsuspected arsonist do for an encore? How could Burke look totally without worry?

"Excellent work," Old Doc said. "I think that settles everything."

The party broke up. She wished she could summon up some enthusiasm. But something inside her had gone up in smoke with the thrift shop. She fretted more now than she ever had before.

Keely took everyone through the house, and Burke trailed along behind them. The hair on her nape prickled with awareness of him. She fought the attraction, a losing battle. Every time she walked into her foyer, she felt Burke's arms around her, comforting her the night of the fire. *Lord, I feel lost. What's wrong with me?*

Old Doc pulled Keely aside while Freda and Gus argued about how wide her walk-in closet was. "How soon can you open a temporary Family Closet? I've got patients in need of clothing. Winter's coming."

Guilt nearly strangled her. Yes, winter was nearly upon them and children needed coats! "We've placed an ad in the next three issues of the *Steadfast Times* begging for donations, especially outerwear for winter. It's bad timing. People are getting ready for the holidays. They're not in a spring-cleaning mood."

"Where will you set up?"

"The Family Closet board has rented that empty storefront next to Kainz's Bar and Grill in Steadfast. We're cleaning and getting it ready as fast as we can."

"I know you're doing your best." Old Doc gave her a hug. "You need to take a rest. I shouldn't have asked you. You looked stressed. I hope you're planning on kicking back over Christmas."

Over his shoulder, Keely saw that Burke's gaze never wavered from her face.

One by one, Old Doc, Gus, Freda, and finally Shane took their leave, going out into the frosty night till only Burke and Keely remained in front of her glowing fireplace. Though enfolded in its lush warmth, Keely shivered.

Why hadn't he left with everyone else? Why hadn't he bolted at the first opportunity? Ever since Burke had arrived at the first school board meeting he'd never stayed with her a minute longer than necessary.

Now Keely stood beside him in the quiet. His presence began to seep deeper inside her, just like the heat from the hearth. Being near Burke Sloan was different than being near anyone else she'd ever known.

When she stood close to him, everything around her became focused, vivid, intense. The lingering scent of vanilla candles burning on the mantel. The flickering light and shadows from the fire. The serene blue of Burke's eyes gazing at her, soothing her. At the same time, all her senses danced to life—all because Burke paused in front of the hearth with her.

❊ ❊ ❊

A LOG IN the fireplace crumbled, making a soft rustling. Burke's heart did a quick thump within his chest. He stared at Keely, the radiance from the fire casting half her fair face in shadow.

Keely's eyes still held the horror he'd seen in them at the thrift store fire. Watching her suffer brought feelings from deep inside him, feelings he barely recognized. *I'm rusty at this. I can't remember how to . . . what to say. Lord, help me out here. Let me lift Keely's spirits and help me find out if there's any chance she might care for me too.*

Harlan's words repeated in his mind: *"Don't waste love."* Burke braced himself. "Keely, I noticed when we did the big tour that you need some painting and wallpaper here and there." He motioned toward the walls of the room.

"Are you . . . volunteering?" She stared at him.

"I'm volunteering Nick and myself for odd jobs the weekend before Thanksgiving. Nick's mom is coming up to see us for the holiday."

Her brows drew together, wrinkling her forehead. "That's thoughtful, but I can't let you use up your time like that."

He saw the hesitation in her large eyes and forgot his own. "I want to help you."

She tilted her head, watching him with wariness.

All the tender feelings he had for her moved him nearer her. The inches between them became charged, alive with energy. He lifted her chin with his hand, her skin velvety against his. Touching her worked on him, deepening his tone, roughening the words in his throat. "Let me help you."

She didn't reply, but he noticed the softening in her eyes. He brushed a few wisps of hair off her smooth, soft cheek. The urge to hold her close was strong. But she had never given him any sign that she wanted more than friendship.

He waited now—not wanting to repeat that first reckless kiss. He'd trespassed then. He wouldn't again.

Keely studied his face as though trying to read him. He lost himself in her luminous eyes. Everything in him shouted to him, "Take her in your arms!" But he fought it. He had no right to hold her, and he realized if he did, he would kiss her a second time.

The wind outside buffeted the windows in a soft swish-hush. It echoed the beat of his heart, the pulse at her temples. They stood in silence, so close.

How do I let you know what I want from you, with you? He cupped both her slender shoulders in his hands, his fingers squeezing, trying to communicate his tenderness toward her through the knit of her sweater.

The moment of togetherness stretched, Burke gazing into the hazel eyes of this lovely, sweet woman. So many misunderstood her—all because of her father and his reputation and clout. How Burke longed to shield her. He didn't deserve her, but he couldn't let this chance pass him by. But would she?

Her only response was a sudden relaxing of the tension he felt in her shoulders. Accepting this sign, he brought her closer, inch by inch. Not permitting himself to embrace her, he bent his forehead against hers. "Keely," he whispered, her warm breath fanning against his cheek, "I want—"

Ring! The phone.

Burke nearly cursed. *No!*

Breaking their contact, Keely reached for the phone on a nearby table. After listening a few moments, she turned to him, not meeting his eyes. "It's the sheriff's department." She offered him the receiver.

Experiencing the sharp sensation of separation from her, Burke took the phone. "Sloan here."

As he listened to the unwelcome news that he was needed to finish a shift for a man who'd come down with the flu, Burke studied her. He hung up. Everything in him yearned to stay here with this woman. If he didn't leave immediately, he wouldn't leave at all. "I'd better be going."

She followed him to the entryway. There he struggled with himself. Should he tell her what he had wanted? No, that talk would need time. He made himself leave her in the doorway—without taking her into his arms.

He glanced back. She stood with her arms folded against the autumn chill, watching him walk away. The image stirred him. Why was this wonderful woman living here alone? His desire to let her know how he felt strengthened.

I don't care if there are fifty fires before I see you again, Keely. I'm not letting Grady, Nick, or anyone else interfere with what's been developing between us. I'm not going to waste any more time. If there's a chance you have feelings for me, I won't play it safe. I'm done being alone, and you should be too.

CHAPTER TWELVE

VERY EARLY ON Wednesday, a blustery November morning at the LF Café, Keely looked across the booth at her father. He'd called and asked her to meet him for breakfast. "Why are you talking to me about this?"

"Grady has been accepted at Hawley College out East. He just has to graduate—"

"I know. I heard you the first time. I'm happy for him." Feeling drained, Keely felt like folding her arms on the table and resting her head on them. "Again, why are you talking to me and not Grady?"

The café had begun to fill up. Toward the front, loud greetings were exchanged as the regulars arrived. The buzz of conversation increased in volume.

Her father glared at her, pressing his lips together as though holding in his aggravation. "You know why I'm talking to you," he snapped. "I need you to make sure he graduates."

She stared at him, trying to believe that he'd actually put this demand into bald-faced words. "I shouldn't be surprised that you are trying to make this my business. I don't really want to waste time arguing with you." *I can't. I don't have the strength.*

She'd expected a rough year with Grady at LaFollette, but nothing like this. Did her father live in a dreamworld? "Grady will graduate if he attends class and does his schoolwork. It's that simple. That's how I graduated from high school."

The bell on the café door jingled and jingled again. Someone thumped down into the booth seat that backed hers. A migraine was gathering strength at the base of her skull.

"You were different from Grady." Her father grimaced. "Girls mature earlier than boys—"

"That may be part of it." She held on to the frayed ends of her patience. "But Grady is in deep trouble. I think he's trying to get your attention—"

"I've given him my attention—"

"Only when he does something like fighting at school or getting suspended."

"It's all that new kid's fault." Her father swept Grady's misbehavior away with a hand.

"New kid? Nick?" Why was she surprised? Of course, blame couldn't attach to a Turner—no matter what!

"That's right. That deputy's nephew. If he hadn't come here, Grady would be doing fine."

The morning waitress was bringing around the coffee-pot. Keely hoped they weren't being overheard. *Lord, please don't let this get out.*

Keely stared at her father, wondering how someone could indulge in that much self-deception. "Did Nick get Grady kicked out of four prep schools?"

Her father's face reddened. "That's *enough.*"

"You're right." She stood up. "I'm not going to argue with you." *I can't afford to waste what's left of my energy.* "If you want Grady to graduate, you talk to him. If nothing else, bribe him." She couldn't help herself; her father's manipulation had pushed her over the emotional edge. Sarcasm tinged her voice. "Maybe a Porsche will do it."

The waitress stopped in her tracks, staring at them.

"I'm not finished talking to you, young lady. I want you to stop seeing Sloan," her father blustered. "He just doesn't cut it with your mother and me—"

She walked away before she said anything else she would regret.

Her father didn't have to tell her to stay away from Burke. She'd already decided that on her own. The county was already arrayed against Nick and Burke. They were convenient scapegoats.

If she showed any interest in Burke, her father would go further and do whatever he could to impugn both of their reputations. There was just too much standing between her and Burke. And they hadn't even talked of romance. Though from the gossip being spread about them, who would believe that?

Outdoors in the brisk wind, Keely's heart thundered in her ears and she felt a little light-headed. She'd suspected all along that her father had set her up as principal; it was the only way he could get Grady through high school and back East—out of his hair. But hearing him say it had landed yet another blow.

If this isn't any surprise, why am I shaking? Lord, forgive me if I was out of line, but I can't take much more. A miracle would be really nice about now. I think that's about what it will take to get Grady to graduate in the spring.

The thought that her own brother might have set fire to the thrift shop, a charity she'd poured her heart and money into, wrapped around her lungs like a tight band. *Could he hate me that much? Or is he just blind to what he might have done?* She couldn't accept this. Grady can't be guilty. *But I don't want Nick to be responsible either.*

Her mind cast around for another likely suspect—

Walachek? Did he still resent her for interfering with his daughter? Had he resented having to help roof the Family Closet? Was this payback? But Walachek wasn't the only one who had a grudge against the outreach and her.

What if the fire at the Family Closet and the ones at school had been set by different people? Burke had suggested that the thrift store fire might have been the work of a copy-cat.

Keely's thoughts leaped to another possibility. Veda McCracken had pointed the finger at Grady. Had she tired of just spying on the thrift shop and taken direct action against the Family Closet? Was that so far-fetched? She'd stolen money from the new-doctor fund last year. And she let no opportunity pass to make trouble. Was her insistence that Grady had set the fire a cover-up to hide the fact that she had set it herself?

Keely opened her SUV door and got in. Resting her forehead on the cold steering wheel, she prayed wordlessly, her wounded spirit moaning.

※ ※ ※

THE SATURDAY BEFORE Thanksgiving, Keely and Burke worked together in her family room. She held the chalk dispenser against the wall at its midpoint while he drew out the chalk line all the way to the other end of the wall from where she stood.

When Nick, Jayleen, Burke, and Harlan had appeared at her door earlier, she'd tried to talk Burke—all of them—out of spending their day helping her. But Harlan had overruled her. So here she was, working with Burke, her resolve to keep her distance from him melting in the late-afternoon sun that splashed gold against one wall. But for the first time in weeks, she didn't feel so . . . alone.

Burke's presence had ignited a glow inside her. A

welcome one—though she tried not to let it show. Matters with this man remained tenuous. But when he was with her, she didn't feel so shipwrecked, so stranded.

Burke had already volunteered to help her with odd jobs around the house, but Keely was still surprised that he had actually shown up. And all the more perplexing, she sensed some change in him.

"Ready?" Burke asked, looking at her down the length of the chalk-coated string, intense concentration on his face.

She took a deep breath. *Ready? Ready for what, Burke?* She nodded, hoping he hadn't noticed his effect on her.

"Okay." He snapped the string and a dusty line of purple chalk marked the wall with a straight line. "Excellent." He straightened up.

Keely echoed, "Excellent." That's how she was feeling—excellent, but excellent while balancing on a tightrope of her attraction to Burke. When would she fall off and break the harmony of the day?

Jayleen's and Nick's teasing voices floated in through the doorway. Harlan was supervising the teens, who were sponge painting her bathroom.

"They sound like they're having fun," Keely commented, trying to hide the impression that she was on the brink of something. What?

"What could be more fun than sponge painting?" Burke gave her a crooked grin. "And at your principal's house too?"

Biting her lower lip, she shook her head. Burke was in an unusual mood. His smile came easily and he talked to connect with her, not just to give or ask her for information. *Burke, what's happening? Are you trying to wear down my defenses to you?* "I hope Jayleen and Nick play it cool."

"Oh?" Burke asked and then his expression sobered.

Could he be so unaware of what was flashing back and forth between Keely and him? The heightened awareness couldn't be just on her side, could it? *I'm not imagining this. He must feel it, too.*

She went on. "Jayleen and Nick need time to mature, put the past behind them. And she still hasn't made a decision about her baby." Keely glanced up and found Burke gazing at her. Her whole being suddenly seemed filled with waiting.

She cleared her throat. "I feel guilty taking one of your few days off. You could have spent more time with your nephew—"

"Actually Nick wanted to come today."

"That's a good sign." She studied Burke. She couldn't figure him out. He was a man outside her personal experience. He never called attention to himself. He did things out of honor, not for selfish gain or public credit like her father. Though he spoke little, he meant every word he said. What was responsible for the change she sensed in him today?

Burke shrugged. "Maybe Harlan persuaded Nick to come. I don't know what he's thinking."

She nodded. She couldn't figure Grady out completely either. Why had he decided to be the model student this week? Had he decided he wanted to go to Hawley next year? Questions—questions and no answers. Never.

Suddenly she couldn't stand worrying one more minute. She relaxed her shoulders, forcing out the tension. *I'm not letting Grady spoil today.* It will be wonderful to have things more "finished" looking, especially for the upcoming holidays.

"Besides, this is entertaining," Burke added.

"Then I'm just glad you call putting up a border in my family room entertainment," she teased. *Burke, you're different today and it's affecting me, loosening up my uncertainty about you.* Wasn't that risky? She found she just didn't care anymore. Months of tension, compounded by an unasked-for attraction to this man. *I've had it.*

She used words to mask her unpredictable emotions. "The idea of doing my own decorating—you don't know how liberating that is to me. Mother always consults an interior designer in Duluth and has workmen come in to do the actual work."

"That takes out all the fun," Burke commented.

"Exactly." She wanted to add, *and I always just accepted whatever my mother wanted. What was the use in voicing an opinion? If I liked something or didn't, it never lasted anyway. I lived in a showroom, not a home.*

"You look sad," Burke murmured. He moved closer and rested a hand on her shoulder.

Before she could stop herself, she brushed her cheek against his hand. The sensation of his wind-roughened skin against her face rocked her to her toes. Shocked at herself, she pulled away and reached for a package of the border. Her hands trembled as she tore through the cellophane wrap of the first roll of border with pinecones on pale green, linenlike paper. *Don't throw yourself at the poor man. You've just had a tense autumn semester!*

"My sister would like this design." Burke came over and helped Keely unwind and drag the roll of pre-glued border through a shallow trough of water.

Keely concentrated on the motion, not on Burke. Or at least she tried. With each of them holding an end of the slippery wet border, they walked in tandem to the wall. Burke pressed down the border and began smoothing it toward her. She held down the end while he manipulated and adjusted the line of pinecones, making sure it butted against the purple-chalk guideline.

Again, she restrained her overwhelming response to Burke. She'd had a few brief romances before, but this was different in magnitude. Burke Sloan had shattered her aloofness around men. Then watching him all day and working beside him had lowered her resistance further. She could no longer deny what she was feeling.

Keely reveled in their working as a team. Did Burke notice how attuned they were to each other—every move, every glance, each nuance? *I'm falling in love. I don't want to, but today I don't seem to be able to stop myself.*

Before she knew it, the other three walls were done. "Finished!" She stepped back and admired their work, her heart full to bursting with Burke's being there, helping her feel the joy, this being in her own home, her own place.

The doorbell rang and she hurried to answer it. Shane stood outside with a large white bag, fragrant with deep-fried onions, in one hand and a jug of root beer in the other. Keely had called and asked him to bring them supper when he finished his shift at A&W. "Step in, Shane. Please put it on the table there."

Pointing toward one of the late Mrs. Armbruster's slender oval tables, Keely opened the front-hall closet and pulled out her purse. Her mouth watered in anticipation. *I'm becoming addicted to A&W!* "How much do I owe you?"

"Everything came to—" he glanced down at a ticket stapled to the bag—"twenty dollars and sixteen cents."

She pulled out a twenty and a five and handed them to him. "Please keep the change."

His face lit up. "Thanks, Ms. Turner."

"Thank you! Do you want to see Nick and Jayleen before you leave?" She watched for his response. "Or would you like to stay and help us eat this?"

"I've had enough A&W today, thanks." Shane grinned. "I'll just run in and say hi though."

Keely waved him toward the hallway.

"I smell onion rings!" Burke came out of her bedroom and headed straight for her.

Seeing him coming toward her, she picked up the warm

bag, hugged it to herself, and held up one hand. "Back!" Breathless happiness bubbled up inside her like root beer over ice cream. "There's enough for everyone, so don't panic."

"Jayleen, Nick, Harlan, come and get it before it's all gone!" Burke called over his shoulder.

After supper Jayleen and Nick decided to drive Harlan home and keep him company. Keely had expected Burke to leave also. Instead, he walked into her family room. He stood with his back to her, staring out into the lengthening autumn shadows outside.

The house was silent, and they were alone for the first time in weeks. Keely moved across the room and stopped beside him. She became intensely conscious of the man beside her—his fair hair shining in the shadows, the square of his broad shoulders, the clean scent of his soap.

Twilight was fading into night. An early skim of ice floated on Loon Lake like a wedding veil, announcing the coming winter. Past the bow window, an elegant pair of deer—a gray-winter-coated buck and a doe—meandered to the lake. The buck had dark antlers, and the doe moved smoothly at his side. Keely was moved by the picture of their lithe beauty and natural intimacy.

"Can they still drink when the ice becomes solid?"

Burke's voice shuddered through her. She drew in the nearness of him, her senses boosting to a higher pitch of sensitivity. How wonderful to share this with him. She knew she'd long remember this sight, this shared moment.

She dragged in air. "There's a spring at my end of the lake and a bit of current as the lake drains to another creek. Deer should be able to drink here no matter how hard the rest of the lake freezes. I wanted this acreage because of that. I'll have wildlife passing by my windows all winter—beaver, raccoon, foxes."

Keely paused and then continued. "When my aunt offered to sell me this land, I couldn't believe it at first." She glanced around her room, thankful that this was her home, her haven. The few touches she'd added harmonized with the wooded setting of her lake home: an antique duck decoy on the mantel, a basket of fresh pinecones by the fireplace, and a throw with evergreens woven into it lying on the rocker she'd bought at the auction. *This is my place, my home, and no one can change anything in it unless I say so. Thank you, Lord.*

A feeling of freedom overwhelmed her, filling her as though she'd been empty before—a human without a place, a home. *I've been a wanderer all these years. I never belonged at my parents' home.* This thought fit tight—a perfect grain of truth—in her heart.

The man standing so close to her triggered another feeling, one of isolation. *I have my place. But I'm still alone.* She tried to tell herself it was enough—but in vain.

"You chose your building site well." He reached over and smoothed a stray hair back from her face.

Her responsiveness to him spiked in her pulse. The low light in the room made her feel protected, hidden from the regular pressures of life. It gave her strength to consider the thought she had forbidden herself. What was she going to do about the fact that she was falling in love with Burke Sloan?

Impressions and images of Burke over the past two months flickered in her mind. Burke that first night at the school board meeting, Walachek pointing a gun at her and Burke's steely voice telling him to lower his weapon, Burke trailing behind her at the estate sale . . . *I can't deny my deep feelings for this man.*

The admission sent a frisson of uncertainty through her. But what about Grady and Nick? What about her father's reaction to Burke? What would everyone say if they knew she was here alone with this man tonight? She suddenly felt afraid, as though she stood on the edge of a cliff. Her midsection felt queasy, almost with vertigo.

"You look worried." He swept his palm over her cheek.

Exulting in the roughness of his hand, she glanced at Burke and found him watching her. *Burke, what am I going to do about you?*

Concern darkening his expression, he turned halfway toward her. He gripped her shoulders. "Don't let the worry in tonight. It's just the two of us here . . . and God."

She nodded. "I don't want to worry." She put her hands up on his where they held her.

Touching him was a mistake. Her hands meeting his sent shivers down her arms. She closed her eyes, gathering her resistance. But the resistance wouldn't come.

"What is it, Keely?" he whispered. "Tell me."

"I care about you," she said softly, unable to hold back the truth.

"I care about you."

His words didn't register at first. She had to replay them in her mind. *Burke cares for me.*

She opened her eyes and found him looking into hers. "I never thought . . . I don't want . . ." Her phrases sounded foolish in her ears.

He tugged her closer.

She reveled in his gentleness. *Stay, Burke; don't leave me without your touch.*

She luxuriated in the moment of closeness, intimacy. "I shouldn't have said it. But it's the truth."

"We've fought the truth long enough," he agreed. "Everything, everyone has tried to push us apart, but we are here together." He leaned down and kissed her forehead, urging her nearer.

Glancing up from her place against him, she realized that his eyes had darkened. "What is it, Burke?"

"I don't want to mislead you." He sucked in air. "I was married before . . . and I wasn't much of a husband—"

"I don't believe that." Her mind raced. Had he been through a divorce? Had his heart been broken? "What happened?"

He tightened his lips together. "We'd only been married a little over a year when Sharon was diagnosed with leukemia. I failed her." He stopped.

She took his hand. "Tell me."

"I couldn't handle it. I mean, I went through the motions with her. Doctor visits, hospital stays, home care. But I bailed out on her long before she died. My body was there with her. But I wasn't."

"You must have been young. It blindsided you."

"I just closed up, shut down." He shook his head. "Afterward, the disconnection spread. I went AWOL as far as my family was concerned."

"It doesn't sound like you failed her. Just because you couldn't face losing her—"

"I was a coward. I couldn't give her the emotional support she needed. I saw how my mom and sister—"

"Don't compare yourself to others. God doesn't. Besides, they weren't losing as much as you were. Didn't you have the right to be human? A right to feel grief?"

He replied with a fierce embrace. "The guilt was too much for me," he murmured into her hair.

"Let go of it. You couldn't save her. That wasn't your job. You did yours. You stood by her. You're not God. Remember that we are dust, grass that withers. God never forgets that."

Burke's chest tightened—even as her words eased a long-tied knot inside him. *Is she right, Lord? Did I load myself with false guilt?*

"Besides, you're here doing everything you can for Nick."

"Fortunately, this summer my dad finally got through to me when Nick needed help. Or I might still be . . . in limbo."

She leaned against him. "Sometimes you still put up shutters. I see you do it and I can't reach you."

"I don't want to shut you out." *Never, Keely. I never want to be parted from you again. You open me to loving, feeling like no one else has since I lost Sharon.*

"I won't let you," she said and then wondered where the courage to say that had come from.

Burke drew her closer within his arms. He wanted to tell her he loved her, but his natural reserve held the words back.

"What about you?" he asked instead. "What happened to your first love?" *Did someone hurt you? Is that why you have kept love at a distance?*

The question startled her, but she leaned closer to him, drawn to him. She shook her head against his plaid shirt, feeling his hard chest under the brushed cotton. "I never met anyone I wanted to be with for life."

"I never wanted to be close to anyone ever again," Burke admitted. "But, Keely, I want to be near you." His voice thickened as he forced himself to put his love for her into words. "So much has happened to keep us upset, to separate us. But could we take some time—try to give our feelings for each other a chance?" He gazed into her large eyes, now reflecting moonlight flowing through the bow window. *Please, Keely.*

"Yes."

❊ ❊ ❊

IN THE ICY blackness of a cold November night, Keely waited while Burke got out of his Jeep. His shoes crunching on Keely's gravel drive, he walked around to the passenger side to help her out. As he drew her out of the car, she murmured, "You're so gallant, Deputy." Though her words puffed white in the chill air, she gave him a teasing smile.

"My pleasure, Ms. Turner." He gave her a slight bow.

She giggled at his formality. It had been such a lovely evening. They'd left all the pressures and responsibilities behind and gone to dinner in the next county at one of Keely's favorite supper clubs and then driven to Minocqua for a movie, a romantic comedy. They'd gotten away from the gossips and whispering.

Burke and she had spent the kind of carefree evening she hadn't had since she finished school in the East and came home. She felt "giggly" as though she were fifteen again. And Burke's dry humor had only made her more so.

"Come in," she invited. "I'll have you light the fire while I make us some Godiva hot cocoa. An old college friend sent me some for my birthday."

"Godiva hot chocolate. That's temptation at its best!" He grinned.

She chuckled and unlocked her front door, the cold making her hurry. Inside, he helped her off with her down coat. His hands so close made her quiver. Stepping out of her warm boots, she slid her feet into the clogs she always left by the door. "I'll go make the cocoa."

"And I'll start the fire." Before she could get away, he pulled her back into his arms and kissed her.

A heady rush of sensation made her cling to him—fearful of losing her footing. "Deputy Sloan," she scolded finally and then grinned at him.

He tucked her even closer. "Do you know how special you are?"

His strong arms around her and his praise filled her cup to overflowing. "Burke, oh, Burke." She kissed him again, basking in the warmth he had loosed within her. *How can this be happening to me of all people?* A needle of cold fear made her pull away. She took a shaky breath. *This is too good to be true. Too good to last! But, Lord, please let it!*

Undeterred, he held her close. "Do I get whipped cream on my Godiva cocoa?"

"Your wish is my command, Deputy."

"Bribing a cop, huh?" He cocked an eyebrow.

"It's only whipped cream, Officer." Glowing inside, she walked to the kitchen. As she filled the mugs with water and heated them in the microwave, she heard the companionable sound of Burke filling the fireplace with wood.

By the time she carried the tray with hot cocoa and cookies into the living room, the flames were blazing, just as her reaction to Burke had intensified tonight. Hiding this, she set the tray down on the coffee table.

Their first real date. A perfect evening. Everything had gone like a dream. But it must be real! It was after midnight, and she hadn't turned into a pumpkin yet. *I'm really falling in love with this man.* She felt warm, cozy, and loved.

He leaned over and kissed her cheek as though he'd been kissing her for years.

But they were taking it slow and enjoying the ride just as they'd agreed.

❀ ❀ ❀

ON THE LAST Friday night in November, the final game of the football season was taking place at LaFollette-Steadfast High.

Burke glanced at Keely sitting beside him. He recognized in her posture and her watchfulness his own concern. This was her school, her responsibility. After what had happened at the last home game, he understood the weight she carried. He'd been on high alert since he arrived. This game was his job too. He patrolled the parking lot periodically. He and another deputy—who was now patrolling LaFollette and the school grounds by car—had inspected all the waste bins before the game. Would their precautions be enough? Or was the fire-setting over at last?

He wished he'd had time to see Keely earlier this week, but he'd been working nights, and she hadn't been able to meet him even for coffee. Unable to resist, he touched her elbow.

She glanced at him, smiled, and then returned to her vigil.

He looked back to the field, too, but his blood surged from her touch. She had the power to move him. He'd crossed the bridge to her and he couldn't go back. He couldn't. He wouldn't.

"Hey! Blackfeather, get a move on!" Veda bellowed behind them.

As usual, Veda McCracken sat high in the bleachers, jeering both teams. Did she do it just for the attention she evidently craved so intensely? Or did she do it to throw the home team off its stride? Burke couldn't decide.

"You're losing it, Blackfeather!" she taunted the teen.

Shane's grandfather turned suddenly and charged up the bleacher aisle straight for Veda. Burke stood up and blocked his way. "Don't," he cautioned the man in a low voice. "Go back and sit down."

"Let me past!" The old man tried to get by Burke. "It's time that old bag got hers." A vulgar description of Veda followed.

Burke didn't budge. "Go back to your seat. I don't want to have to arrest you and make you miss the end of this game. Can't you see that's what she wants?"

Shane's grandfather glared at Burke. But after venting a stream of profanity at Veda, he returned to his seat.

Burke sat down beside Keely again. "Doesn't she realize that she could be making herself a target? Someone might decide to shut her up."

Keely shrugged. "I don't think she's smart enough to figure that out. Or maybe she doesn't care."

"Hey! Patsy!" Veda jibed. "Your granddaughter's turning out to be a cheap runaround just like her mother!"

"Shut up!" Freda, who was sitting near Keely, shouted at Veda. "You have the same filthy mind you had in high school!"

A chorus of agreement and applause broke over the stands.

❧ ❧ ❧

KEELY GLANCED BACK at Veda. The woman's face was red from shouting, and she looked like she was in pain. The woman's stomach must be churning with acid. Why did Veda come? What motivated her to such antagonism? Why had people let her get by with it for so many years? Had Veda really seen Grady set fire to the Family Closet? Keely inched closer to Burke's side.

On the field, Shane recovered a fumble from the Minocqua team and charged down the field. A Minocqua player tackled him. The LaFollette stands groaned.

"LaFollette, Minocqua's kicking your . . . !" Veda sneered—loud and clear. "Hey, Deputy!" Veda taunted. "Think you're gonna marry the rich girl! Don't bet on it! Big Man Turner will have something to say about that!"

Keely tried to shut out the rest of Veda's invective. Two weeks had passed since she and Burke had stood together in her living room and confessed that they cared for each other. Whenever she thought of that evening while they'd watched the pair of deer watering at the lake, love swirled up inside her.

But she and Burke couldn't avoid being seen together forever. Then the gossip would heat up! What would her father try?

Grady popped into her mind. Where was he? He'd been here earlier. Had he left? And Nick, who'd sat on the team bench, had disappeared into the locker room area. Had the coach kicked him off the bench? Nothing more had happened in the weeks since the Family Closet burned to the ground. Had the storm passed?

But the last quarter of the game was going as disastrously as it could for the home team. Keely's sympathy went out to her players and coach. They'd done their best; yet it didn't look like it would be good enough.

Suddenly Nick, in full football gear, appeared in the huddle. Keely looked at Burke. He sat forward on the bleacher. The coach waved to them. Nick was being allowed to play! Keely felt a thrill. Burke reached for her hand.

The huddle broke up and play resumed. Nick caught a short pass and began running—the Minocqua team in hot pursuit. Keely squeezed Burke's hand, feeling her spirits climb.

Boom!

Explosion rocked the air, sending out shock waves. Flames shot high beyond the athletic field in the direction of the parking lot.

The stands erupted—everyone was screaming, shoving, shouting. Keely was jostled and bumped from behind in the stampede to the parking lot.

"Hang on to me!" Burke shouted in her ear.

She clung to him like a mast in the storm. Moving against the tide, he dragged her along with him higher into the bleachers.

Curses. Screams. Yells. Angry shouts. Shrieks of fear and pain. *Dear God, don't let anyone get hurt! Please don't let anyone get hurt!* Keely had no clear idea of what was happening—just crowding, pushing, screaming all around her.

"Freeze!" Burke's voice, magnified by his handheld

bullhorn, roared over the frenzy below them. Keely huddled close beside him, grateful that he'd brought this device with him. "Halt!"

He raised his gun to shoot as though prepared to release a warning shot into the air. The crowd below lost its momentum. Bewildered faces—illumined by the field lights, looked up to them. "Everyone, stay calm! Return to your seats. Walk at a normal pace. No rushing. Now!"

The crowd began to obey him.

"I'll go out and assess the damage," Burke announced over the horn. "If there is a need, you will be instructed to leave by the rear exit. Until I give the word, remain seated and await instructions! Keep moving bac—"

Boom!

Another explosion. Burke pushed Keely down. He remained calm and pulled Keely close to his side. Still screaming, the crowd ran back toward their seats.

Burke managed to get his phone out of his belt. "Get Rodd out here!" he shouted into the phone. "Someone's blowing up cars in the parking lot!"

CHAPTER THIRTEEN

LEAVING THE CROWDED stands, Burke ran toward the parking lot. Someone might need help! And he had to put a stop to the explosions if he could!

A sheriff's siren whooped, and the other deputy swerved to a stop at the street side of the parking lot. *Great! Backup!*

Keely was at Burke's heels. He turned to her. "Go back to the athletic field! Get both coaches to help you!" He handed her the bullhorn. "Keep order!"

She didn't argue but took the horn and swung back. "Don't worry. I can handle it!"

Hating to leave her, Burke ran on. Ahead, he saw the flames still shooting skyward. The car that had exploded was parked cockeyed in the middle of the street, not in the lot. How had it gotten there? Another car, parked nearest the first, also blazed, sending up billows of orange-gold flames. Burke felt the heat on his face.

An anguished scream echoed through the crisp night air. "Help! Help . . . me!"

Burke recognized the voice and raced toward it. He spotted Grady lying on the parking lot asphalt. He ran to him and dropped to one knee. "I'm here."

He reached for Grady's wrist and stopped. The teen was burned on the arm and wrist he'd been intending to grip. The same side of Grady's blackened face was burned; it was red and blistered. Burke took the other wrist and felt his pulse. It was rapid. Burke scanned Grady and saw no other injuries. "Were you out here when the car exploded?"

"How do you think I got burned?" Grady shouted. "It hurts! Hurts!" The kid began swearing.

The other deputy appeared at Burke's side. "The ambulance is on its way—"

The sound of the fire engine cut him off. Blasting their air horn, the crew pulled up and began running the hose to the nearest hydrant.

"Check the athletic field," Burke instructed the other deputy. "Ms. Turner may need help to keep everyone inside the stadium and out of the firefighters' way. If not, come right back."

With a nod, the deputy jogged away, talking into his cell phone.

Grady moaned loudly.

"Don't worry. Help is coming," Burke assured him. "Did you see who did this?"

"*I* did this," Grady snapped. "I pushed the old bag's car out in the street and set it on fire—"

"Hold it," Burke stopped him. "I'm a police officer. Everything you say can and will be used against you in court. Don't tell me anything you don't want me to know."

"*I did it, you dumb jerk!*" Grady yelled at him. "I wouldn't have had to do so many tricks if you'd been smart enough to catch me!"

"You *wanted* to be caught?" Burke stared at Grady. The kid reeked of gasoline and was clearly in intense pain and maybe shock. *Hurry up with that ambulance!*

"I wanted to get out of this hick town! I thought my dad

would have to send me away if I got in enough trouble! What's wrong with you? I dug holes, shot out windows, set the bleachers on fire . . ."

The teen's ready admission shocked Burke. Hearing this would kill Keely. Could he believe her brother, or was he just talking crazy? "Grady! You're confessing a whole string of crimes to me. Are you sure you're in shape to be talking like this?"

"Don't you get it?" Grady bawled. "I want out! I want out and I don't care how I do it!"

As the man who loved Grady's sister, Burke wanted to stop her brother from saying another word. As a police officer, he had to keep this kid talking. Taking a deep breath, Burke did his job. "Why did you dig the holes?"

Grady spat out the name of a girl, followed by several derogatory terms. "She wouldn't go out with me. I wanted her to take the fall, but that other girl hit the holes first." Grady swore loud and long, groaning and twisting on the asphalt.

"You say you set the bleachers on fire," Burke said. "Did you also set the fires in the waste bins?"

The other deputy returned but hung back, listening. He'd be Burke's corroboration.

"Yeah, I found out I kinda like setting fires." A ghost of a smile lifted Grady's pained expression. "It was fun watching them. And then all the excitement. I liked watching, hearing about the fire." Grady screamed, "Help me!"

"Why did you set the Family Closet on fire?" Burke continued the questioning. The truth had to come out. It would hurt Keely, but this would be over—finally. "Everything else was done on school property."

"I was just going to pay back my sister for making me work there. It was like having to work at the Salvation Army!" Grady cursed again and called his sister a name.

"Don't say another word against your sister!" Though his hand itched to slap the word out of Grady's mouth, Burke kept a lid on his anger.

"I didn't mean for the whole place to burn down," the kid whined. "I just wanted to burn the back porch." Grady writhed with the pain, moaning. "So I started the fire and then tried to call the fire department to report it. But my cell phone's battery was dead. I just had to make a run for it!" He screamed again, "Help me!"

The ambulance roared into the parking lot. Burke stood up and waved his hands. "Over here! Man down! Burns!"

Pulling up, the EMTs jumped out of the ambulance. Burke stepped back beside the other deputy to let them surround Grady.

As he watched them work on the teen, he thought about Keely. The mystery was solved. Nick was only guilty of letting air out of tires, setting off firecrackers, and fighting with Grady. Everything else Grady had admitted to. Burke took off his hat and raked his hair with his fingers. *Keely, I would have done anything to save you this. Oh, Lord, help her. Help this kid.*

※ ※ ※

KEELY STOOD IN the brightly lit room at the clinic. Fear rampaged inside her. Her baby brother lay limply on the gurney, with reddened and blistered skin and blackened, shredded clothing from the blast. He'd been in the parking lot when the car exploded.

This fact loomed inside Keely, making it hard for her to breathe. *Grady, does that mean you set the explosion? Dear Lord, help me. I've dreaded this and now it may be true. What more could I have done?*

Burke had his arm snugly around her. "Hang in there," he whispered in her ear. "It's not as bad as it looks."

"He's right," Dr. Doug spoke up. "Your brother's only got first- and second-degree burns. And I don't see any problem with his lungs."

Grady lay on his back staring up at the lights overhead without expression. That wasn't like her brother. He didn't take pain well. Even though the EMTs had given him medication immediately, she'd expected him to still be complaining. But he just lay there, silent and immobile.

"He's in shock," Dr. Doug said as though reading her mind. "And the morphine is taking the edge off all his reactions, not just the pain."

"What . . ." she faltered, "what . . . treatment will he have to have?" The unreality of everything since the explosion seemed to be slowing her own ability to think.

Burke tightened his hold on her.

She wanted to say something to him, but the words couldn't get past her lips. She felt disconnected, cut off, abandoned.

A powerful voice boomed through the quiet clinic. "Where's my son?"

Keely stiffened. Her father had arrived. She pressed closer to Burke.

Her parents hurried into the examining area. "What happened?" her father thundered.

Wendy Durand, the sheriff's wife on duty at the clinic tonight, hovered near him. "Mr. Turner, please quiet your voice. We have patients—"

He pushed past her and went to the doctor. "Tell me."

Dr. Doug turned away from the chest X ray he'd been examining. "Your son was burned in a fire at the high school."

"Fire? Another fire?" Her father sent Keely and Burke a scathing look. It shouted, *This is all your fault!*

Why is everything my fault? I still can't believe Grady's responsible! How could he expect me to stop Grady? Even as Keely thought this, the shock was dulling her reactions.

Dr. Doug began, "He was in the parking lot when a car exploded—" Suddenly, Dr. Doug called out, "Catch her!"

Wendy caught Keely's mother as she fainted. Burke left Keely's side and helped Wendy get the woman safely into a bedside chair.

"You!" Turner launched the word at Burke. "Where were you when this was happening to my son? If the sheriff doesn't get rid of you—"

"Mr. Turner," Burke replied, "I was at the game when it happened. I had just patrolled the parking lot not ten minutes before the explosion. We had no way of knowing that someone was going to blow up a car."

"That nephew of yours has gone too far this time!" her father continued. "This isn't just a misdemeanor—"

"Father, Nick was on the field playing football when the explosion happened." Keely refused to let her father get away with false accusations. "He couldn't have done it."

"A timer!" Turner snapped. "He must have set a timer!"

Burke shook his head. "The sheriff is examining the crime scene himself right now. But I don't think we'll find anything that elaborate."

Missing Burke's warmth, Keely folded her arms around herself.

Burke picked up Grady's unburned hand. "I can smell the gasoline on his skin, can't you?"

"You can't put this off on *my* son." Her father's face was deep red now. "You better watch yourself!"

Keely felt tears coursing down her face. "Burke told me he's admitted it, Father."

"The initial car blown up was Veda McCracken's," Burke continued, not letting her father break in. "She informed against your son for the Family Closet fire. That gives him an excellent motive—"

"Everyone hates that old biddy," Turner replied.

"I don't hate her," Grady mumbled. "I hate you."

The words stilled everyone. They all turned to stare at Grady.

"Why did the other car blow up?" the teen asked. "I only fixed it so the old lady's car would blow—"

"Grady, you don't know what you're saying," his father interrupted.

"Yes, I do. I hate you and I blew up McCracken's car."

"Grady," Burke said, "I've cautioned you repeatedly and I've read you your rights. Remember, anything you say can and will be used against you—"

"My son is no criminal!" Turner roared.

"Mr. Turner," Burke said in a patient but implacable tone, "your son obviously wanted to be caught. Doesn't that tell you something? He needs help and he's trying desperately to get it."

"You never found any evidence when I set the other fires, did you?" Grady asked, his voice weak and devoid of emotion. "My old man thinks I can't do anything right, but—"

"Grady," Turner ordered, "shut your mouth!"

"Will he be scarred?" Keely's mother asked in a plaintive tone. She'd come around and was finally able to speak.

"Only my soul, Mother," Grady said with a sarcastic twist. "Give me some more drugs. I'm floating."

Mrs. Turner began weeping.

Keely felt like she were floating, too, in a nightmare. She wished she could wake up and all this would disappear.

"Grady may have to have some slight plastic surgery," Dr. Doug answered as though unaware of the potent currents in the room, "but he should heal fine. He needs to stay here until he's well enough to go home in a few days. He was lucky he was far enough from the blast that he only got a lick of the flames. At least, that's my guess. If he'd been closer, it would—"

"I ran as fast as I could," Grady went on in that odd voice, still staring at the ceiling. "But the flames just went so fast on the gasoline trail I made to her—"

"Shut up, Grady!" his father ordered. "Don't say another word."

His son looked at him. "What's the big deal? You can buy the old lady another car. The one I blew up wasn't worth anything. If I'd realized how fast the flames would eat up the gasoline—"

Turner pushed Burke out of the examining area. "Out! Out! I'm calling my lawyer!"

"Your son needs help," Burke urged. "Some kids use suicide attempts. Some use setting fires—"

"I won't listen to you," Turner raged. "You aren't the one to lecture me!"

Burke stared at him. "Don't try to move your son out of this clinic." His voice sounded firm and cold. "He's to stay here under guard until the doctor releases him, and then he will be charged with arson."

Turner tried to object.

"Father," Keely said with as much force as she could muster, "just let it go now. Let it go."

For once, her father subsided.

Burke went to wait at the clinic entrance for Rodd to arrive. Keely watched him walk away and felt as though he'd left her completely. She and Burke had just begun drawing close. Now she couldn't even imagine the attraction that had refused to be ignored. *Burke, what's happening? What will happen to us?*

Keely and her parents sat in the doctors' lounge. Dr. Doug had let them use it while he finished treating Grady's burns. Later, they'd go to see him settled in his room.

"This is awful," her mother cried. "I can't face anyone."

"Grady didn't do it," her father maintained.

Keely looked back and forth between them. They were acting just as she'd expected they would, so that must not be upsetting her. What was it? What had snapped inside her? "This is a terrible shock to all of us."

"Grady didn't do it," her father repeated.

"How will I ever face anyone in this town again?" her mother moaned.

Keely closed her lips. Her own shock was too fresh. What could she say to them? She felt both her mother's shame and her father's denial flowing inside her. She tried to hold back tears but couldn't. Why had this happened? She'd worked so hard. She'd prayed in such earnest. What hadn't she done right? And what would be her father's next move? Would he be able to keep Grady from being prosecuted?

"Father, I have only one thing to ask you," Keely said in a voice that trembled. "How can you keep denying this? Grady admitted it in front of witnesses."

Her father didn't even react.

Burke was right. Grady was shouting for help. But would her father ever listen?

※ ※ ※

"KEELY, THIS IS Burke. If you're there, please pick up."

It was the next afternoon. Still in her pajamas, Keely sat in her family room, overlooking the lake. She stared at the phone.

"Keely?"

She didn't move. He hung up.

All the feeling had gone out of her. The sound of Burke's cold voice as he'd repeated what Grady had told him had started the freezing of her emotions. How could her brother have done all of it?

She'd suspected him herself, but not of everything! Not of burning down the thrift store! Did he have any conception of the wrong he'd done? What were people thinking? What was her father going to do? He was capable of going to any length to protect his own.

Burke, Burke, we knew this wouldn't work out from the start. Why didn't we save ourselves from this pain?

I should get up and go to the clinic and see Grady. But her resolve to go on had somehow withered. She slid onto her side on the sofa and closed her eyes.

❋ ❋ ❋

EARLY THE NEXT Saturday morning, a bright cold day, Keely drove into the Kainz driveway, dreading this meeting. But she had to come. Both Penny and Jayleen had asked her to be present. *Why do they want me? I have nothing to do with this.*

She parked her car and got out. The Weavers' minivan was already here. Patsy Kainz had invited Penny over to talk to Jayleen about Rachel's future. At Jayleen's request—it was to be just the four women. Bruce would stay home with Zak. *What do they think I can do? I can't even run my own life. Everything I touch goes up in smoke.*

She considered all she'd learned this past week. Grady had pushed Veda's car into the street, opened the gas cap, and poured a trail of gasoline from the car to the curb. Then he'd dropped a match. Imagining him doing this while she and Burke sat inside the athletic field hit her as unreal.

Not only had Veda's car exploded but also the car nearest it. Evidently, it had had an undetected crack or the first explosion had cracked its gas tank. Three other cars had been destroyed by the ensuing fire. Fortunately, Veda's tank had been nearly empty or it could have been much worse. Keely's father had already been served with papers suing him for loss of property.

Keely had taken Monday and Tuesday off. She hadn't wanted to face the crime scene. But she'd forced herself back to school on Wednesday, just as she had forced herself to answer Burke's next call that same day. But she hadn't been able to make herself talk to him since.

Each day it became only harder, not easier, to get out of bed and go to her office. Her deep sense of loss became heavier and heavier. She told herself she wasn't responsible for what Grady had done. But she didn't think that was what was dragging at her, weighing her down.

Nightmares plagued her every attempt at sleep. In her murky dreams, she'd be standing outside the Family Closet as it blazed. Someone was inside—someone needed her, but she couldn't move. She couldn't get the person out! She'd waken, her heart pounding.

Keely walked over the newly frozen ground. Her exhaustion making her more susceptible to the chill, she knocked on Patsy's bright red door.

"Hello!" Patsy greeted her and ushered her inside. "It's getting cold out there! We'll be getting snow before you know it!"

"I hadn't noticed," Keely said in all honesty, sitting down at the table in the kitchen where Penny and Jayleen already waited. Her knees shook she was so tired. December had arrived. The fund-raiser and the holidays loomed ahead, and she couldn't work up an ounce of enthusiasm over anything. *If I could just get a full night's rest!*

Patsy bustled around the red-and-white kitchen, pouring tea and putting out sugar cookies shaped like turkeys. Watching the older woman's energy only heightened Keely's fatigue. The scent of the apricot tea and the sugar-cookie sweetness was cloying.

"We have to finish these up. Time to bake Christmas cookies soon!" Usually Patsy's upbeat liveliness charmed

Keely. Today, she really couldn't take very much of anything. *Can't we just get to the point?*

Finally, Patsy sat down and looked around the table expectantly. "Jayleen," she said, "why don't you tell Mrs. Weaver and Ms. Turner what you want to say."

Keely felt a spasm go through her. *Why do I have to be here? Jayleen looks like she's going to be sick. Penny looks like she's attending her own execution.*

Jayleen looked at Penny, and then her eyes slid to Keely and back to Penny again. "I talked with my social worker about Rachel."

They waited.

"She says," Jayleen began again, "that I need to decide if I want to try to get Rachel back before she gets much older. That the older she is, the harder it will be for her to leave her . . . to leave you, Mrs. Weaver."

Patsy nodded, encouraging her granddaughter.

"We've been afraid—" Penny cleared her throat—"that the social services office might decide to move her to a different foster home. We'd started adoption proceedings. . . . When you returned, that was put on hold. . . ."

"I never wanted to lose my baby." Jayleen stared at the vinyl tablecloth covered with a pattern of golden fall leaves. "But I did. Then I thought I'd never see her again."

"You tried to get Rachel to me," Patsy reminded her granddaughter. "How could you have known the car would blow up?"

How could I have known how far Grady would go? Keely put both of her chilled hands around the hot mug of tea.

Jayleen wiped a stray tear away. "I still have two years of high school to finish and then . . ." The girl shrugged. "I want to help out at the clinic. Dr. Doug was telling me that they need nurses' aides and you need training for that."

Another pause.

"Go on, honey," Patsy encouraged.

"I'm not going to seek custody of Rachel." Jayleen's eyes lifted but immediately looked back down at the pattern on the tablecloth. "I think she should stay with you and Pastor Weaver."

The words took Keely's breath away. Feeling Jayleen's hurt rise, lapping around her, Keely's own suffering deepened. *Oh, Jayleen! I'm so sorry for you.*

"Jayleen," Penny said, "Bruce and I don't want to rush you into anything. We'd be happy to help you regain custody of your baby."

Keely understood Penny's reluctance. How could anyone feel joy in the midst of the tragedy Jayleen had survived and must go on surviving?

Jayleen scraped her chair back. "No, I want you two to raise her. I don't want to mess up her life any more than I did." The girl looked into Penny's face. "I could have gotten her killed!"

Jayleen's voice trembled, rising. "She could have been blown up in that car! Anything could have happened to her! I love her. I'll always love her, but I can't be her mother. I'd make a mess of it." She rushed from the room.

They watched her go. Keely couldn't bring up any word of comfort to share.

"Patsy," Penny said, "we don't want to rush her."

"You're not. This has been heartbreaking for me. I want that baby. I wanted my granddaughter to be able to raise her own child." The grandmother shook her head with certainty.

"But my granddaughter wants what's best for her baby. You'll raise Rachel like your own, and we'll know where she is and that she's safe. We'll watch her grow up right here. It's not like giving her away and never knowing. That would be the hard part to me."

"She's made this decision?" Keely asked finally. "What does her father say?"

"We all told Jayleen that this was up to her. Rachel's her baby."

"I just feel . . . ," Penny faltered. "I . . ."

Patsy patted the pastor's wife's hand. "It's better for Jayleen to make this decision and get on with her life. She has thought and thought about what would be best for little Rachel—until I've seen her sick with thinking. She's made her decision. Now let's help her go through with it."

Penny nodded, still looking devastated. "I pray we will be able to."

Then Patsy turned over the latest *Steadfast Times*. The front-page headline blazoned: "Turner Son to Be Charged with Arson."

"Now I'm not bringing this up to hurt you, Keely," Patsy said. "But I won't say something behind someone's back that I won't say to their face. If your father hasn't got the message yet, he'd better. We're not going to stand for him trying to hush this up. Your brother's a danger to everyone, including himself."

"But that's not Keely's fault," Penny countered.

"No one in the county thinks that it is," the older woman agreed, reaching over to pat Keely's arm. "If your father had any brains, he'd have listened to you. Everybody knows you've done your best."

The pain quivering around Keely was too much. She stood up. "Well, I think I'll be going then. Penny, you and Bruce will make lovely parents for Rachel."

Patsy tried to send a plate of cookies with Keely. She managed to escape without them and fled, feeling her sorrow cresting.

Outside in the cutting wind, Keely opened her car door and got in. Behind the wheel, she broke down, sobbing.

Was God's will being done here? *I wanted to do more for Jayleen, Lord. The Weavers will be excellent parents for Rachel. But Jayleen will have to live with this decision for the rest of her life. I should have done more.*

Finally, Keely forced herself to drive away. Her eyes were swollen and her head hurt from thinking. Her emotions felt as though they'd been beaten and mangled. Maybe the right decision had been made. Who was she to judge? *I can't think. Why can't I think clearly?*

She focused on driving back home. That was all she could cope with now.

At least Jayleen was taking care of her daughter in the best way she thought she could now. If only Keely's parents were doing that much for Grady. Her mother hadn't left her home even to visit Grady at the clinic. She just called Keely and wept on the phone. Her brother's lack of remorse and how much help he'd need had hit Keely so much harder than she'd ever imagined.

※ ※ ※

KEELY SAT IN the back of the high-ceilinged courtroom feeling physically sick. Grady was being arraigned on charges of arson. Their mother was still hiding at home. Keely wished she could have, too, but her conscience wouldn't let her leave her brother to face this with only their father at his side.

The courtroom was packed. Watching the proceedings against a Turner had drawn a crowd, mostly retirees who looked grim. A few of them had nodded politely to her as she entered. Most glared at her father's back and whispered heatedly. Keely recalled Harlan's warning to her father. Would it have made any difference if he'd heeded Harlan then?

Looking combative, her father sat behind Grady and their family attorney at the defense table, seemingly unaware of the hostile crowd. The bailiff called for all to rise as the black-robed judge entered. They all took their seats with a rustling of jackets and thudding of boot soles. It had snowed today.

As the arraignment started, Keely tried to follow the legal procedure, but her own reaction to this awful moment interfered with her ability to comprehend it.

Burke Sloan and Sheriff Durand were both in the courtroom. To give evidence? She remembered Burke's calm recitation of the clues against her brother at the clinic that night. How did her father expect to nullify Grady's confession in front of witnesses?

In the glaring light of the large room, she gazed at Burke's profile, and she felt as though she were a different person. It was like she'd died and had been reborn with someone else's emotions. Just a week ago, she'd felt so close to Burke. Now she felt distant, removed. And her nightmares had gotten worse.

Numbly, she waited for the grim-faced judge to charge her brother and set the trial dates. Grady had gotten lucky; this wasn't the judge who had released Walachek early. But after much discussion, the judge agreed to a private conference in his chambers.

Grumbling swept the gathering as Keely watched her father accompany Grady and their lawyer along with the district attorney through another doorway. Burke and Rodd walked out too.

Keely felt the eyes of everyone boring into her, and she could almost hear their thoughts: *The fix must be in. . . . Turner pulled some legal trick. . . . Do you think he bought off the judge?* Her stomach clenched.

A few minutes later, the bailiff came to her. "Ms. Turner, the judge wants you to come in too."

"No, please . . . I . . . ."

The man gestured her toward the door. "Don't keep the judge waiting, miss."

Rising, she went to the door and knocked. Hearing permission to enter, she walked in. All faces turned to her.

"Thank you for coming in, Ms. Turner," the judge said and indicated a chair for her. "I want you to hear what I'm going to say to your father and brother, since as a family member, this will affect you too."

She sat down on a maroon leather chair, not making eye contact with her father. She nodded to the judge.

"These charges are serious—," the judge began.

Her father tried to interrupt, but his lawyer laid a hand on his shoulder. Her father subsided.

"I don't want to go through a long court battle. I don't want to drag the Turner name through the mud. But something has to be done. Franklin, your son is a danger to this community and to himself."

Again, her father tried to speak.

The judge held up his hand. "Don't interrupt. Your family and mine have been in this county forever, so we both know that I'm trying to do what is best for everyone. We can go ahead and prosecute Grady and send him to a correctional facility. I don't want to do that. Though fire-setting can be a seductive addiction, I'm hoping that he can be rehabilitated. Now, Franklin, do you want to get your son the help he needs, or do you want him incarcerated? He's still a minor, thank heavens, or I'd have little latitude here. What do you say?"

Their family lawyer spoke up. "What are you proposing?"

"Grady needs more than just counseling. He needs to be committed to a private hospital that can meet his needs and better serve the needs of this community. Franklin, if you will send Grady to one of the facilities that the DA has in mind, I will give Grady a suspended sentence—on one condition."

Tingling with surprise, Keely couldn't believe her ears.

"What's the condition?" her father asked in a voice that was nearly a croak.

"That he not be released until the DA and I are shown proof that he is no longer likely to offend again. We refuse to hush this up here and send him off to do the same elsewhere."

"And if I refuse?" her father asked, his face red.

"Then I will keep him in custody until trial—no bail. The community has made it quite clear that they don't want an arsonist on the loose. Popular opinion doesn't usually sway me, but in this case I agree. If your son goes to trial—given his admission of guilt—he will most likely be convicted and sentenced to a juvenile facility."

"I need time." Her father's complexion had whitened now.

"You have until tomorrow."

Keely wondered why she had been included in this. What would her father decide? Would he fight it or accept it? Knowing him, fighting would be more likely. She headed to the door, not wanting to have to deal with her father and his lawyer.

After leaving the judge's chambers, the family lawyer had detained Keely's father on the steps of the courthouse. That had given Keely the chance to drive off to the rear of the Black Bear Café. She sneaked in the back way and slid into a booth. If she went home or to the school, her father, who had been motioning for her to wait, would catch up with her. *I can't face you now. I can't face all this—any of this!*

The waitress came back with a pot of coffee and poured a cup for Keely. The scents of cinnamon rolls and buttered toast and bacon woke her stomach. Realizing that she hadn't eaten anything since lunch the day before, she ordered a late breakfast.

Then from her purse she slipped out the Christmas card that she'd received this morning. Opening it, she studied it. The snowy New England scene on its front took her back to her days at college. She read the note from her friend on the inside again and then slid it back into its envelope. Maybe she should take advantage of her friend's offer. Holding her cup in her chilled hands, she closed her eyes.

"Ms. Turner, can I talk to you?"

Keely's eyes flew open. Walachek. She sat up straighter and started to slide out of the booth.

"Please!" He held up a hand. "I need help with Carrie."

"You'll have to speak to social services about that." Keely stood up.

"I did. I have. Lots of times and I've done everything. Help me. Please."

She paused. The conversations around her had ebbed. Everyone had obviously noted Walachek approaching her. She'd come in the back way and had wanted to leave the same way, barely noticed. That, however, was not to be. "Okay," she gave in and sat down. *Why does everyone think I can do everything? I can't.*

He sat down across from her. "I've done all the stuff I was supposed to. I went straight through anger-management counseling. I started AA and I did that community service. But Carrie still won't speak to me. What do I do?"

"Mr. Walachek, I don't know what to tell you." *Why does everyone turn to me? I couldn't even help my brother!* "Abuse has consequences."

The man looked like he might cry. "I let everything fall apart after my wife died. I didn't drink too much until she got sick. Then I just couldn't leave it alone. The trailer was empty without her. How do I get Carrie to talk to me?"

Keely pushed aside her coffee cup. "Have you talked to her aunt?"

He nodded. "But she says she doesn't know how to get through to my girl either. My sister-in-law accepted my apology for what happened back in August." He shook his head. "She said that she hoped the Family Closet program would help Carrie, but . . ."

But now it's crippled until we can get the insurance money and decide what to do about a new facility. Carrie wasn't the only one who needed the Family Closet. Children were going without winter coats this year. Keely's head ached. She pressed a hand to her forehead.

Burke walked through the front door of the café.

Keely panicked. She couldn't face him. She slid to the edge of the bench. "I'm really sorry, Mr. Walachek. I don't know what to tell you." Keely found it exhausting just forcing out each word. "Carrie has to see the need before she makes a change. We can want it for her, but she has to want it first. I wish I could do more."

Dismal, dismal advice. How had she thought that opening a thrift shop could turn lives like Carrie's around? The girl was headed for disaster and even Carrie's own father could see it! And he was helpless to stop it. *So am I.*

The waitress was talking to Burke and looking back toward Keely's booth. Burke turned and headed her way.

Lord, please, can't everyone just leave me alone? I need time to think. I can't think! Keely considered making a run for the back door but gave up the idea. She'd been ducking Burke's calls all week. She'd have to face him—here and now.

"Walachek?" The one word was a clear challenge. Burke stood beside the booth. He said no more, simply stared at the man, waiting for an explanation.

Walachek stood up, palms open. "I was just asking her for help with my daughter. I wasn't making any trouble." The man looked to Keely.

"That's right," she agreed. "And I'm afraid I was unable to help him. Good luck, Mr. Walachek."

"Will you . . . would you . . . talk to my daughter?" the man asked.

"I have talked to her, Mr. Walachek, several times. She hasn't listened to me either." Keely gave him what she hoped was a sympathetic look. The man walked out the back door and Burke took his place across from her in the booth.

"Do you think your father will do what the judge proposed?" Burke asked without preamble.

Keely grappled with her flattened emotions. She shrugged. *I have no idea what my father will do.*

"You look like you haven't been sleeping well."

The concern in his voice didn't ease her. It made her tighten up. "I'm fine," she lied.

The waitress brought her breakfast. But Keely had lost her appetite. She took a sip of coffee, stalling.

"I've been concerned about you. I want to help you get through this."

She stared at him. How could she explain how drained, how lifeless she felt?

"Things should settle down now."

His words came to her as though from a long way off. *What's he saying? That everything will be fine now that my brother's guilty? That everything's okay now that the Weavers are getting Rachel for good?*

"I'll be quiet and let you start eating." Burke gestured toward her untouched plate.

She looked down at the pancakes and bacon. She thought of the Christmas card again. "I'm not hungry now."

Burke moved forward, his hand reaching across the tabletop.

She moved her hand out of his reach. If she let him touch her, she'd break into fragments and blow away.

"Keely, you need a break. I'm worried about you. Won't you let me help you through this?"

Tears filled her eyes. "I can't talk about it now." She slid out of the booth. "Stay and eat my breakfast. I'll call you." She rushed out the back door. She'd left her car in the alley, so she slipped inside and headed away. Burke stepped outside, but she drove by him.

Lord, I don't feel like me. What's going on?

CHAPTER FOURTEEN

ON THE NEXT Sunday morning already deep into mid-December, Burke sat between Nick and Harlan in a rear pew of Steadfast Community Church. The pews were crowded as though people had come for comfort, solace after an autumn of fires, runaway gossip, and just plain shock.

But the service had been a blur to Burke—just as the days after Grady's arraignment had been. Keely hadn't shown up in court the next day. The arrangements for a suspended sentence and Grady's transfer to a private institution had been carried out.

Grady's complete shock over this turn of events had demonstrated just how disconnected the kid had been from reality. Grady had kept demanding that his father "fix this." But Franklin Turner had sat stolid and silent, unable to "fix" anything.

Over the intervening days, Burke had kept picturing Keely in the café booth and hearing her say, *"I'll call you."* But she hadn't called him. And she hadn't come to church this morning. He ached to see her, talk to her, touch her. *Lord, am I going to lose her, too?*

"I usually don't do this." A change in Bruce Weaver's

voice broke into Burke's introspection. "But I want to address what has just happened in our community."

A wary hush fell over the congregation. Burke looked up.

The young sandy-haired minister stepped away from the pulpit. "We all know that Grady Turner admitted responsibility for the fires at the school and the thrift shop."

Instantly, Burke's mind took him back to that night when he'd knelt on the cold asphalt parking lot while Grady had alternately cursed, screamed in pain, and confessed. That memory would never leave him.

"We don't know what drove this young man to do this."

From that night, Burke knew more about what had driven Grady than most. In the ER, Keely's parents hadn't even asked about their son's physical condition! What kind of parents were they?

"But we can all be grateful that no one was seriously injured. Only Grady was burned by the fires he set." Bruce paused. In the first row sitting on Penny's lap, little Rachel clapped her hands, playing patty-cake.

Bruce smiled. "We all know that, thank God, now Grady will be getting the help he needs. In a situation like this it's easy to pass judgment. But none of us has lived a sinless life. We need to remember Grady in our prayers. And examine our own lives. Are we doing right? Have we set fires of unkindness, disobedience? fires of gossip?" Bruce stared into the congregation.

Next to Burke, Nick stirred restlessly. Since the night Veda's car had been burned and the coach had let Nick play ball, his nephew had been quiet. Grady had gone the length with his anger. What would Nick do? Was this really over or should Burke prepare himself for round two with Nick? *Lord, help me.*

Then Bruce lifted his black leather Bible off the pulpit and flipped to a bookmark. "I want to read to you what Paul had to say about God's love in Ephesians 3:14-19. It's what I wish for each of you, for all of Steadfast.

"'When I think of the wisdom and scope of God's plan, I fall to my knees and pray to the Father, the Creator of everything in heaven and on earth. I pray that from his glorious, unlimited resources he will give you mighty inner strength through his Holy Spirit. And I pray that Christ will be more and more at home in your hearts as you trust in him. . . . May you have the power to understand, as all God's people should, how wide, how long, how high, and how deep his love really is. May you experience the love of Christ, though it is so great you will never fully understand it. Then you will be filled with the fullness of life and power that comes from God.'"

The young pastor closed the Bible. "That's what I wish for all of you, all of Steadfast and LaFollette, as we go into another Christmas season. I want Christ to be more at home in your hearts. I want you to know God's love and to share it with others."

Beside Burke, Nick scrawled one word onto his church bulletin. Keeping his eyes forward, he slid it onto Burke's lap. It read: "Sorry."

Sorry. For the first time this autumn, Burke hadn't had to force the word from his nephew. A mighty tide of relief rolled through Burke, almost leaving him weak with gratitude. *Thank you, Lord!*

Burke took the pen from his nephew's hand and wrote: "Forgiven."

Nick met his gaze. Burke offered him his hand. They clasped hands. Harlan reached over and laid his gnarled hand on theirs. Warmth filled Burke. He hadn't lost Nick after all.

"Let's all rise for the closing hymn," Bruce said. "Turn to 'Just As I Am.'"

The three men stood and shared one hymnal. "'Just as

I am, without one plea,'" Burke sang. "'But that Thy blood was shed for me. And that Thou bidd'st me come to Thee, O Lamb of God I come! I come!'"

Lord, bring Keely back to me. You brought Nick. You brought Jayleen. Bring Keely back to me!

⁂

THAT EVENING, BURKE sat alone at the kitchen table, staring at the dishes he'd promised to do. A pinging on the windows heralded an early snow and sharp wind—a good night to stay indoors. Harlan and Nick had gone into town to help decorate the church for Christmas.

Burke hadn't felt like company. Maybe sitting quietly and praying would give him some idea of what to do about Keely. They'd come so far. How had Grady's guilt torpedoed their relationship?

Rodd walked in Harlan's back door, slamming it against a cold gust of wind.

His brow creased, Burke looked up. "I thought you'd be at church tonight."

Shrugging out of his jacket, Rodd pulled out a chair and sat down. "I was at the church. But Harlan said I needed to be here."

Burke looked at his friend with a quizzical lift to his eyebrow. "Here?"

Rodd nodded. "Harlan said you were here alone." He paused. "You and I have something in common."

"We have a lot in common." *What was Rodd up to?* "We have for a lot of years. What's your point?" *I don't want a pep talk now or platitudes.*

Rodd gave him a half grin. "We both love women who are givers."

Burke glanced at Rodd. *Love?* He hadn't said anything to Rodd or to anyone else about his feelings for Keely.

"Now don't act like you're not in love with Keely Turner. Everyone in the county knows it."

Burke gaped at his friend. "Everyone knows?"

"You two have had a rough time this autumn—your nephew, her brother, her father!" Rodd shook his head. "But I think the Family Closet burning to the ground was what really did her in. Keely's the one who bought that house and got the area churches busy setting up the outreach. Single parents needed help and this county really needed a thrift shop."

"Keely?" Burke wondered why she hadn't told him. "I thought Penny Weaver—"

"That's because Keely didn't want it known. But she bank-rolled the place and kept it going. If the thrift shop had been burned due to an accident, she probably would have bounced right back. But that brother of hers doing it. That hurt."

Rodd grimaced. "And I don't know what's going to happen to him in the future. He's out of our hair now, but I don't know how much even a private institution will help him. Being Keely Turner, she probably feels responsible, guilty."

"That doesn't make any sense. Her brother's trouble is not her fault. Surely she can't think that," Burke objected.

"Will she talk to you?"

"No, I've tried. I've called and called her. But she won't have anything to do with me. I don't understand it."

"I do. I told you. We both fell in love with women who are givers. That's good, but the problem with givers is that they give and give and finally they run out of gas. Keely's run out of gas."

Burke stared at Rodd. Of course Keely was a giver. Anyone—even he—could see that. "But what do I do? How can I make her see that Grady's guilt doesn't have anything to do with how I feel about her?"

"That's not really the point. You were at church this morning."

"Yeah." *I sat right behind you, old friend. Thanks for nudging me back to church this year.*

"Well, I think Bruce planned his sermon for Keely, but she didn't come."

"You mean the story about Elijah?" Burke tried to link the Old Testament prophet to Keely. Again, he recalled the moment of unity Nick, Harlan, and he had shared at the end of the service. Nick had been smiling all afternoon. He'd even called his mother without being told to.

"Yeah," Rodd continued, "remember Elijah took on all the prophets of Baal, defeated them, and then ran away from Jezebel's death threat? Keely's like that. She's poured herself out for this community and her family, and she's empty now. So it isn't that she doesn't still care for you. She just wants to run away and hide."

"How do I get through to her? I'll take any advice you have to offer."

"This is no time for standing around wondering what to do. You have to get her attention. Convince her you love her no matter what or you're going to lose her."

Burke traced a pattern on the tabletop. "I thought I'd give her some time and try again—"

"You don't have time for that. I said she wants to run away. I just heard that she's going to leave."

"Leave?" Burke stiffened.

"Gus Feeney called Harlan. Said Keely has turned in a letter of resignation and she's putting her house on the market in January."

"What?" Burke sat up. "She wouldn't sell that place!"

"I couldn't believe it either, so before I came here, I drove over to Gus's house and talked to him. He said that Turner is putting the mill up for sale, and he and his wife are going to spend the winter in California. May retire early there."

"What has that got to do with Keely?" Burke asked, his mind reeling.

Rodd shrugged. "I asked Gus if she's going with her parents, though I didn't think that was likely. He said he got out of her that she has a friend starting a private school in Vermont who wants her to come out and be part of getting it off the ground."

"Vermont?"

"Yes, Vermont." Rodd leaned forward. "You better get your act together if you don't want to have to chase her all the way out East."

Burke stood up and headed for the back door.

"Hey!" Rodd called to him. "She's not at home. She's at that storefront the church rented to be the temporary Family Closet. She's there working with Jayleen."

***

KEELY STOOD STARING out the dusty window of the empty storefront. The darkness outside reflected her mood. Closing her eyes, she pictured the snowy hills of Vermont. The image was lovely, but she felt herself tearing up.

"Ms. Turner, I have the wash water ready."

Jayleen's voice called her back to the temporary quarters of the Family Closet on Main Street in Steadfast. Keely turned. "Oh! I'll finish this." She quickly swept the last corner of dust into a pile and stooped to coax it into the dustpan. "Okay, you can start mopping."

Jayleen approached with the wheeled industrial-type mopping bucket and dipped the string mop into it. "Why are you leaving?"

The teen's question brought Keely up sharp. "What?"

"Mrs. Weaver told Grandma at church that you put

your resignation in. She told me when I stopped there on my way here to help you. Why are you leaving?"

Keely turned away and began spraying glass cleaner on the large front window. "I need a change. That's all."

"You're running away just like your parents," Jayleen accused her. "But you're not like them."

Not taking the bait, Keely kept on cleaning the window, listening for Jayleen to start swishing the mop over the vinyl floor.

"You are leaving, aren't you?" Jayleen insisted.

"This doesn't really concern you."

"Yes, it does. You're my principal, and you're the one who started this thrift shop—"

"It was Mrs. Weaver's idea—"

"Do you think we're all stupid? Everyone knows that you're the one who put up the money to buy the house for the thrift shop."

Keely looked over her shoulder. "What?"

"And we don't want you to leave. Just because your brother is crazy doesn't mean you have to leave."

Keely felt her eyes smart with tears. "I don't really want to discuss—"

"Maybe I understand that better than anyone else, and that's why I'm saying this."

Keely turned and faced the girl, who stopped mopping and leaned on the mop handle. "What do you understand?"

Jayleen frowned. "Mrs. Weaver came out and talked to me again . . . after that day I said I wanted to give her my baby. She talked to me like you did that day in the thrift shop—about God's forgiveness and how we just have to ask for it. We can't earn it. It's just there for us to take."

Keely's mind whispered that passage from Ephesians: *"God saved you by his special favor when you believed. And you can't take credit for this; it is a gift from God. Salvation is*

238

not a reward for the good things we have done, so none of us can boast about it."

Jayleen shrugged. "But it's hard to take it when you feel . . . so . . . like you don't deserve any of it."

Keely waited, understanding what Jayleen was getting at but unable to free herself of the same ache. *I don't feel worthy, Lord. I know you've saved me by grace alone. But why don't I feel it?*

"Carrie thought Grady was cool because of his money and car," the teen began. "And some people say nasty things about you just because. They're jealous because you don't ever have to worry about money. They said—why shouldn't you set up the Family Closet? You owed it to everyone."

Jayleen's expression darkened. "But that's not right. You tried to do something good and it got wrecked. Just like I tried to get my baby safe to my grandmother. It didn't work out, but God doesn't hold that against me."

"That's right." Keely felt her emotions being stirred again. She'd felt so lifeless since Grady's arraignment. "That's right," she repeated. *I know it, Lord, but how can I make it sink deep down inside me?*

"But the Weavers," Jayleen continued, "can take care of and raise Rachel really fine, so then I can feel that I did my best for her. And the Family Closet can be here until the new one gets built and your brother is going to get help."

Lord, is there help for Grady? Keely felt a tear trickle down her cheek.

"So why do you act like it's your fault that your brother messed up?" Jayleen looked at Keely. "You don't even have to ask for forgiveness because you didn't do anything wrong. Does that make sense?"

Jayleen had put her finger on the sore spot. *Why do I feel like such a failure, Lord?* "Everyone was depending on me."

"Rachel was depending on me. You said God would forgive me. What about you?"

What about me? Am I running away because I don't want to be left holding the bag for my parents? Is that my real reason? "I need time to heal, Jayleen. I just need a break—"

The back door burst open, letting in a blast of cold wind. "Hello!" Burke's voice carried from the back room. He walked in.

Keely's heart beat wildly. The sight of him moved her away from the window. She set the glass cleaner down on a step stool. After days of feeling nothing but packed-down pain, her love for this man rushed up from her toes to the top of her head. "Burke? Why are you here?" Though longing to run to him, she backed away.

"I want to know what you think you're doing," he protested. "Heading for Vermont without saying a word to me."

Keely dropped the rag she'd been using.

Doing an about-face, Jayleen retreated at a rapid pace, pushing the creaky, wheeled bucket ahead of her toward the back room.

"How does everyone know?" Keely cried in frustration. "Can't everyone just leave me alone? I need time away!"

Burke inched closer. "I think Gus Feeney's called half the county, telling everyone about your trying to resign from your position as principal."

The look on Burke's face made her remember his arms around her and his warm lips coaxing hers. "Well, he shouldn't have." She fell back another step. "I just wanted to leave quietly—"

"No." He kept heading toward her. "I don't want you to leave."

She kept retreating. Exhilaration cascaded through her, breaking up the skim of ice inside her. "I can't face everyone—"

In one long stride, he was close enough to gather her into his arms. "If you're leaving, then I'm leaving. I'm not letting you get away."

"Burke, I just want to be alone—"

"Too bad. I spent over a decade alone and I don't recommend it." He kissed her.

Sensation exploded through her—warmth, love, longing. She kissed him back, then pulled her head away to speak. "Burke, I can't face everyone—"

"I'll be right by your side." He kissed her once more. Again, Keely kissed him back—his arms banded around her, his fresh-soap scent teasing her senses, his soft lips on her mouth. She knew now that she'd wished for him to hold her like this all these lonely days and nights.

She pulled away. "Burke, you don't want me—"

"Will you marry me, Keely Turner? Say yes. Please." Then he sealed his proposal with another kiss.

Keely felt her knees weakening. His kisses were like sweet waves of peace, draining away her shame and reluctance, her feelings of failure. She clung to his warmth. "Burke," she breathed against his lips, "you don't want to marry me." *I'm not worthy, Lord. I wasn't able to save my own brother!*

His hand claimed the back of her head while his other arm gave her welcome support. "If I thought," he murmured, "that you had one real reason that we shouldn't become engaged, I'd give in. But you don't."

"You don't want me—"

"I do." He kissed her again, short and urgent. "God can take care of your brother, your parents, the thrift shop, the school—everything. I need you and I want you to be my wife." He tilted her head back slightly. "Do we see eye to eye on that?"

Tears flowed down her cheeks. She had to make him listen! "I failed Grady."

"Grady failed you . . . and everyone else."

"He hurt so many people."

"Still has nothing to do with you." He massaged the tight muscles of her neck.

"I feel so guilty."

"False guilt. I told you I failed Sharon."

"But you didn't fail her—"

"That was the false guilt. I see that now," he agreed, overriding her. "I stayed with her to the end. I thought I failed her because I didn't feel up to what happened to her. What froze me inside was the fear of losing her. And when I did, the ice inside me stayed."

He took a deep breath. "But I'm older, and I understand God's love better now. Losing Sharon didn't mean he'd turned his back on me. And being frightened of losing my wife was no sin. I carried unnecessary guilt for years, and I shut myself away until my family forced me to see that Nick needed me."

He cradled her face in one hand. "If you were guilty of anything, I'd tell you so and we'd face it together. But believe me, I won't fail you. I won't freeze up on you."

This made her smile through her tears. "How can you be so certain that you're right? We've only known each other a season. And we've been through one crisis after another."

"Maybe that's why I'm so sure I want you to be my wife. We've been through so much together. That makes me feel like I've known you for years. I've seen you show compassion, forebearance, kindness, strength. I love you because I've seen that you are a wonderful woman."

"But—"

"You take a lot of convincing, lady." He kissed her again. "But I can keep this up all night," he teased. "In fact, it would be my pleasure."

She laughed out loud, the heaviness inside her, lifting, lifting! She suddenly felt free, liberated. "Is this how you question a suspect?"

"Never." He grinned. "Just say the word and I'll let you go."

"Don't. Don't ever let me go." She kissed him, exulting in the sensation of cheek against cheek, skin against skin.

He folded her into a tight embrace. "I don't deserve you, but I'm never letting you go to Vermont . . . or anywhere else. God brought me back from the numbness, from being dead inside. I'm not letting you go there."

Tears filled her eyes. That was how she'd been feeling— numb, dead inside. But no more! "So you do understand," she whispered. She tucked her head into the cleft between his jaw and shoulder. She wished this closeness, this embrace, could go on forever. Then she realized that it could! "I love you, Burke Sloan, and I accept your proposal."

Hearing this, he took his time and gave her the kiss he'd been wanting to give her for over a week. He caressed her lips, drawing her deeper and deeper into the kiss, this exchange of affection, a physical symbol of all he felt for this woman, this wonderful, exciting, challenging woman. *As long as you and God are with me, Keely, I'll never be alone again, cut off, and I'll make sure you never are either.*

"I love you, Keely Turner, and I'll thank God every day for you for the rest of my . . . *our* life together."

EPILOGUE

IN BRIGHT DECEMBER sunshine, light, fluffy snowflakes cascaded from the sky with abandon. They reflected Keely's generous state of mind. She and Burke strolled arm in arm down the main street of LaFollette. His love surrounded her like a shield against the cold, against the harsh words about her brother that some still muttered.

The Day on the Town fund-raiser was in full swing. Shoppers clogged the streets, laughing and calling out, "Merry Christmas!" Carolers walked along the curb, singing "Joy to the World!"

Nick and Jayleen walked on the other side of the street, Shane and Harlan behind them. Bruce and Penny pushed Rachel in a stroller while their son skipped and hopped beside them. Veda McCracken entertained herself by driving up and down the street in the new car Keely's father had bought her before leaving town. Veda honked her horn at everyone, and even this Keely found amusing.

Old Doc met them at the jeweler's door. "Season's greetings! I hear that you have your own tidings of great joy."

Keely blushed.

"You heard right. June wedding. Everyone's invited!"

Burke said, tugging her even closer to his side. "We're going to go in and buy the ring now. Waited till today so 10 percent would go to the new-doctor fund."

"Excellent! I hope it's a lovely ring for a lovely lady. Let me congratulate you both and wish you all the best."

Keely's parents were already in California; Grady was in a private hospital near Chicago. Keely prayed that he would find the help he needed there. She and Burke would visit him during the Christmas break. Keely felt sorry for Grady, but Burke's love strengthened her. *God loves me—I can't earn that love and I can't lose it.* She began to hum along with the carolers: "The wonders of his love, the wonders of his love!"

Burke shook Old Doc's hand. "Bet you're looking forward to that new doctor?"

"I am. She'll be here just about the time you two tie the knot."

"Great."

Old Doc chuckled. "My sentiments exactly. Old Doc out. New Doc in."

A Note from the Author

Dear Reader,

Families can be our greatest strength and joy and our greatest weakness and sorrow. Both Keely and Burke struggled with the issue of connection versus disconnection. Years before, Burke had disconnected from his family and now was fighting his way back to them. Keely had been fighting *for* her family for years and was about to give up and disconnect. In God's wonderful way, he brought them together just when they needed to see themselves in a new way, a new relationship.

I hope that you are fighting *for* your family and are doing whatever you can to strengthen the bonds of blood and those of love. It is never easy, but it is always a good idea. If we can't love our own family, how can we love anyone else with credibility? (1 John 2:9)

The next book in the series, *Summer's End*, will see the fruition of the county's years of fund-raising to bring a new doctor to the clinic. But of course, nothing is ever for sure in this world or in Steadfast, Wisconsin.

Take care! God bless!

Lyn

About the Author

Born in Texas, raised in Illinois on the shore of Lake Michigan, Lyn now lives in Iowa with her husband, son, and daughter. Lyn has spent her adult life as a teacher, a full-time mom, and now a writer. She enjoys floral crafts, classical music, and traveling. Lyn and her husband of over twenty-five years spend their summers at their cabin on a lake in northern Wisconsin. Lyn writes and her husband telecommutes for his company. By the way, Lyn's last name is pronounced "Coty."

Autumn's Shadow is the sequel to *Winter's Secret* in the Northern Intrigue series. Lyn's novella "For Varina's Heart" appears in the HeartQuest anthology *Letters of the Heart*. Her other novels are *Finally Found, Finally Home, Hope's Garden, New Man in Town,* and *Never Alone* (Steeple Hill); *Echoes of Mercy, Lost in His Love,* and *Whispers of Love* (Broadman & Holman).

Lyn welcomes letters written to her in care of Tyndale House Author Relations, P.O. Box 80, Wheaton, IL 60189; online at l.cote@juno.com; or through her Web site, www.booksbylyncote.com.

Turn the page for an exciting preview

of book 3 in the Northern Intrigue Series

SUMMER'S

End

AVAILABLE FALL 2003

ISBN 0-8423-3558-7

www.HeartQuest.com

SUMMER'S END

Excerpt from Chapter One

How did I get myself into this? Kirsi Royston turned onto the state highway toward Steadfast, Wisconsin. Breezes played with the hair that had escaped her long ponytail. Usually that was a carefree feeling. Today it was just irritating.

She'd flown from L.A. into Minneapolis two nights ago. Yesterday she'd bought this used Jeep Wrangler. Today she'd driven across the wide Mississippi River and up the bluffs overlooking it. Now May sunshine warmed her face. But that didn't ease her taut nerves. *Well, things change. Situations change. Mine has, and the clinic will just have to understand that.*

Kirsi's stomach didn't buy that, and she turned back to watch Wisconsin roll by. Mile by mile, the scenery along the lonely highway had continued to astound Kirsi. She was accustomed to rocky Pacific beaches, soaring mountain slopes, green canyons.

Wisconsin had sounded so tame, so dull. But it had turned out unexpectedly beautiful—like the Rockies, without any mountains. Just thick forests, meandering rivers, and small, clear lakes.

Grandfather had tried to prepare her. "Don't underestimate the Midwest, Kirsi. This is a beautiful country. Every part has its own splendor."

You were right, Gramps. Sorry I doubted you. I should know better. Thinking of her grandparents gave her a warm but lonely feeling. How circumstances could change in just six months! She'd never expected her grandparents to offer her such an opportunity.

A sign snagged her attention: State Park, Stalker Lake. Her Jeep turned off the highway as though on autopilot. *Hey!* Kirsi scolded herself. *This is just plain stalling and I don't do that!*

She drove over a gravel track into the wooded park and followed the sign to Stalker Lake anyway. She found the parking lot and then left her Jeep. It wouldn't hurt to take a brief stop. Her legs could use stretching.

Excuses. *I'm just putting off facing Dr. Erickson and I know it.*

The lake was bigger than she'd expected and had a wide sandy beach. She pictured families on the sand and kids splashing in the water. She shivered though. Wisconsin's May wind had a chill to it, especially here in the shadows of the pines.

The breeze rustled the evergreen boughs, and a bird she didn't recognize called in the stillness. She shivered again. Feeling as though someone was watching her, she glanced around. No other cars were parked nearby, but the eerie feeling persisted. Her complete isolation dawned on her. This was something else she rarely experienced in California.

Was someone watching from the dense pine forest? She tried to push away the irrational fear but couldn't. She folded her arms around herself and jogged back to her car. Turning on the ignition, she backed out and drove to the highway.

Before she knew it—the main street of Steadfast zipped by her. She slowed, U-turned, and drove the length of it again. Black Bear Café, the *Steadfast Times* office, Steadfast Community Church, Foodliner, and Harry's Gas Station— she let the quaint names sink into her mind, hoping they would calm her nerves. Then with a ragged sigh, she followed the sign that said Erickson Clinic.

In the lot outside the clinic's emergency-room entrance, Kirsi parked and glanced around. Only a few vehicles were parked nearby—not a busy place on a Friday afternoon in May. Pushing down her hesitation, she jumped out and headed straight inside. *Time to face the music.*

The emergency reception area looked deserted, but she could hear sounds . . . voices from down the hallway.

From behind the counter, a gruff voice spoke. "Hi." An older woman's gray head appeared. "I was picking something up off the floor. Didn't see you there. Do you need help?"

"Not really." The moment had come. Kirsi had to declare herself. Hesitating still, she offered her hand to the plump woman.

Eyeing her, the woman took Kirsi's hand and gave one strong shake. "You're a stranger. What can we do for you?"

Kirsi sized up the woman's no-nonsense face. *Get it over with.* "I'm Dr. Kirsi Royston—"

"The new doc?" The woman reached over the counter and claimed Kirsi's hand again, giving it another firmer shake. "I'm Ma Havlecek. I'm volunteering today, answering the phone. We're expecting an ambulance any second—"

The sound of an ambulance siren drowned out the rest of the woman's words. Out of the nearest ER suite hurried a nurse with short golden brown hair. A tall doctor with dark hair followed her, rushing past Kirsi toward the doors.

From the opposite direction, the ER entrance, a teenage boy came in strapped on a stretcher. Struggling against restraints, he spat out a string of curses.

Kirsi sized the young patient up. His agitation was all

too familiar to her, but here? He couldn't be suffering from . . . not in Steadfast, Wisconsin.

Well past her, Douglas Erickson, MD—she recognized him now from a photo she'd been sent of the clinic staff—paused and looked back. "Dr. Royston!" he blurted out her name, looking shocked. But immediately, he moved on. "When did you get here?"

"Just a minute ago. I drove over a day early." *To have a day to get acquainted with you before I tell you what's changed.* She hurried to catch up with him. "I just wanted a chance to look around—"

"My grandfather will be delighted that you're so eager to get started." He reached the wheeled stretcher and began questioning the EMTs.

Well, yes, she was eager to get started—in spite of everything.

As the new patient was wheeled to the examining area, Kirsi trailed Dr. Erickson. "I'll just observe you for a few minutes," she said, "if that's all right."

"Fine." The doctor's attention was on the writhing patient. The EMTs hovered, waiting to release the patient from the restraints. The nurse tried to soothe him. No success.

The teen became frenzied. Screeching. Twisting. When Dr. Erickson tried to examine his pupils, the kid managed to butt the doctor's chest, nearly knocking him off his feet.

Erickson grabbed the youngster and thrust him back down. "Wendy, did the school say anything about what this kid was doing before this came on?" The doctor bit out the words, interspersed between the teen's yowls.

"The principal said he was found in one of the rest rooms." The nurse raised her voice. "From the odor in the room, she thought he was smoking marijuana."

With violent twists, the teen bucked against the gurney. It rocked, tipped. The nurse yelped.

Kirsi leaped back in time. The stretcher flipped on its side and hit the floor. Erickson stumbled and nearly fell. The EMTs surged around the patient, righting the stretcher.

"What's wrong with him?" From behind them, the older woman receptionist shouted. "He's havin' a regular fit!"

Kirsi waited for Erickson to give the obvious answer, but he was too busy helping the paramedics get the stretcher righted.

"This looks like meth to me," Kirsi said. "He probably soaked the marijuana cigarette in it first."

Both Erickson and the nurse cast worried looks toward her. "We've rarely had a meth overdose here—"

The teen jerked and went limp.

Erickson yelled, "He's coding!"

Automatically, Kirsi turned to the wall dispenser and pulled out a pair of plastic gloves. Without waiting for an invitation, she helped the nurse hook the kid up to the cardiac monitor.

"His pupils are dilated!" Erickson pronounced.

The nurse pulled over the crash cart. Kirsi began an injection to stimulate the heart. All her own worries vanished as she fell into the familiar routine.

The nurse finished hooking up the blue bag and pumped air into the patient's lungs. Frantic moments—Kirsi worked with the other two trying to get the teen's heart beating again. Without luck.

"Clear!" Erickson shouted, paddles in hand.

Kirsi and the nurse stepped back, their gloved hands suspended in air. The jolt jumped the teen's limp body. Kirsi stared at the monitor. Still flat-lined.

"Clear!" Doug shouted again.

"Wait!" Kirsi held up a hand, her focus on the monitor. The welcome beep . . . beep started. "We have a heartbeat."

"Thank God," the petite nurse breathed.

Kirsi echoed the thought. Her own heart had been pounding with adrenaline. That had been a familiar response. It gave her confidence. Things weren't really so different here in Wisconsin.

With his eyes tracking the etching line on the monitor screen, Erickson put the gray paddles back in their racks on the sides of the red metal crash cart. He looked up at Kirsi. "Meth? You think this was a meth overdose?"

"It didn't have to be an overdose. That stuff can kill a kid like this the first time. It's lethal." Then she felt it. Her words released it, a pall—spreading, hanging over them like a funeral drapery. Crack, crystal meth—deadly poisons. "Meth's everywhere nowadays."

Erickson nodded. "You're right. This is just the first case like this with a teen that we've had."

"But that doesn't mean," the nurse agreed, "it hasn't been around." She turned to Kirsi. "Dr. Royston, I'm Wendy Durand. We're glad you're here."

Uncomfortable with the welcome, Kirsi took the nurse's hand. What would their reaction be to her news? "Thanks." Trying to switch the focus from herself, Kirsi took a step closer to the patient and glanced down at him. "We'll have to see if he comes around soon. This isn't over."

"Ma," Erickson said, "call the hospital in Eau Claire. We may need the Medi-Vac chopper later."

"Is Eau Claire the closest?" Kirsi asked, peeling off her gloves as she walked beside the doctor.

Erickson nodded. "The helipad is out that door." He pointed down a short hall.

From the photo she'd seen of the clinic staff, she hadn't been particularly impressed with Doug Erickson. But he was one of those men who had a presence that a photograph couldn't convey. It wasn't just that he was good-looking. He had an aura of competence and personal force that was instantly appealing. His square jaw had a determined look to it, and he had a lean, muscular build, uncommon in a doctor. Trying not to appear to study him, Kirsi heard the opening swish of the automatic doors to the reception area. Another patient?

A woman's voice shouted, "It's Rachel, Ma! Is Dr. Doug here? I think she's having convulsions!"

Shedding his soiled gloves into a biohazard container, Dr. Erickson left the nurse with the teen and headed toward the voice. As though pulled by an identical string, Kirsi followed him, grabbing fresh gloves. She handed him his pair.

Their pace quickened at the sight of a distraught woman holding a little girl obviously convulsing in her arms. The doctor took the child from her. He ran toward the other examining area. "How long has she been like this?"

The mother jogged behind him, trailed by a little boy. "I was driving home and she just started gasping and then this! I drove right here! What is it?"

The question went unanswered as the doctor laid the convulsing child on the examining table. Kirsi began hooking her up to the monitor. The sound of an ambulance cut through the intense examination.

The doctor let out a sound of impatience. "Not another emergency! What's going on?"

"I'll get it." Kirsi swung around and headed toward the emergency entrance. She met the EMTs at the back of the ambulance. "I'm Dr. Royston," she announced in a firm voice.

"The new doc?" One of the men looked up.

Kirsi nodded. "Who's the patient?"

"Veda McCracken." He and another EMT exited the ambulance with a large older woman on the stretcher between them.

"Go on," Kirsi prompted them.

"Her heartbeat is erratic. She's semiconscious—"

The patient railed at them in an angry mumble.

The EMT continued, "The postman saw that she hadn't picked up her mail for the past two days so he looked in the window—"

"She lives alone?" Kirsi asked, taking the woman's pulse and wondering where to take her. The two emergency suites were already occupied.

"Yes."

"And he only checked on her after two days?" Kirsi asked, letting her disapproval come through her voice. This wasn't L.A.! Didn't people in little towns look after each other?

"Today he looked in the window," the EMT continued, ignoring her comment, "and saw her on the floor of her living room."

"Let's get her into that examining room." Kirsi nodded toward the suite where the teen and nurse were. It would be tight, but Kirsi could tell by the woman's sunken eyes that she was probably severely dehydrated. "I want her hooked up to an IV—stat."

The EMTs obeyed her, but they filed out of the room as soon as they lifted the older woman onto another examining table.

Kirsi looked around and found that she was alone with the patients. Why had the nurse left?

Kirsi called out, "Nurse?" She pulled an IV pole toward the patient and began to try to locate a vein in the woman's arm for the IV needle. But the woman was so dehydrated Kirsi knew it would be difficult to find a vein.

Wendy Durand reentered but hesitated just inside the door. "I've paged the nurse in the other wing. She'll be right here."

This struck Kirsi as odd. But since the cardiac monitor

was already in use on the drugged teen, she went on trying to find a vein. "You're not the only nurses on staff today, are you? Please get this patient's pulse."

Wendy approached the older patient as though she might explode and gingerly took her wrist. "No, but we are having trouble with scheduling—"

The patient, who had been staring at the doctor, now turned to the nurse. The older woman started yelling and thrashing ineffectually on the table, trying to pull her arm from the nurse's grasp.

"Ma'am, you're going to be all right." Kirsi spoke clearly and with authority. "You're at the clinic. We're—"

The woman managed to throw out her foot and nearly kick the nurse. The nurse evaded the attack. She continued trying to take the woman's pulse even though the patient fought her efforts. The older woman flailed on the table like a landed tuna. Incomprehensible words and cursing came out in spurts.

"We better restrain her," Kirsi said, setting the woman's hand at her side and reaching for the straps at the sides of the table.

"No," the nurse said, "this is about me. She wants me to get away from her. Her pulse's elevated." Wendy dropped the woman's wrist, went to the teen, and without explanation wheeled him and the monitor out into the hallway.

What? Kirsi looked after the nurse, dumbfounded. Her patient moaned and contorted herself more. Kirsi grabbed both of her patient's hands. They were large-boned with dry, roughened skin.

Kirsi squeezed them and then leaned close to the woman's face. "Ma'am? Ma'am? I'm Dr. Royston," she repeated this until the woman finally stilled and met her eyes.

"I'm going to take good care of you," Kirsi continued. She repeated this reassurance two more times. "Do you understand me? I'm the new doctor here at the clinic. I'm going to hook you up to an IV and take your vitals. If you understand me, can you squeeze my hand?" Kirsi waited patiently while urgent sounds still floated to her from where Dr. Erickson dealt with the little girl. Where had the nurse gone?

Finally, Kirsi felt a slight pressure on her hands. She gave the patient a warm, encouraging smile and squeezed the patient's hands in return. "Don't worry. I'm going to take good care of you."

The woman sighed, relaxing limply on the table.

Taking the woman's faint pulse, Kirsi began to murmur reassurances and explanations of what she was doing as she went about taking care of her patient. But no nurse came, and Kirsi fought the increasing irritation this fact sparked. There had to be some logical reason for Wendy to have left her and for no other nurse to arrive. Right? But she couldn't think of one.

❖ ❖ ❖

As the crisis with baby Rachel eased, Doug's thoughts split between preparing his patient to be admitted and dealing with the arrival of Dr. Kirsi Royston. Seeing the new doctor with her long black hair, tanned skin, and black eyes had taken his breath away—literally. His heart had felt like a heart in a cartoon character—nearly bursting from his chest!

Of course, he'd seen pictures of the new doctor and spoken to her over the phone. But his grandfather had handled the face-to-face interview six years ago. That was when Kirsi Royston had answered their ad about receiving financial help to pay for her medical-school expenses. In return for the money, Kirsi would practice medicine in the county for six years—now after just finishing her residency in California.

"Will Rachel be all right?" Penny Weaver, the local

pastor's wife, asked him. She stroked her little foster daughter's dark curls. Little Rachel looked wan, weakened.

A different question came to mind. Would Dr. Royston—fresh from a California residency—fit in here, in isolated, very-small-town Steadfast? He'd been praying so for over a year now. But he had no peace about it. Would he be able to help the new doctor adjust?

Doug brought his mind back to his young patient. "I think Rachel experienced a febrile seizure. It's not uncommon in childhood. Usually due to high fever. But I want to keep her here overnight just to be sure."

Penny nodded. "I'll stay with her."

Doug touched Penny's shoulder. "Of course. I'll ask Ma to call your husband to come and get Zak for you. Wendy will be in soon and take you through admitting Rachel."

In the midst of trying to smile, Penny bit her trembling lower lip.

"Rachel will be fine." Doug squeezed Penny's slender shoulder. "I just want to make sure the fever is going to stay down."

"I believe you. It just scared me."

"Don't be scared, Mom," Zak, Penny's five-year-old son, spoke up. "Jesus will take care of Rachel."

Just outside the ER suite, the new doctor was waiting for Doug. He took a deep breath. Before long, he'd be accustomed to her dark exotic good looks. But right now, he needed to remain professional, watch how he showed his reaction to her.

She stepped close to him. "I need to talk to you in private—now." Her voice was laced with irritation.

What had happened to upset her? He'd been so busy with Rachel he had only been aware that she was handling Veda McCracken. What had the old woman done already to upset the new doctor? Veda was capable of anything.

"Certainly." He nodded. "Let's go into the doctors' area. This way."

He led her down the hall to the small suite, which included a table and chairs and a bed and full bath that were used by the doctor on overnight duty. He switched on the light and closed the door behind them. He motioned her toward a chair at the table. "I'm sorry you had to face Veda McCracken alone—"

"I want to know—" Kirsi looked directly into his eyes—"what happened to the nurse . . . her name was Wendy, right?"

"Happened to her?" He cast back in his mind. "She was taking care of the teen—"

"That's right, but before that, she was helping me with my patient, and then she just up and left me!"

Doug frowned. He wasn't surprised that Veda had upset everything. That was her lone talent. But how could he explain Wendy and Veda McCracken and . . . everything else right now? This wasn't the opening conversation he wanted to have with Kirsi Royston. He stalled. "You admitted Veda?"

Kirsi nodded. "Yes, she was seriously dehydrated. But you're not answering my question. Wendy left me and said another nurse was coming—"

"Sorry. I did get that message but didn't have a chance to pass it on. We had another patient here who needed the other nurse." He took a deep breath. "We were spread kind of thin today. And Wendy—"

A knock sounded at the door. At his word, it swung open to reveal Wendy. She stepped inside, her expression downcast. "Dr. Royston, I apologize for leaving you like that." Wendy's voice quavered. "But you didn't understand that my being in the room was what was upsetting Veda."

Doug nodded, but he knew this didn't satisfy the new doctor. Her expression was succinct.

"Why would she be upset?" Kirsi asked, studying Wendy with a furrowed brow.

"It's a long story, Doctor," Wendy replied, obviously holding back tears. "But Veda is an angry woman, and I've been a target of that anger all my life." Wendy drew in a ragged breath and then looked at Kirsi. "I didn't leave because I wanted to get away from her but because she would only have gotten more agitated if I'd stayed."

Doug's heart went out to Wendy. She was deeply embarrassed to have to expose this to the new doctor on her very first day at the clinic. *Poor Wendy.*

Wendy gave an apologetic shrug. "My shift is over now, so I'll be going. Welcome to Steadfast, Dr. Royston. We're very happy you've arrived." Wendy left them, closing the door behind her.

Kirsi looked at him. "I don't get it. What's going on here?"

Visit www.HeartQuest.com for lots of info on
HeartQuest books and authors and more!

www.HeartQuest.com

HEART QUEST.

HEARTQUEST BOOKS BY LYN COTE

Winter's Secret—Standing to the side of the battered door, Sheriff Rodd Durand eased out his gun in the icy stillness. "Police! Come out with your hands up!" He expected no answer. This lowlife criminal preyed on the most defenseless—the elderly who lived out in the country and alone. Righteous anger swept through Rodd like flames.

There's only one unlikely link to the crime spree in this sleepy Wisconsin county: Wendy Carey. But the threat to the community is nothing comapred to the threat Wendy poses to Rodd's heart. . . . Book 1 in the Northern Ingrigue series.

For Varina's Heart—What says romance more than a handwritten letter from the one you love? Suddenly finding herself tied to a man she does not know, Varina treasures her heart's dreams while hanging on to each letter that arrives from Gannon Moore. This historical novella by Lyn Cote appears in the anthology *Letters of the Heart*.

HEART QUEST

CURRENT HEARTQUEST RELEASES

- *Magnolia,* Ginny Aiken
- *Lark,* Ginny Aiken
- *Camellia,* Ginny Aiken

- *Letters of the Heart,* Lisa Tawn Bergren, Maureen Pratt, and Lyn Cote

- *Sweet Delights,* Terri Blackstock, Elizabeth White, and Ranee McCollum

- *Awakening Mercy,* Angela Benson
- *Abiding Hope,* Angela Benson

- *Ruth,* Lori Copeland
- *Roses Will Bloom Again,* Lori Copeland
- *Faith,* Lori Copeland
- *Hope,* Lori Copeland
- *June,* Lori Copeland
- *Glory,* Lori Copeland

- *Winter's Secret,* Lyn Cote
- *Autumn's Shadow,* Lyn Cote

- *Freedom's Promise,* Dianna Crawford
- *Freedom's Hope,* Dianna Crawford
- *Freedom's Belle,* Dianna Crawford
- *A Home in the Valley,* Dianna Crawford

- *Prairie Rose,* Catherine Palmer
- *Prairie Fire,* Catherine Palmer
- *Prairie Storm,* Catherine Palmer
- *Prairie Christmas,* Catherine Palmer, Elizabeth White, and Peggy Stoks

- *Finders Keepers,* Catherine Palmer
- *Hide & Seek,* Catherine Palmer
- *English Ivy,* Catherine Palmer
- *A Kiss of Adventure,* Catherine Palmer (original title: *The Treasure of Timbuktu*)
- *A Whisper of Danger,* Catherine Palmer (original title: *The Treasure of Zanzibar*)
- *A Touch of Betrayal,* Catherine Palmer
- *A Victorian Christmas Keepsake,* Catherine Palmer, Kristin Billerbeck, and Ginny Aiken
- *A Victorian Christmas Cottage,* Catherine Palmer, Debra White Smith, Jeri Odell, and Peggy Stoks
- *A Victorian Christmas Quilt,* Catherine Palmer, Peggy Stoks, Debra White Smith, and Ginny Aiken
- *A Victorian Christmas Tea,* Catherine Palmer, Dianna Crawford, Peggy Stoks, and Katherine Chute

- *A Victorian Christmas Collection,* Peggy Stoks
- *Olivia's Touch,* Peggy Stoks
- *Romy's Walk,* Peggy Stoks
- *Elena's Song,* Peggy Stoks

- *Chance Encounters of the Heart,* Elizabeth White, Kathleen Fuller, and Susan Warren

HEART QUEST

COMING SOON (SPRING 2003)

› *Lady of the River,* Dianna Crawford
› *Sunrise Song,* Catherine Palmer

› *Happily Ever After,* Susan May Warren

HEARTWARMING ANTHOLOGIES FROM HEARTQUEST

A Victorian Christmas Collection—Now available in one volume, four delightful Christmas novellas from beloved author Peggy Stoks: "Tea for Marie" (originally published in *A Victorian Christmas Tea*); "Crosses and Losses" (originally published in *A Victorian Christmas Quilt*); "The Beauty of the Season" (originally published in *A Victorian Christmas Cottage*); and "Wishful Thinking" (originally published in *Prairie Christmas*).

Letters of the Heart—What says romance more than a handwritten letter from the one you love? Open these historical treasures from beloved authors Lisa Tawn Bergren, Maureen Pratt, and Lyn Cote and discover the words of love that hold two hearts together.

A Victorian Christmas Keepsake—Return to a time when life was uncomplicated, faith was sincere . . . and love was a gift to be cherished forever. These three Christmas novellas will touch your heart and stir you to treasure your own keepsakes of life, love, and romance. Curl up next to the fire with this heartwarming, faith-filled collection of original love stories by beloved romance authors Catherine Palmer, Kristin Billerbeck, and Ginny Aiken.

Sweet Delights—Who would have thought chocolate could be so good for your heart? A cup of tea and a few quiet moments are all you need to enjoy these tasty, calorie-free morsels from beloved romance authors Terri Blackstock, Elizabeth White, and Ranee McCollum. Each story is followed by a letter from the author and her favorite chocolate recipe!

Prairie Christmas—In "The Christmas Bride," by Catherine Palmer, Rolf Rustemeyer can hardly wait for the arrival of his Christmas bride, all the way from Germany. You'll love this heartwarming Christmas visit with friends old and new from A Town Called Hope. Anthology also includes "Reforming Seneca Jones" by Elizabeth White and "Wishful Thinking" by Peggy Stoks.

A Victorian Christmas Cottage—Four novellas centering around hearth and home at Christmastime. Stories by Catherine Palmer, Debra White Smith, Jeri Odell, and Peggy Stoks.

HEART QUEST

OTHER GREAT TYNDALE HOUSE FICTION

- *Safely Home,* Randy Alcorn

- *Jenny's Story,* Judy Baer
- *Libby's Story,* Judy Baer
- *Tia's Story,* Judy Baer

- *Out of the Shadows,* Sigmund Brouwer
- *The Leper,* Sigmund Brouwer
- *Crown of Thorns,* Sigmund Brouwer

- *Looking for Cassandra Jane,* Melody Carlson

- *Child of Grace,* Lori Copeland

- *They Shall See God,* Athol Dickson

- *Ribbon of Years,* Robin Lee Hatcher
- *Firstborn,* Robin Lee Hatcher

- *The Touch,* Patricia Hickman

- *Redemption,* Gary Smalley and Karen Kingsbury

- *The Price,* Jim and Terri Kraus
- *The Treasure,* Jim and Terri Kraus
- *The Promise,* Jim and Terri Kraus
- *The Quest,* Jim and Terri Kraus

- *Winter Passing,* Cindy McCormick Martinusen
- *Blue Night,* Cindy McCormick Martinusen
- *North of Tomorrow,* Cindy McCormick Martinusen

- *Embrace the Dawn,* Kathleen Morgan

- *Lullaby,* Jane Orcutt

- *The Happy Room,* Catherine Palmer
- *A Dangerous Silence,* Catherine Palmer

- *Unveiled,* Francine Rivers
- *Unashamed,* Francine Rivers
- *Unshaken,* Francine Rivers
- *Unspoken,* Francine Rivers
- *Unafraid,* Francine Rivers
- *A Voice in the Wind,* Francine Rivers
- *An Echo in the Darkness,* Francine Rivers
- *As Sure As the Dawn,* Francine Rivers
- *Leota's Garden,* Francine Rivers

- *Shaiton's Fire,* Jake Thoene